<u>EXCURSION</u> MIGHT HAVE BEEN BARRED, BANNED, OR BURNED A DECADE AGO.

It boldly presents the amorous adventures of an insatiable, lost ballerina. Jabbing, staccato, shocking, it sweeps across Europe as Janet Hunter searches for a sexual encounter that will reveal to her the meaning of her life—and the meaning of love.

"Miss Hunter hops sprightly from bed to bed, sometimes failing to ask the name of her lover, and once foiling a mass rape by four peasants by the simple expedient of cooperating." *Greensboro Daily News*

"Describes what happens to a nymphomaniac . . . a bizarre, comical crew of lesbians, queers, sex-maniacs and just plain bums." *Boston Globe*

"A talented, intelligent, and sensitive writer."
The New York Times

Other SIGNET Books You Will Enjoy

EXCURSION

by Francis Pollini

A Signet Book

Published by The New American Library

Library of Congress Catalog Card Number: 66-20291

*This is an authorized reprint of a hardcover edition
published by G. P. Putnam's Sons.*

SIGNET TRADEMARK REG. U.S. PAT. OFF. AND FOREIGN COUNTRIES
REGISTERED TRADEMARK—MARCA REGISTRADA
HECHO EN CHICAGO, U.S.A.

*SIGNET BOOKS are published by
The New American Library, Inc.,
1301 Avenue of the Americas, New York, New York 10019*

FIRST PRINTING, JUNE, 1968

PRINTED IN THE UNITED STATES OF AMERICA

For Gloria

Dancing is an action, showing outwardly the spiritual movements which must agree with those measures and perfect concords of harmony which, through our hearing and with earthly joy, descend into one intellect, there to produce sweet movements which, being thus imprisoned, as it were, in defiance of nature, endeavor to escape and reveal themselves through movement. Which movement of this sweetness and melody shown outwardly (when we dance) with our person, proves itself to be united and in accord with the singing and with that harmony which proceeds from the sweet and harmonious song or from the measured sound we are listening to . . . the art of dancing is for generous hearts that love it, and for gentle spirits that have a heaven-sent inclination for it rather than an accidental disposition, a most amiable matter, entirely different from and mortally inimical to the vicious and artless common people who frequently, with corrupt spirits and depraved minds, turn it from a liberal art and generous science, into a vile, adulterous affair, and who more often in the dishonest concupiscence under the guise of modesty, make the dance a procuress, through whom they are able to arrive stealthily at the satisfaction of their desires. . . .

GUGLIELMO EBREO, *William the Jew of Pisaro*

(Italian dancing master of the Renaissance)

man the beast
hairy beast
ugly, vile, cruel, horrible beast
nature's abominable beast
supreme horror beast
conceal the beast
seek ever to conceal the beast

absurd appendage
dangling

THE BEAST

1

FRED—"

When she had the letter read she whispered his name, sensing him close to her, the dark maleness of him upon her, caressing her, kissing her neck and breasts and shoulders, whispering to her, whispering sweetly to her, and finally, marvelously, asserting itself . . .

Delicious, timeless, agony of movement, moment, sweet sounds and movement, moment . . .

Being, torn out of moments, the night singularly withdrawn, looked down at her, gently, mocking her, enfolding her . . .

. . . of course! . . . An excursion . . . lovely excursion! . . .

Unknowingness masking silence, savage, blissful silence . . .

. . . in Canterbury . . . in the heart of Canterbury . . . the Cathedral . . . lovely, white cathedral . . . steeple . . . oh lovely steeple . . . sweeping . . . thrusting . . . pure and lovely . . . upward . . . strong and lovely . . .

Before the mirror, opening her eyes, seeing herself there, reflecting what could only be enshrined inviolably from pathways strewn with memory, blackened memory, pulsations salvaged and discerned in memory . . .

. . . absurd thing . . . lovely . . . long hard round thing . . . lovely . . . pink thing . . . hot velvet pink thing . . . plunge into me . . . penetrate . . . seek . . . deep . . . into me . . . the core of me . . . touch . . . very core . . . Soul Of Me . . .

Flesh, offspring of memory, streaming, screaming, ubiquitously, substance seen and known, held and relinquished, the molten dawn, molten red dawn, looming, damn dawn, doom dawn, damned doom dawn, consort, whore-herald of newness, false, False newness . . .

. . . in the heart of . . .

"My God—" white hands, red-tipped, pressed tightly to her face, "What am I going to do—*What*—"

And next day. The letter, fiercely clutched . . .
"Why, he was just a *little boy* when I—"
No when, only wonder, reaching for the wonder of it . . .

Holding on, sweet faces, swirling . . .
 . . . she wears but ruffled red . . . and light rose she is a light rose so light rose . . . Jeanne, sweet poor Jeanne . . . can't she mix one just one properly ever . . .
Parties.
. . . I love parties . . .
Pantie parties . . .
Why
"I hadn't the bit vaguest really—idea—Why what a surprise really!" And, "When, dear?"
"Next week."
Lear.
. . . elancer . . . oblique . . .
"How lovely! Lovely!"
"Isn't it lovely?"
. . . glisser . . .
"I think you're right."
You know . . .
Warmth, within, sudden, flaring quickly, spreading—
. . . there . . . that is where . . . Touch Me There . . .

He wants, he does want, *now scream*, just wants, *laugh, do scream, hysterically, now, just now, this is now, how, oh now* . . .

She drifted. She was with him, drifting. She asked him, *"Who are you?"* It was her voice. *"Where are you?"* He spoke. There it was, his voice, the words, forming, now, reaching out for her, now, closing in on her . . .

"Oh Fred!" *Silly boy.* "My Fred!" *Silly silly boy.* YES FRED!

"YES FRED!"

My boy . . .

All derision. Again, before the mirror, lovely white body, white breasts, in the mirror . . . Gently, feather fingers, brushing her breasts . . .
. . . my breasts . . . lovely breasts . . . when did you caress my breasts . . . did you . . . oh did you . . . caress, fondle my breasts . . . when, precious, sweet, precious . . . rosebud tips . . . my breasts . . .
She turned, slowly. She stroked them, gently. She raised her arms, she was smiling, turning, on tiptoes now . . . her eyes closed . . .

. . . in the white light, sur les pointes, the music taking her, brilliant white light, in the white light, turning, her arms above her, beating, two wings beating, gently, slowly, in the white light, caressed by white light . . .
A boy—he's just a boy—
I was great—
It's what they call . . .
Don't they call—
Robbing The Cradle
Laughing now, softly, lightly, at it.
Don't They . . .
Silent now.
Only . . .

In the dying, only in the dying, in us, each day, death of everything, will you know, each day in us, flown years, flying years . . .
Her mirror. Lovely mirror. Lovely body. White lovely body. In the mirror . . .
Oh God.
Fred
GOD.
She saw him. He was naked, under the sheet, with her. She felt of him, she was fondling him. He was caressing, kissing

her breasts. She whispered, screaming in the whispering, *Oh God,* TAKE ME, *will you, Will You,* PLEASE TAKE ME . . . And the hard thing, long, round, hard thing, velvet-tipped thing, lovely warm thing, In Her, went Into Her, deep, deep, Into Her, and she hung on, a mad ride, lovely mad ride, with it, careering with it . . . She screamed, loud and high, to it, agonized adoration of it, sweet pain, exquisite pain, and ecstasy, screaming to it, *Deeper, darling Deeper,* OH MY DARLING *Sweet Sweet Darling yes my darling*

FIND ME

Late day dress
white silk.
Bib necklace, shaded from gray to white.
En
chanting.

Simply.

_____2

. . . *H-Bomb, A-Bomb, Gas-Bomb, Buzz-Bomb, and best of all, the Was-Bomb. Best oh best the best of all* The Was-Bomb . . .

  . . . *And the Beast within us, in each and all of us. The Beast Deep Deep Within Us, part of us, ever, born in us* . . .

  And these things, products, offsprings of the Beast within us . . .

FETTER THE BEAST WITHIN US

She looked out at the valley. She looked out at it, falling away from her in deep swoops of green and rusty brown. She looked out at it and saw the shadows swallowing it all up now. Relentlessly, greedily, all up now . . .

. . . Why? Who is he? I have to run now? Haven't I
known all?

Where is dawn, if morning plunges madly . . .

. . . and all?

Oh was it.

. . . The spurt. Oh spurt . . .

Be it.

. . . excursion . . . lovely, long excursion . . .

Oh Be it.

. . . Janet darling . . . may I call you darling . . .

Be It?

Scream, ubiquitously, fix the stars, grasp one, swoop,
breathlessly, with it, ascend, ever, ever, with it . . . BE IT
. . . I—can you name me—consecrate me—palliate me—my
god elevate me—I say—may I say—do let me say—Pene-
trate Me . . .

. . . Jan I love you . . .

Love me.

. . . listen Jan I love you . . .

Loves me.

. . . Hot hands on my breasts, his lovely hands on my
breasts, love me . . .

He Loves Me!

She veered back to her father.

"Hircine! I say you are hircine!"

"What?"

She laughed, hugged him.

"You don't know that one."

"No!"

"I'll send it to you. Cut it out and send it to you."

"Spell it—"

She did so.

That night, he looked it up . . .

In the morning, floating on fluff.

"I'm not at all that, you know."

Remembering, laughing, now not laughing.

"Oh? Is that so? Really so?"

. . . I, woman, surrender to man, open my lovely body to
man, receive the vulgar, brutal, bestial thrusts of man, in-
corporate man, for just that scalding fragment of a
moment . . . Destroyer Man . . .

I LOATHE MAN

Screaming, hysterically, epicenely, to the night, lying, rag-
ing, between cool sheets . . .
Her night . . .

She opened the letter quickly. She scanned it, eagerly . . .

Are you mad? Dear boy. *My dear boy!* Dearest boy. *Fred!*
Darling boy. *Oh Fred!*

sweetest boy . . .

*Can breasts be said to present, represent, configurations
prefigurations (oh) tending definitely toward—amelioration?
(Thunder applause. My dear. Dear dear. Who knows. Who
In Truth can know?) (Stoke the phantasies.) But really, can
they, even under sheer, light, ever so light, oh light! fineries
. . . What seeker of sex, I say dear, confronting such tender
and mere shifts, can believe that? Honestly conceive that? My
dear!*
A swimmer, exhausted, crawls from the pool . . .

oh pool

dear
dear pool
my dear
darling
an echo bounds amidst the ruins.
Oh Ruins
darling
oh darling
have you got
(I've got)
the rag on.

3

Why? An accident, my dear, purely. Fortuitous. *He came to the party.* Who had invited him to the party? *Who ever invited anyone to these parties?* My dear. He came. With Raymond. *Raymond had in fact in point of fact in fact my dear a fact it is a fact told you about him.* He came.

. . . swinging in and out of the rose room green room mirrored room there were perhaps thirty of you. Too rich. Bitchy rich. Worthless rich. You. All of you . . . She saw him, silent, watching, apart from the others. She saw him, and halted, sipping her drink only, her eyes upon him, watching him, *Raymond nearby, engrossed in a sparkling pre-*fait-accompli, *charming lovely, demure young lovely . . . slovely . . . I saw him, my eyes would not leave him. In my spying, bored spying, oh god I saw him . . . His hands now touching an elegant long-stemmed plant, what was that plant, how is it you know so few plants, examining its leaves, there now, fine, wide, suddenly tapering leaves, standing there now as I walked over to him, I said walked over to him, serious, thinking face, here, my god, yes here, oh my god, you do mean here,* oh yes, here, yes my God

—Hello

. . . turning, abruptly, his eyes upon me, dark, lovely eyes upon me . . .

—Hello

. . . Smiling, no not smiling, only the eyes upon me, the eyes, fully on me . . .

—Well—have a drink—How are you? Friend of Raymond's?

. . . No answer, do you recall, there was no answer, only the eyes you know gripping you, you felt them gripping you, they knew, oh yes, they saw you, at once you knew, within you . . .

He stayed late . . . what? You talked . . . what? . . . You talked a long time . . . what? . . . what? . . talked I said talked do you know what that means could you possibly have any idea vocal chords that's what they're for what they are

*for you understand how could you understand . . . what?
. . . to hell go to hell Rot . . .*

He came as invited, the following afternoon.
There was a hunger in her, unconnected with flesh.
She swore: *Unconnected with flesh.*
A whirling, desperate urgency. Violence assaulted:
subdued . . .
—Let me show you my paintings.
Pause.
—You paint?
Dark eyes enveloping her, seeking her.
—Yes.
Little laugh.
—in a way, you see—I just make copies—anybody I hap-
pen to like.
—Picasso?
—Shall I try?
Laughing, taking his hand, leading him into the room,
hotly aware of his presence, within a pounding, blood surg-
ing, fragrance, fragments, whirling . . .
   *. . . Odette floated, held high . . . slowly, descending,
floating, touching, turning . . . sway, hold and sway . . .
held by the Prince, in his arms, to and fro, swaying . . . the
music . . .*

. . . I Was a Great One . . .

—You're very rich, aren't you?
Surfacing, abruptly, turning, meeting his gaze now.
—What do you mean? Really.
Shrugging.
—*I mean, you don't have to work—you can do what you
like—go where you please—when you like—*
Silence.
Long, long silence.
Looking at him, looking fully at him.
He was turning, slightly, away from her
Softly,
—*I'm sorry*
—*You needn't be*
—*I'm really sorry*

—It's all right. All right now. Come on . . .

Gently, urging him . . . He came then. She showed him her work then . . .

—Degas—yes, well, when you consider . . .
What?
What, then. Motility? Enshrined proclivity?
—once
—yes

Aware, suddenly, surely, he wasn't listening, perhaps *hearing . . . Not Here*, the moment hovering, fixed forever, on her, part of her, directing her, eyes turning from whatever canvas, *well what was the canvas*, eyes on his eyes, upon them, seeking, trying . . . *not of flesh not*—touching his hand, fingertips just brushing his hand, and then moving, gently, slowly, upward, and then tugging, barely just barely tugging . . . *whispering*

—hey

And

—you're not listening—you're not even listening—here—come over here—now . . .

Pulling him towards one of her own, *Woman in Red*, two more weeks might complete, just might, her whisper now upon him, close, next to him, audible only in terms of immured movement, sustained, held there, movement . . .

—I'm here—you know—listen—we met at the party—you remember the party?

He was turning, looking at her, eyes upon her, *dark eyes, there*, upon her . . . smiling . . . *he was smiling, do you remember the smile, you remember, right there, here, it was here, and the knowing, within, tugging at you, you may remember, try, do try, remember . . .*

The eyes on an inner world, *they see you but they are on that inner world, touch that world, share, know that world, part of that world . . . inviolate . . . cannot . . . sacred . . . I cannot, I know I cannot, just possibly cannot . . . there, within him . . .*

"Darling! When?"

"I thought you knew."

"Not really! *Knew?*"

"Monday. Most likely. Monday."

"How thrilling! Absolutely! We'll see you off. Shall we?"

Do that . . .

DO DO THAT.

The pale light, discerned.

bit . . .
BITTY BITCH

In the pale light, discerned, reflections vanishing, reversing, ever, before her . . .

. . . an old lady, don't you know it, how could you not know it, you can count even, know it, it is not here, no, now, not at all, not now, never more, and he is a boy, a mere boy, is that your voice, you know, your voice, do you know, your own voice . . .

TELL ME

_____4

She was downstairs shortly. She was going to a sort of—farewell party. Dorothy was giving her this "farewell party." *She heard a waltz, the life-beat of it, coming to her now, from somewhere. Now its melody. Muffled, drifting.* She walked. Her dress rustled with each step. She heard her dress rustling. She loved it rustling.

. . . white breasts . . .
why am I going to this damn party
. . . my lovely breasts . . .
"All packed, dear?"
Dear dear
Her mother across the room, elegant, ugly, in brown dress.
. . . bitch witch . . .
The sun, behind her, lurking . . .
"Yes. Just about. A few odds and ends yet." Pause. "You know."

you knew
The smile, slipping, falling with a crash, near her.
"Do have a nice time. Dear."
Scream, plunge headlong into the scream . . .

WON'T YOU

. . . hasn't it —*yes* a long time —*it's been a long long time* is this necking —*what do they call it* can't you see — *what do they call it* I don't know —*Do you care* I don't care —*I'm an old woman* my dear dear an old—*white breasts* How old are you —*I don't know* Kiss me —*I don't know* Kiss me—*my God* Jan please —*I'm an old woman* Please I want —*old* Please—*I want to be*—

Upon her. Loving him upon her.

Time, dissolving, flowing away, from her, from them . . .

Fragments, only, brushing the evening . . .

In her white automobile they were driving somewhere.

Gentle, warm night, they were driving somewhere. They were driving near the sea, now along the sea. In the open car the warm breeze caressed them, held them. They could hear the surf, breaking and bubbling, sliding . . .

. . . his face next to mine, whispering, to me, surf whispering, warm night, love night, I am the love night, I, heir-progenitor to stirrings, know the stirrings, when, oh when—do you know me? what do you know of me? I love you—what do you love of me? I love you—my God oh my god my god—I love you—you can't no you can't oh you can't . . .

One night:

—I've got to go away for a while. Uncle Sam wants me to play soldier for a while. It won't be long. You come with me. You can come with me. You can live near the camp, wherever in hell it will be. *You can marry me. Come on, marry me.*

Pause, long enough to die in . . .

—*No.*

Come on.

—No.

—Then wait for me. Promise you'll wait for me.

—What are you writing?

—A play.

—Send it to me.

—I'll send it to you.

—*I'm an old woman.*

—Wait for me

—Terribly terribly *old woman*

—Promise you'll wait for me

—my god, can't you see, *Can't You?*
—Stop that

my god
Fred

white rose

Fred

MY
WHITE ROSE

———————————————— 5

Mr. and Mrs. Hunter were about ready for bed.

It had been one of those evenings both hated to endure and—which neither would miss for the world.

Mr. Hunter's brother John, *Judge John Carlton Hunter,* had "dropped" in. Mrs. Hunter hated the sight of him. Mr. Hunter was a chorus of acclaim, nay, éloge, for him. He was convinced brother John was the Cream of the Crop. Of four brothers, after all (whereabouts of two, at the moment, unknown), he was the only one who lifted a finger to earn his own living. The words had a noble ring to his ear, nearly.

Holy, really . . .

"Well, dear Linda." He sighed now, observing his wife's breasts emerging from her rather intriguing bra.

"Well," Mrs. Hunter sighed, slipping out of her panties.

"Hee Hee!" cried Mr. Hunter, observing the scanties.

"Oh God, Really! Harold, how old are you?" she said, facing him. "Just how in the world old are you, tell me?"

"I'm sorry, Linda," he murmured to her.

"I should think so, yes, well think so," she said, pulling her nightdress on now.

Silence.

Mr. Hunter stepped into his pajamas.

"Nice of Jack to stop by," he ventured.

Adding, "How did he know Jan was going?"

"He has eyes everywhere. He knows everything. You ask him. Your dear brother. Just ask him—" She flung at him.

"Really dear—" he started.

She stared stonily.

"I do wish—" he attempted.

"You wish!" Mrs. Hunter exploded. "Listen—can't you ask him to phone next time he plans to—stop by? God! At least that way—at least"—Pause—*"I can disappear!"*

Mr. Hunter was pained, but he let it glide by. He would not be shaken . . .

He said, "She's gone. God knows how long—or where."

"Where?" Mrs. Hunter raised her eyebrows considerably, "To Europe—what can you mean—don't you *know?*"

He sighed, "Yes."

"Then why in the world—"

"Damnit, dear, figure of speech—only—"

"You've used that word again!"

"What?"

"It's frequent with you now—you know? Do you know?"

"For sweet—"

"Harold!"

Her face hovered before him, precariously.

"Hard days, sweet," he murmured.

"I should think you'd apologize."

"Forgive me—"

"That hardly sounds convincing—"

"Forgive me, forgive me, forgive me—" he sighed, easing into bed . . .

Mrs. Hunter frowned . . .

He said, "I should go to work."

A moment of absolute silence.

"What? What did you say, Harold?"

"After all, my father—"

"But, darling—" She was nearly, very nearly laughing . . .

"What?" he demanded.

"Well—"

"Don't stop! Say it."

"No. You'll only pop off again."

"Yes—start *that* again—"

"I'm not starting a thing—"

"Then what's so funny? Can't a man work? *Didn't* father work? *Didn't he?* Now, *your* people—"

Her laughter receded quickly. Now, a touch of hysteria, "Never mind *my* people! I know—that damned brother of

yours—he influences you incredibly! Incredibly! You pick
up everything he offers—As for *your father*—"

"There! *That's* what you had in mind—"

"He was a *man!*"

"There! Damnit! Damnit! DAMNIT!"

Mrs. Hunter, hotly, "Don't! Don't! I won't have it! Won't,
won't have it!"

"I'm not a man? *You ought to know if I'm not a man!*"

"Stop!"

"Damnit!"

"Stop! Stop! *Stop it!*"

His big blue eyes opened fully and saw her powdered violence, her clenched hands, her trembling hands . . . A wave
of panic struck him . . .

"Linda," he said to her, uxoriously tender, touching her,
stroking her, "my darling baby Linda, you know I didn't
mean that, you know—you—"

She sobbed, suddenly, forestalled tears, great tears, slipping, rolling, over complex makeup, one phase removed. He
drew her to him, speaking softly, caressing her. She snuggled
on his shoulder, hot tears there finding sanctuary . . .

--6

. . . my excursion . . . lovely excursion . . .

On the train to New York, where she would board the
liner, she tried to concentrate on a new edition of Baudelaire.

The moments, hovering, swooping down on her . . .

*. . . rustling . . . faint rustling . . . rhythm . . . expanding
. . . melody . . . and white and white clad figures about her,
lovely corps about her, moving, turning, gliding, now making
way for her, forming lines, turning . . . making way for
her . . .*

Silence.

Looking out at early autumn bronzeness.

A tear, quivering in the corner of an eye, breaking free now, falling . . .

. . . you . . . was that you . . .

. . . tourner . . . splendid . . . élancer . . . resplendent . . . shimmering white light . . . you in the white light . . .

In passing, overwhelming her, muting her, offering only a glimpse of the die, long ago, cast long ago, ever . . .
. . . Must tell him . . .
She should tell him.
. . . Write and tell him . . .
She would tell him.
. . . Write and tell him . . .
She would write . . .
. . . Tell him . . .

7

Mr. Hunter, musing:
Why?
It was so nice to have her. For two whole years we had her.
Suddenly—
Like last time.
Don't think of last time . . .
Is she going back? Is it possible she's going back?
Just the thought makes me feel good.
My Janet.
We started as a little girl, we practiced, we studied . . .
Lived it, all day, nothing else mattered, because you were good, putting it mildly, eh, Jan darling?
I knew immediately. They *all* knew, later . . .
First of the whole lousy clan ever to have any talent.
I mean *talent*.
You made the top.
You were the top.

And then—
OH CHRIST!
Mr. Hunter stopped.
He tried to go on, but could not.
A massive wall had sprung up, within him, cutting him off from himself, there, within him . . .
Mrs. Hunter, brooding:
Look at him! As if he cared for her! *I'm* the only one who's ever cared for her. All he was interested in, *all any of them ever were interested in* was her dancing, *her career as a dancer.* What good did that do her? I'm the only one who cared. She didn't know, still doesn't know, that *I'm* the only one who cares. The dancing never meant anything to me. She is *my daughter.* I care about her as *my daughter.* Gone. Didn't say why, must be good reason. Always good reason . . . How long for . . . *she'll write . . . I know she'll . . .*

He let her. He doesn't care. He thinks she'll go back, *start again.* That's all he wants, that's all any of them want. He's wrong. *Quite wrong.* Always wrong, Ruined her. He, they, *ruined her. He and his kind ruined her.* Poor dear. Poor poor dear . . .

RUINED HER

Mrs. Hunter sighed, yawned, and fell asleep now . . .

_____ 8

She had written him—a sweet, feminine note, her tiny hand-writing ebbing, flowing, across the paper which opened up, book-like, one face adorned with a tiny sketch, an ocean scene, the ocean, leaping, and early dawn, silence. The envelope now, addressed to him at his camp, somewhere in the southwest. She had looked it up. St. Louis was near there . . .

Long, deadly years, concatenate with time now, summers, long ago, passing so slowly, swiftly, so swiftly, *now . . .* unknown, petulant, veering relentlessly, toward tergiversation, entombed, once, forever . . .

Encounter three.
We await three . . .
What will be left?
A tree?
. . . darling . . .
Autumn redolence, tender autumn redolence . . .
Bonecase, caldron, seething . . .
. . . you want me to marry you? Did you ask me to marry you? I couldn't have heard right. Did I hear right?
Pen halting, abruptly, cold shivers, suddenly. And delight, brief spasm, only . . .
. . . My god what are you writing you shouldn't be writing . . .
Writing.
. . . I'm going away for a while. I'll be in Europe. If you want to, here are a few addresses you might write to. Going to get around a bit! So many people I haven't seen in years . . . Am I running from you? Is that what you think? Perhaps I am. Darling, perhaps I am. I should be running from you . . . Keep up your work . . . no matter . . . Affectionately . . .
A sudden rush—
. . . he could write, we could see the ends of the world, no need to sell, darling, wouldn't even need to sell, my darling . . .
. . . great lake, shimmering in early morning sun. Pines, falling away from it, following the slope, upward now, gently, at last one vast mass of greenness . . . murmurings among the pine smell, sudden awakening in early morning sunlight . . . Italian hills, villa facing southeast, white stone, pink roofed, handsome white stone . . . swift blackness, swooping, taking her . . . line of dancers now, before her, swaying, turning, and the movement upon her, the music and movement through her, taking her . . . Firebird . . . she was the Firebird . . .

Gone.
Now . . .

9

New York.

. . . my mad city . . .

which for some time, some long time, she had not seen.

She stood, remembering.

And chose—

Sought to forget.

. . . Bernice, American angel, my angel. America Beautiful. Hellfire. I hold memories sustained by Hellfire. Dear Uncle . . .

She watched the city.

. . . moonlight . . . I burst open in moonlight . . . my breasts, splendid, white, in moonlight . . . Burst Open In Moonlight . . .

Bernice.

. . . dearest . . .

"Where have you been?"

She shrugged her shoulders.

"What are your plans?"

Eyes, upon her.

"Don't you have plans?"

Scream.

"Must I have plans?"

She would scream.

"Yes. I think you should."

"I don't."

"How long will you be gone?"

"I don't know." Adding, "It's an excursion."

Silence.

Bernice, surveying her . . .

"An excursion?"

She turned from Bernice. She turned to look out the window. In the distance, the great buildings rose, probing the night sky, glittering against the night sky . . .

"Bernice—"

Near her.

"Bernice—"

Blackness, swiftly, swooping on her, rushing, pounding blackness, hanging on in the blackness—

"BERNICE!"

"Hush—hush now—there now—"

. . . Her mother, standing, held an infant. She held out the infant. She was offering it to her. She stretched out her arms to take it . . . She backed away, quickly. The infant was dead . . . the line swayed, beckoned her . . . she floated, a part of memory now, suddenly, dead within her . . .

. . . The Prince, leaning over her, kissed her. She, Aurora, awakened, slowly . . .

MY GOD

Slowly . . .

_____10

Snug in her cabin in the liner, she saw the porthole. How she loved the porthole . . .

She wrote him again. Not a long letter, but she tried to explain, tried to come somewhere near explaining, *her excursion . . .*

. . . you are a young tree . . . reach for the sun . . .

oh
sun

The steward, a handsome young fellow, was there.
Who had rung for him?
She couldn't recall ringing for him.
She looked at him.
His eyes wandered over her.
She let them.
. . . my breasts now . . .

He brought her order, a nice drink. Such a young fellow. Handsome young fellow . . .

"How old are you?"

"Twenty, miss."

Pause.

"*Janet.*"

That evening, in her cabin, they lay, near one another, white breasts in his hands, fondled, caressed by his hands, adored in his hands . . . He took her, she loved it, loved his lunges, deep, vigorous, crying out, his hand on her mouth, her teeth into his hand, mad with his lunging, her nails dug his back, scraped long, deep, down his back . . . She screamed . . . at last . . . with his lunging . . .

. . . in an old room a piano was playing. The class had just started. They were limbering up, at the barre. *She saw herself in the mirror. Exquisite, she loved herself, in the mirror. Lovelier than any of them, she knew, in the mirror. And better. Better than any of them . . . In the mirror . . . she bent back, her foot describing small circles on the floor. She felt her muscles pull . . . She heard the mistress,* Développé now—fine, lovely—Janet—battements—yes—now everybody, again—everybody—again—again étendre—Helen—Dear Helen—port de bras! now then . . . On. Ever. Forever. At the barre . . . She was sweating. All were sweating. Still, on, the barre . . . A short break at last, and then, quickly, they moved to the center of the room . . . Mistress clapping her hands. Piano. The music seemed from Giselle. But was it? Not easy to tell. Not exactly being played too well. Well . . . Giselle. Definitely, her Giselle . . . Mistress' voice, Arabesque—Anna—the foot—yes—bit more—just a bit more— yes—yes yes—now—Entrechat! Développé! Lovely! Lovely! Développé—Janet—watch your arms, darling—yes—fine— yes—lovely—Nora, drop your instep—ah yes—leg higher— bit—not too high—that's it—no no—too high—en arrière —saute—sur les pointes—quickly—everybody now—quickly quickly—sur les pointes—lovely—Janet—those arms—yes— lovely—ah, lovely—tourner—élancer—adagio—so lovely . . . All morning. Day. Was it day. What day . . . She reached the danger point. She felt she would drop. Every bit of her wanted to drop. The room swayed. The music was a clatter of noise now. She would drop. Sure she would drop. On. And on . . . Drop . . . Janet . . . the voice . . . Those*

*arms! . . . She responded to the voice . . . Janet! . . . She
caught herself, she hung on . . . Stop flopping those arms!
. . . All right now . . . she was all right . . . soaring . . .
she was out of herself, no longer at all part of herself . . .
She watched herself. Bizarrely, she watched herself. She was
soaring, high up, now, watching herself . . .*

"Ah—Janet—*Aha*—"

*. . . She, Odette, led her swan maidens . . . magic music
of night . . . They floated, hovering over all, touching only
the edge of a moment's decline, turning, gliding, defying time
. . . They followed, circled the clearing . . . They danced,
exquisitely, in the night . . . white night . . . The Prince appeared . . . They fled . . . She remained . . . Tender, lovely*
pas de deux . . . *the music flowing . . . she swayed in his
arms, gently,* sur les pointes, *to and fro, feather gently . . .
The hour struck. She trembled. The sorcerer was at hand
. . . She was pulled away, out of the Prince's arms . . . He
tried to hold her. He could not . . . Trembling,* sur les
pointes, *back, back . . . the sorcerer's great power . . .*

"You are so cleverly handsome."
"Thank you, Janet."
"Is your back bleeding much?"
"Now it has stopped, Janet."
"Why aren't you in films?"
"Ah, Janet—"

Devoured. Next night, that night, and next . . .

She was smiling, watching him. The years, reeling. The let-
ter enshrined, part of her. She was hearing. Aware she was
hearing—
"We can live in the south of France—if you would agree!
You know, Janet, it is warm all year there. Think of it! Ah, I
can think of that!"
He was so handsome, she lay there, smiling, watching him.
"My town is there—well, not very far from there. That is
where I come from."
He was quite carried away by it, she heard him.

"Lavreaux—a big man, Janet—has an estate there."
He lay near her, murmuring to her—
"He has been trying to sell for years, oh yes, you know—"
She kissed his ear.
"He'll sell very cheaply now, *mon cher*—I can tell you, just take it from me, you know—"
"And how long have you lived there?" she murmured now.
"All my life! Except—of course—when I went out to take this job—"
"You should have tried the films—"
"Are you in films?"
She laughed.
"No no, not at all, oh no—my dear—"
He kissed her now.
"Wouldn't you like to, with me—"
He was a pet. She stroked his neck.
"He'll sell very cheaply—" he began, again . . .
She lay back now, smiling, just watching him . . .
Her voice now, strange, and distant,
"Do we dock tomorrow, my dear?"
Pause.
"Friday—"
"Friday—" she echoed . . .

"Good-bye, André—"
She watched the rage.
"You are so handsome, André—"
She watched him, never wavering, countering the rage.
"You've been so good to me. So very good to me—André—"
He was near her. He stood still, very near her.
"I'll throw you off the boat, Janet."
A pause. She sipped her drink. So cool in the pause.
"They'll only rescue me, André . . ."
Sweet pause.
"Dear André—"
Never pause . . .

Hamilton Upwind, M.D., physician *and* surgeon of no mean caliber, cousin of Janet, mother's side, was trying out his new British sports car.

Mr. Hunter sat next to him, for he had coaxed him into coming along for a little ride.

"Not bad, huh?" said Hamilton, taking a corner at seventy.

Mr. Hunter said nothing, but after a few more of these did manage to persuade his cousin-by-marriage to pull in somewhere for a cup of coffee.

"Pretty good, huh?" said Upwind, screeching to a championship halt.

"I—" said Mr. Hunter, *"My God!* Take it easier going back, will you, Hamilton boy?"

"Whatsa matter?" Upwind laughed. "That's what they're made for! Ask Janet—she's out there now, right? Ask her—"

Mr. Hunter lapsed into silence.

"How's she getting along? Hear from her?"

Mr. Hunter lit a cigarette, shifted around somewhat.

"Linda did, today," he answered, finally.

"She did? Hey, she never told me! You better tell her off for me—buddy!"

Upwind, now, for some reason, laughed aloud.

Mr. Hunter, staring, casually, sipped his coffee.

Upwind descended, "How is she, anyhow?"

Mr. Hunter mumbled, "O.K. I guess. It was only a brief note. That's all."

Upwind leaned in, growing confidential.

"You know something?" he said. "You really want to know something?" he added.

Mr. Hunter waited.

"I'll tell you something." Pause. "Harold, old buddy." Another pause. "I'm going to *tell* you something."

He paused. Reflected. A long time, he reflected.

Mr. Hunter wondered, and waited, for something.

Finally, "Harold, boy, I think the way it all ended, the ballet stuff I mean, I think that was good, a very good thing. The best thing that could ever have happened to her. I tell you. Harold, that's a lousy life, what kind of a life is that, anyway? Don't look at me that way, Harold boy, someday you'll see

33

what I mean! Put her face to face with life, that's what it did!
Hell, what did she ever know of life? Living that way—how
many years—do you know how many years? Ever since I remember, since she was a kid! That's almost the whole of it,
her life I mean. *Unnatural. Dreamworld.* No sir. I'll always
maintain it. That's why they're nutty—almost all of them—or
going nutty. Don't get me wrong—I don't mean Jan girl. I
mean, you can't live *that* way *forever* and *not go* nutty. Get
me? And for what? Look, a few years in the limelight—if
you're lucky—and then? What then? Look, I'm not kidding,
it's a damn good thing it went that way. Better it happened
sooner than later. She's still young! Heck, look at me—Am I
Old? You wait, she'll come back from London with a sweetheart. Ha Ha! You wait. I bet she does. *Sweetheart!*"

Mr. Hunter, politely, sipped his coffee.

Upwind plunged on, "I just hope she doesn't come back
with any Socialistic Ideas. Christ! How long will she be there?
That Socialized Medicine and all that crap—that's the *end,*
buddy. Just hope she doesn't come back contaminated with
that, old buddy! That's all we need, huh? Jesus! Make the
goddamn country even lazier than it is already! Hell, we got
the best medical services in the world, know-how, personnel,
the works. People bitching all the time about bills—so forth
—the way it goes, huh? They expect us to work for peanuts?
Why the hell don't they go out and Make The Dough, instead
of bitching? Maybe they'd like to be in our shoes—*one day*—
Just *one* day, that's all it would take, right, Harold buddy?
Lazy bastards. Yeh, that's all we need, I tell you. We'll never
see it here though, I guarantee it. By God we won't. The
American Public just ain't *That Stupid,* buddy! We do what
we can to educate them on the matter, inform them, let them
know all the ins and outs, what's going on about the matter.
Vigilance! That's it, Harold buddy. Goddamn, with all those
pinkos running around Washington these days you can't have
too much of that! On your toes, that's it, we got to be! Free
this, free that, everything free, yeh, coddle everybody, sure,
that's the way to make the Nation great, oh yeh, isn't it? How
in hell you think we got to be the Greatest Country In The
World? Huh? Answer me that one! Boy, I'll tell you, the day
they bring in Socialized Medicine—whatever the name the
smart pinkos give it—*God forbid!*—That's the day *I quit
practicing medicine!* Yeh, I mean it! *Pack up and Quit!* But
don't worry—we'll never see it. Never. See it. That's all we'd
need! Yeh That's All We'd Need!" He paused. "Buddy." He
halted, lapsed into a long silence . . .

"Let's go, Hamilton," Mr. Hunter suggested, quietly, after a
while . . .

I WANT TO BE NICE

Out of time, her own cry, storming down the years, part of time, all time, forged there . . .

London, cool and wet, gray, dear, *dear London* . . .

She wrote of this to him. A postcard for aesthetic natures, it bore a reproduction of a Van Leyden. A man, long, unhappy face.

—*brrr—letter follows—*

"Oh, don't be silly now—we have *tons* of room!"

Jane, whom she had called, would of course not hear of her staying at a hotel.

"Well, all right dear. All right."

"Splendid! Well, come along then. Hop a taxi! How are things? How's the big bad man in Wilmington? Has Poppa bought the White House yet?"

Laughter.

Such sweet laughter . . .

Olive was there.

"What's kept you away so long?" And, "Oh, darling, we *do* understand!"

Janet, smiling, so pleased to see them. She loved the English!

"We'll have fun now!" Olive was saying. "Jane has some *smashing* boyfriends now—young darlings, really—you'll see."

"So young—you'll see—"

"Well—"

"This is your first stop? You haven't been to Paris?"

"Have you seen what's coming out of Paris? I mean—"

"*Fantastic!*"

"Yes—"

"*Really!*"

"I haven't been to Paris—"

"Do they really expect—"

"*Really!*"

"I can't think—"

35

"Tsk Tsk!"

Squealing with laughter, three of them . . .

"Oh well."

"Did you get to the wedding?" Janet inquired.

"Oh yes."

"Quite nice."

"Did she look nice?"

"Quite nice. Really."

"What an affair."

"Rather."

"Quite quite."

"Now for some babies."

"They should have nice babies."

"Oh well."

"*Lovely* babies."

"Yes."

"Here we are now."

"*Where* now?"

"Oh, *Janet!*"

Hugging her, both of them hugging her . . .

. . . soft whispering, turning, touching, only touching . . . passing, quickly . . .

Evening. All wrapped in white chiffon. Enchanting, really. White Chiffon. Loving herself in chiffon. They were to have dinner, *the young darlings,* Jane's darling young darlings. Dinner, dancing, soft lights . . . light soft night, *la la, London night* . . . There. She was there. And wasn't. Laughter, music, bubbling around her. Good Anglo-Saxon head of the young man, *darling,* beside her . . . bubbling wonder stuff, glasses of it . . . *the party, somewhere in the house, had been going on for some time now . . . from her room she could hear it . . . laughter, music, from somewhere, drifting up the long, curving staircase, along the hallway, her room . . . Occasional footsteps passing her door. She was excited . . . new thing, recently ripened thing . . . alarmed, loving it . . . She had longed for it . . . Now, vulnerable . . . she knew she was vulnerable . . . She didn't mind being vulnerable . . . All women, vulnerable . . . right thing into her . . . She longed for the day it would go into her . . . It frightened her sometimes . . . What would it leave in her? She was terribly afraid of the things it might leave in her . . . She couldn't get to sleep . . . the party . . . thinking of things . . . sudden flurry of*

*things . . . Carl, asleep in his room, farther along the hall
. . . Parties had never kept her awake before . . . so far off,
could barely hear, really . . . yet, she couldn't sleep . . . she
lay there, excited, listening, wishing she could do more than
listen . . . not too far off, parties, many parties, for her . . .
she knew . . . Carl . . . She loved her brother . . . She was
aware only of love for Carl . . . my breasts . . . two treasures
. . . He was just a year younger . . . She loved him near her
. . . When she practiced, he watched her . . . he always
watched her . . . he played the records for her . . . He would
sit, quietly, watching her . . . dark eyes, quiet, lovely boy, she
stroked him . . . Often, she stroked him . . . She loved to
stroke him . . . He let her . . . Quiet boy . . . So fond of her
quiet boy . . . She had always loved him . . . he didn't go out
. . . teachers came here, to his room, the study, different
rooms, for him . . . quiet Carl . . . dark-eyed, lovely Carl
. . . her love for him . . . the warmth, in the night, her love
for him . . . the party, the night, the warmth of her love for
him . . . He loved her too. She was sure he loved her . . .
She smiled, felt so warm, good, thinking of him. She was
aware only of love for him . . . In bed, in his own room, he
could hear the party too. She would ask him tomorrow, first
thing, when he came to see her. Did you hear the party? and
What did you think of the party? He would answer, quietly
. . . A few words, those dark eyes on her, quietly . . . She
sighed, turned over, hugging her pillow . . . Footsteps, halting, just outside her door. Her heart skipped. Was it—No. It
wouldn't be. She knew it just wouldn't be. Couldn't be . . .
She smiled, nevertheless, wishing it might be . . . Footsteps
moving on. Down the hallway . . . She tried to sleep. She
snuggled deep, trying so hard to sleep . . .*

She danced with the young man.
Good, Anglo-Saxon man.
Nice young man.
She looked at him and thought, *What a nice young
man . . .*

She liked the young man.
She was close, whispering sweet things to the young
man . . .

Laughter, much laughter at the table. And someone—

someone was saying, "Do you know, Jan dear, Janet dear,
here in England, Our England, we have a countess, Dowager
Countess, who is a coal miner?"

"No less? No less now?"

"Oh, I'm quite serious!"

"She is that, indeed she is, Jan."

"But I believe you!"

"She goes down into her pit, private pit, three hours a day—"

"Such a short shift."

"But of course, she's quite old—listen—she's found a
unique way of extracting gas from coal—listen—it will—rev-
olutionize the country—"

"Industry."

"Quite, quite. Industry."

"Marvelous!"

"The National Coal Board has given her permission—"

"But of course—"

"How else could she?"

"My dear!"

"Dear dear."

"Dear dear dear."

"The old dear."

"A nice, long toast to the old dear!"

"Rah, rah, the old dear!"

"Bless the old dear."

"Long live the old—dear."

Much champagne later, Janet asked, "Is she related to
you?"

Jane, unsteadily, "Who, dear?"

"Countess."

Jane, coming ashore again, "Really?"

She let it go at that.

She just

let it go at that . . .

Jane said, "Want to get out of here?"

"What?"

"Out of here."

"I like him."

"He'll come with us."

"Well, well—fine, then."

"Didn't you know he'd come with us?"

"Why not? He came here with us."

"That's—"

Jane lapsed into silence.

Thinking.

The young man turned to Olive.

He whispered, "Who is she, anyway?"

"Who?"

"Janet—"

"Janet?" She burst out laughing. "You don't know? You really don't know?"

The young man was quite peeved.

Olive leaned close to him. She said to him,

"Janet Hunter."

The young man thought about this.

He looked over at Janet and thought more about this . . .

"I say now!"

"Yes."

"I *do* say now . . ."

"Oh yes . . ."

A pause, refreshing . . .

"Fancy that now!"

They went to a jazz club. It was packed to the rafters, but they squeezed in somehow. People were jumping all over the place. The band was wound up in a terrific surge of melody and rhythm. It reached out, seeking the night. It found the night, fused instantly with the night. And everybody. It gathered them in, made them one, with it, and the night. Its pull knew no bounds. Its contact with life told them now. Without words, it told them now. All now. It swelled and swayed, and all were clapping now. Great clapping of hands, and shouting, and laughing, beating the rhythm now. A mighty roar, shaking the building, the very heart of the building. On and on. Janet was so happy. They were all happy. It would never end. It seemed it would never end . . . Abruptly, brilliantly, the band brought the piece to a close. Pandemonium. Screaming and laughing and hugging. All hugging.

"That was the Greatest! Oh, Oh, The Greatest!"

Janet heard her voice saying this, trying to say this.

She applauded fiercely, a long while, a long long while . . .

A drink was before her.

She was wondering, *Who put all these drinks before me?*

Young man holding her, kissing her, sweetly kissing her. She loved him kissing her . . .

Olive staggered, fell. Squealing, laughing, they helped her. They all held her . . .

They left the place, finally.

They drove off.

In the back of the car, the young man cuddled her.

She closed her eyes, spinning, she murmured . . .

"Do you masturbate?"

"No—no masturbate."

"Never?"

"Leaves you flat."

"Never?"

"Never never."

. . . scion . . .

"Venus Books? Lovely—*Venus Art Books?* White—Tony
—gorgeous white—plump, upright—*oh Ripe Ones*—Black
panties?—fine so fine *black*—brief brief—*suspenders*—stock-
ings—*Tony?*—Oh Ripe Ones!"

"Never . . ."

They arrived somewhere . . .

Scion.

Sitting there, swaying, now trying to raise himself,
sweet scion . . .

"Do you *really* want to see London? I say! Janet?"

. . . Oh, Scion! . . .

"What's your name again?"

"When?"

"Your name again."

"Anthony—Percival—Reginald—Mar—"

"Tony! Enough now! My goodness! Now!"

But he went on. She clapped a hand over his mouth. She
was laughing, all the while laughing . . .

"Enough now!"

— — — — —
— — — — —

"Yes."

"Yes?"

"But only the slums, Tony dear—"

"Slums—"

"The slums."

"I know."

"OH!"

"Look: we take the boat. See out there? A boat. My boat.
Downriver, Tower, even farther—coming?"

"Slums."

"Come on."

"The slums!"

"Right. O.K., the slums. Let's go! Save the Queen. Queenie! I say—QUEEEEEN"

"EEEEEEE"

It was near dawn. They stumbled out . . .

They reached the point where his boat lay and climbed in, not without some difficulty. Tony got it started after a while. There was a loud cheer. They discovered Olive and Jane were there. But only Jane's young man.

"Where's he gone?" Olive asked.

"I can't think!"

The boat, with a roar, under Tony's firm hands, started off down the Thames.

"Full speed!"

"The slums!" Janet ordered . . .

"Who wants the slums?" Jane just moaned.

Tony flourished an arm, "Houses of Parliament."

"That was quick."

"Who cares?"

"Uncle's in there!"

"Oh? Now? Is he there *now?*"

"And how . . ."

Speeding along, weaving, under the bridge, narrowly missing one pillar, spray flying.

"We'll get a ticket!" Jane shrieked, hanging on, her young man stretched out on the floor of the boat.

"Never fear! My cousin—"

"The slums!" Janet yelled, hurling herself at him.

"Hey! Hey, Watch Out!" he shouted, battling her off.

More bridges.

"Hail Waterloo," Tony announced.

"Hail Columbia!" Jane revealed.

"Hail Somerset Oh House!" Tony bellowed, throttle full out.

Olive, "Nothing more lovely—Janet—whole, whole of London—look, Janet!"

Down the Thames, weaving, roaring . . .

Lovely Somerset House—

Guide Tony . . .

Sirens.

Police boats after them . . .

They cheered, long, in the night, racing along, chorus of cheering . . .

"The Tower! We made the Tower!"

Tony informing . . .

The bridge, starkly, looming, before her, and, to the left, sprawling Tower, grim, ancient Tower . . .

"Chop chop! Chop them all off!"

Tony, roaring, laughing and roaring . . .

. . . *Lady Jane led to the block, neck resting on block, large masked man near her, witnesses gathered, staring, sawdust-filled basket before her, ax raised, swift flash of steel in the sun . . .*

Janet screamed and fell, hitting the deck with a thump . . .

She heard the cry.

————————————————————13

. . . *when the sun shines then you will know . . . know, know . . .*

She tried to sleep. Everything was turning, over, over. Now she was turning, floating, falling. Faces. Voices. So many voices . . .

She tried to sleep, seeking release from the turning, the voices. They pressed in on her. She ran among them . . . She dreamed she was running among them . . . Lost, turning over, among them . . .

. . . *long, long circle . . . white blurs . . . turn . . . Giselle, betrayed by her lover, sought her mother . . . circle of faces about her . . . die now . . . circling, circling, ever widening the circle . . . faster . . . turning . . . the music . . . flow into the music . . . furiously, about the circle . . . sword . . . hands uplifted, sword in her hands . . . into her . . . one last turn, seeing him . . . and now her mother . . . Giselle, near her mother . . . one scream, falling . . . blackness . . . and falling . . .*

————————————————————14

Judge John Carlton Hunter, pillar of society, was at his post this A.M., doing his duty.

He was restless, yet—worn out. The trial, concerning the murder of a well-known young man by his younger brother (it was alleged), dispatched via a rather ingenious form of garroting (it was known), had been going on for thirteen days. The Judge wasn't very superstitious, but he was doing his best to prolong the trial just one more day, if possible—even though, at this point, it ran directly counter to his most overpowering desire, to wit: to sleep. *Lie down, forever, Sleep* . . .

Not that the trial didn't fascinate him. He was, indeed, spellbound by the rather intriguing details of the case.

But they had been unwound, and rewound, and now it was just a matter of time, a matter of certain attorneys letting off whatever steam and hot air still remained in them. One more day. Yes. After that—the verdict. *And sentence.*

For there was no doubt in John Carlton's mind, and he would see there was no doubt in the Jury's either, the younger brother, the Accused, was Guilty. He was certain the first moment he had laid eyes on him . . . He liked to believe, though, that he had become certain only after hearing hours and hours of irrefutable testimony . . .

The Judge, just now enduring some especially agonizing and pointless direct examination of the Accused by his attorney, stayed awake by reconstructing the more endearing aspects of the case.

Item: The relationship between now kaput older brother and mutual sister, aged fourteen and one half.

Item: Bizarre relationship between Deceased and Accused, when neither was either, note.

Item: Wild rage of the Accused on unearthing nature of Relationship between Deceased and said mutual sister.

Item: Masterfully ingenious planning of Demise, mode of Demise.

Item: The "Little hut in the woods."

Item: Flawless (1) snaring (2) collaring (3) slow dispatch of Deceased—*a record, surely*—in presence of mutual sister.

Item: Who, unfortunately, could not appear. She had gone mad. *Promptly.*

"Promptly," the Judge said, aloud.

All eyes turned on him, wondering what he could have meant.

"Sir?" queried the defending attorney.

John Carlton, clearing his throat, replied gruffly,

"Carry on. Just carry on."

They did, and he returned to his reverie . . .

That was the snag in the case, he thought now. Only snag. No Sane Witness to the *fait-accompli.* But—never fear. Whole mass of damning evidence had been reconstructed, ac-

cumulated, fabricated, lubricated, and presented, *brilliantly,*
by the *brilliant* prosecuting attorney, a future Governor one
day no doubt . . . and his Team.

Item: The *corpus delicti.*

Oh *delicti!*

The Judge was elated. He subdued the voice, just about to
escape, somehow . . . *That's something I've never seen! A
Garroting!*

Now, the thought of this interesting mode of dispatch
uplifted the Judge, in fact, inspired him. He felt good. He
came to life.

—If only we could use it in our capital cases!

His mind fastened on this and raced along, fascinated by
the prospect.

—That would deter them! Really deter them! By God it
would deter them! Brilliant idea, No? Ho! Ho! How can I get
that point across? Maybe, just maybe, at the next Conference
—yes, that would be the place to start it—

Though, thinking further on this, he became unhappy.
There'd be opposition. Especially Hawkins, Peters, Jim Larm-
er—that fine trio of blind namby pambies! They'd spear-
head, organize the opposition. Hell, without them—God,
without them—might just be—place would go wild for it!

He had a vision of the Conference adopting his proposal.
He was elated. But then, again, fell from his pinnacle.

—That damn Legislature! That crowd of worthless do-
nothings and dumbbells! Those public pansies! How would
we put it across there?

Now, indeed, he became quite unhappy. And soon, disgusted. It was clear that in the present context of things his
idea had little more than meager prospects of adoption.

He became sleepy again, and began to slip away from
things. Once in a while he was jerked back by the sudden rising or falling of the voices involved in the interminable pro-
ceedings going on below him.

—Poor fool! What's he trying to prove? Everybody knows
he's had it! God oh God what agony! One more day, *and then
the sentencing!*

It would be worth it though. In this State they used the gas
chamber. And John Carlton made it a point to attend as
many sessions there as possible. It was pretty fair. He chuckled—*everybody thought it was The humane way to do it.
Painless, nice and easy, Fun, almost.* But the Judge knew.
Yes, he really knew . . .

*None of that hood over the head and drop through trap in
the floor business, like in hanging. What could you see?*

In the gas technique, you could see everything. *Everything. You stood outside those nice big glass windows and saw everything.* That was the beauty of it! *Man's head, or woman's, dropped.* Certain amount of shuddering and twitching. Stillness. *But the heart kept on beating! Sometimes, for a long time it kept on beating!*

The Judge sighed . . . Of course, the Chair had its points. *The sensationally beautiful heave and thrust against the straps at the first jolt. Smell of singed flesh. Second jolt . . .*

He wondered if, at least, he couldn't get a motion through recommending a change to the Chair . . . Once or twice, on a courtesy visit to colleagues in neighboring States, he had seen the technique in action.

He looked at the accused.

He pictured *his* little session.

He felt good, his penis tingled with forepleasure.

By God What A Session!

He lost it. Completely. He wandered around, blank, within himself . . . At last, he stumbled across another part of himself. There, he found Janet . . .

It pained him, really, to think of her. He used to be so proud of her. She had been the one *true* bright spot of his life. Better even than sessions! She was something he could *always* be proud of. His own children gave him no pleasure. Just now he was working on getting them off their fourth charge of "Peddling and Receiving Pure Marijuana." As for his wife—he stifled a curse, thinking of her . . .

In recent months, he had once again been toying with the idea of divorce—*or at least a separation*—thus shaking off *the whole bunch* . . . Whole painful bunch . . .

Janet.

Ah, Janet!

Who had been *his honey, his treasure, his pride and joy forever!*

Who had been

—Prima Ballerina Assoluta of these whole United States —The World! Acclaimed by all! The darling of all! Sought, pursued by all! A marvel, a delight to all! A heaven on earth to see, to be transported by, far away by, in her moment, her glorious, supreme moment! Moment of moments!

Who had been . . . Who had . . .

—And then . . .

AND THEN—

"*Goddamnit!*"

The Judge exploded, rapping his gavel sharply, once, twice, startling the whole courtroom, freezing it into a silence rarely, if ever, even in that hallowed atmosphere, surpassed.

All eyes upon him, there before them, gavel half-raised, face frozen in attitude of so recently delivered oath . . .

Moment passing.

People shifting in their seats, feet scraping, mumblings, and soft, titillated laughter, women's laughter, he was especially aware of women's laughter, and now subdued rumbling, men's laughter, rising, slowly, surely, rising . . .

John Carlton recovering himself, rapping fiercely . . .

"Silence! Enough now! Order! I'LL CLEAR THE COURT!"

Silence finally . . .

My Janet . . .

"Proceed, Counsel. When you're through we'll adjourn until tomorrow. Prepare your summing-up for then. Both of you. All right, proceed."

I'll fix the earliest possible date allowed by law . . .

His gaze fell now on the Press gallery. He saw Pent, *that Crusader* . . . He boiled. The fellow had been doing a series on some "celebrated" case of a prisoner in one of the Federal penitentiaries who had been kept in solitary confinement for forty-three years. *What was his complaint? Lucky to be alive,* That was it! *People like Pent caused a lot of damn trouble. Stirring up ignorant public hysteria on matters which should be left strictly in the hands of Responsible Officials.*

He glared at Pent.

What does a fellow like Pent know about that?

Print anything, just sell his rag . . .

What Does He Care About?

———————————————————15

. . . lord Tweedie-pounder . . .

After all, oh, when you think of it—
   summer elegance
   Lanvin castillo model belted at true waist
   scarf drape instead of collar
   nylon and silk patterned fabric
   white pearls throwing shadows on pale blue water . . .
   Oh Hoo!
   oh do

My Dear!
do do
oh dear   That One   red hair Round That One
White gloves
elbow length . . .
Elegant!
Quite.
What does it matter?
. . . *milk breasts, understand that, darling, lovely milk*
breasts, do you know that . . .
Beside her.
Handsome young man, beside her.
Still, somewhat—
Stoned . . .
She mused over him, saying his name.
She was sure, absolutely, it was his name . . .
Well spent.
Oh—night—
Well spent . . .
Nijinsky . . .
My God!
What a
Leap . . .

She stroked the young man, Prince Siegfried, beside
her . . .
She laughed, softly, she kissed him . . .

. . . *suckling them* . . .

At the dressing table, staring into the mirror, seeing him,
still on the bed, reflected there, and herself, her dressing
gown partly open, her breasts, soft, round, white and
lovely . . .
Loving.
Touching—
Her mother's breasts.
Stroking them . . .
they fed the two of us   did they   two of us   didn't they
She hung on, staring into the mirror, only.
She saw Carl, suddenly . . .

What Does It Matter Now

The young man was stirring. It was near noon. She would get him up now.

he was playing with it   he had taken it out of his pants and was playing with it   it was so small   silly small
IT WAS SMALL
wasn't it

why was he playing with it

She giggled, softly, suddenly, in the mirror . . .
Janet! Get him up now! The young scamp Scion, look at him! Up now! Give him your breast now. He needs your breast now. There, go on! Now!
She moved over to him. Somewhat unsteady, but, over to him.
. . . let him partake of your breast now . . .
She shook him, gently.
. . . that's what he needs now . . .
He was turning, moaning. She leaned over him. She lifted his head. She bared her breast and supported it before his mouth. She was smiling. She eased the nipple into his mouth. He, perhaps half-awake, began sucking now . . .
She was murmuring,
"There, *there now* . . ."
His hands moved to her breast.
They touched, held her breast.
Held, fondled, soft mother breast . . .

. . . she held him. Her mother held him. In the kitchen. She had seen her pick the little boy up, caress him, and kiss him . . . Janet stared . . . he was suckling, her mother had undone her blouse, her breast had come out . . . the baby sucked eagerly, happily, greedily . . . she smiled at him . . . she saw her mother smiling at him . . . she was cold . . . suddenly, all over, watching her . . . she stood silently, staring . . . her mother seemed unaware of her . . . she was there, she knew she was there, must have known she was there . . . ice cold . . . now she was ice cold . . . she tried to speak . . . breast, baby, mother . . . so cold . . . she tried to move . . . it would be all right . . . move . . . why

couldn't she move . . . now move . . . she couldn't move . . .

In Camden Town, they had a time of it. Jane took them all to a party there. She had friends there. In Camden Town, they were all there. From all over the world, everywhere, There! A great place. By the canal, rows and rows of buildings were boarded up and caving in. Some rows, only half boarded up. People lived in the other half. But that was the canal. The rest, a thriving, bustling place. Some places, maybe ten, fifteen shared a flat. *Cozy!* Not bad. Really. Very cozy! At this party, they had a time of it. Wonderful dark skins there. Sexy, supple Jamaicans, mainly. And Indians. Lots of friendly Indians.

Students, scholars. Some of them.

In the cozy flat, they had a great time. They danced and drank, wonderful music, all night.

She loved their walk, their talk . . .

"Huh honey? O.K.? *Now* honey—"

—*Tony!*

—Try a black one. *Jan!* You've never tried a black one?

Uproarious laughter.

Thumping.

Jumping, laughter . . .

"Good Good—Ho Jan—Real Good!"

—*Jan!*

—Well you said

—*All Night?*

—You

—*Did I?*

—Way!

—*Did I?*

—Go Way!

—*Jan*

—WILL YOU!

_____16

. . . near the place.

Not for a million years near the place. Nowhere. Ever

never again absolutely never ever than this to the place. What use to me? Absolutely what ever use now oh now To Me?

But she was near. Not even knowing . . . Walking.
And
In the place . . .

They were rehearsing. It was *Sleeping Beauty.*
. . . when, darling . . .
She saw her.
Her heart leaped.
Lovely.
She loved her.
Still lovely . . .

She tucked herself in the rear of the place, well out of sight. It was empty, save for the musicians and those in charge.

The music, rising. Aurora in *arabesque now*, turning, beautifully, perfectly . . . now . . .

. . . when, darling . . .

She closed her eyes, she leaned against a wall, in the shadows, the music coming to her, making its way deep into her. It found its roots there . . . She swayed . . .

. . . Rose-colored tutu, silk, embroidered with silver, ring of flowers about her hair . . . leap now . . . now . . . into the garden . . . the Queen caresses me . . . kisses me . . . her arms about me . . . four Princes seeking my hand, bowing, deeply, they dispute who shall be the first to kiss my hand . . . smile . . . my lovely smile . . . sur les pointes . . . turn, slowly, beautifully, conclude en arabesque . . . darling . . . Jan, Janet, Jan darling, arabesque . . . Spanish Prince, supported by him, series of turns, arabesques . . . the music, flowing . . . lift me, easily, high, touch the air, arching white arms, my white arms, lovely arms, above my head . . . descend, slowly, gently, touch the ground . . . turn, flee from the garden . . .

She opened her eyes.
She left the theatre.
Weak, trembling, she made her way out of the theatre . . .

HOW NICE

Janet, in bed, musing . . .

What, after all, my dear, oh you dear, is the essence of femininity? The absence of masculinity? The rudiments (vestiges?) are there. Darling! There. Observe the functional utility, will you, of the rod, rammed home, deep, deep home . . .

My darling . . .
The rammed, the rammers.
Revolves life, dance eternal en suspensio . . .
Oh Suspensio!

Save in the sadness, only in the sadness, learning in sadness, there, finally, all sadness. All in sadness. Death sadness. Stiffness. Final stiffness. Inevitable. There, where the saddest of sadness . . . someone dear . . . so near . . .
How Dull Life Without A Joy A KICK Really!
The rod . . .
Femininity adores the rod.
Desperately needs the rod.
Lures the rod . . .
Plunge, Plunge Deep The Rod!
Engulf.
Retain the rod . . .
Love Rod!
Fragile issue of flesh. Precarious, so fragile issue . . .
You knew . . .

Once you knew!

My God
My
When Will I

CAN I BE ALIVE AGAIN

51

She was supposed to meet Jane and Olive for dinner. But she forgot about it. She wandered the streets, alone. She felt good, though sad, *herself,* alone. She walked slowly, dusk, shadows growing, all around her . . .

A young couple, kissing, nearby on a bench. Young man's hand caressing the girl, tenderly, stroking her, so tenderly, touching her breasts . . .

She turned from them . . .

Cool, clean, August night. She reached Waterloo Bridge. She walked halfway across it. She stopped. London skyline, lovely skyline, Somerset House, she stared at Somerset House, lovely, loving Somerset House . . . A sudden gust of wind caught her. She shivered, drew her coat closer about her. Big Ben tolling the hour. She turned to see. Turned, slowly, to see . . .

. . . A little girl, she had come to Europe for the first time. She stood with her parents and heard the great clock. She asked, "Who winds it up then, Daddy?" He had smiled, briefly, had explained to her, carefully, tenderly . . . Her mother, leaning against the railing, murmuring, half smiling, turned to him . . .

Time, urgently, cruelly, whispered to her, a voice bred in stillness, timeless, surging out of stillness, relentless offspring of stillness, circling, seeking her, swooping and touching her, resting its hand on her . . .

She moved off the bridge now, retraced her steps. She was very sleepy, suddenly. She wanted nothing so much as to lie down and sleep now . . .

A man, walking toward her, stopped her. In the streetlight she saw him. He touched the brim of his hat. He smiled. Trim moustache smile. She looked at him.

"Can I be of assistance, miss?"

For a long moment, quietly, she looked at him.

She drew her coat closer about her.

She turned.

She moved on, past him . . .

—Darling:
How are you? We all think of you. Only a little card? My my! I wrote to Clarise about you. We are all well. Poppa sends his love. I'm sure he will write you . . . Take care of yourself, dear . . . see Ned—dear Ned . . . he's still up there—Cheshire—near Budworth—grand place—Shall I write him?

Dear Mother.
She held the letter, after reading it, a long while, staring blankly at it, into it, through it . . .

Ned, go to hell . . .
Clarise—*God!*
oh god
She laid the letter aside.
She chased her aunt from her thoughts . . .

A brief note, from him:
—What are you doing over there?
I'd like to hear from you . . .

. . . beautiful, haunting, ever-quickening. High, high she leaped, yet so gracefully . . . they floated together, through the still air, with the waltz, part of the waltz . . . gradually, slowly, the music died . . . she was again in her chair . . . the room was empty . . . she picked up the rose . . .

She held the letter.

In a chair, near the window.
She sat quietly, looking out of the window . . .

At a coffee bar, an interesting coffee bar, tucked away in charming Soho, she sat with Jack, an American around thirty.

She loved Soho. It was one of her favorite parts of London. Of course, one had to watch one's step there. But—how fascinating!

She had landed here, one night, after some party.

She had met Jack.

They had gone to many galleries since.

He was studying here.

He was going to be a great painter. He had told her that. His father was in oil, Texal oil, he hated his father. He had also told her that. He had taken one degree at Columbia, another at Cambridge. What in—wasn't quite clear to her. Now —here—he was studying—

"What are you studying?" she ventured, sipping her coffee.

There was just a pause.

"The beginnings of things," he replied, lighting a cigarette.

She let it go at that.

He lit a cigarette for her.

"You certainly are beautiful."

"Well, thank you."

He studied her.

"Yes, sir, really beautiful."

"Thank you."

"Let me paint you."

"Of course—only—"

"That's all right—it won't take long—!"

"Well, that's good, now."

" 'Course it's good now! You've got Soul, gal, you're all Soul! You know that?"

"Do I have to know that?"

They were silent a while.

She smiled at him.

"You shouldn't be here," he offered, soberly.

She waited, puffing her cigarette. Interesting specimens, coming, going, some waving to her. Someone, below, was strumming a guitar.

"I know all about you."

She knew that.

"Wrong place, absolutely wrong place for you."

The coffee bar.

"The British are a pack of bastards."

Not the coffee bar.

"Absolute, complete—*pack of bastards*."

They were silent. She stared at him. He took a deep breath. His eyes were upon her, bright, deep eyes upon her.

"Nastiest, crumbiest bunch of people you'd want to hope to run into anywhere. Why are you here? Don't let anyone kid you about the wonders of their culture, personal freedom, integrity, et cetera et cetera bullcrap. All sheer bullcrap, absolute bullcrap."

He took a long sip of coffee.

"Look at your so-called middle classes, the so-called 'bulwark,' 'framework,' or 'backbone' of the nation. You ought to get to know them. I've been here long enough. More selfish, insulated, insular bunch of bastards you'd have a hard time running across anywhere, but anywhere! They stink, from head to toe, very bottoms of their toes. My God, what critters! Listen, Janet, I wouldn't give two cents for the bunch of them! I mean, all of them—lower, middle, middle middle, upper—all of them! You want to know something? If they want to test H-Bombs, why don't they do it here? Right here! The bastards! Lousy bunch of hypocritical bastards!"

Curling, the smoke held her, fascinated her. It turned this way, that, hovered, traced back on itself, and, finally, dispersed itself.

"I see," she said, finally.

And, gently,

"Why don't you leave then?"

He sighed a long sigh, a bitter sigh.

"It's worse over there, Jan, you know that."

A bass, clarinet and piano had started up in the place, in the basement. The tones reached her, caressed her.

"Why not the Continent?" she ventured.

"France—" she added.

His hand went through his hair. He stroked his forehead. He sat back in his chair, staring downward.

"I've thought of that, seriously thought of that," he muttered.

"You know where I think would be the place, though?" he shot at her.

She waited.

"Spain."

She showed her surprise.

"Yes, Spain. Why not? There, at least, they make no bones about it. They're Fascists, and know it, and nobody pretends otherwise. There, everybody's out in the open with it."

He paused.

"And, you can live dirt cheap there," he added . . .

He fell silent.

The jazz tune came to her, felt so good to her. She felt the quick surge within, responding to it. She leaned back and smiled to it, tapped out the rhythm to it . . .

"You remember Shanty?" Jack said.

She tried to think. She remembered.

"Oh, yes."

"He's doing scripts for TV now—"

"Still bobbing, though?"

They laughed.

The fellow had a way of bobbing up and down before you, when talking to you.

"He made me seasick. You think I'm kidding, Jack boy?"

"Nice fellow, though. Don't think he'll be going back. He likes it here!"

"There you are, now."

Jack was grinning, "Yeh. Screwed now."

"My goodness! Jack boy!"

He brightened. He had hold of things.

"Listen, though—I'll tell you one thing here I'll miss, really miss—"

"What's that, then?" she queried.

"The women!"

"Oh?"

"Oh ho! The young ones especially! I can tell you, confidentially: *they know what it's for.* They *love* what it's for!"

Pause.

Janet, "What's it for?"

He studied her. She laughed, softly, at him.

"I'm not kidding, Jan!"

"I know you're not."

"They don't care who they do it with. Black, yellow, Turk, Indian—these gals are great ones! Liberal, wholesome, lovely gals. Jesus, though, I feel sorry for them! Just think, look what most of them have to wind up with! Keerist, Holy Mo! Lucky ones are those who marry the darkies, or Indians—hell, they're the ones, the Indians—poor gals, the jerks they wind up with! If you ask me, that's the way to straighten out this lousy island—marry off all these sweet things to the darkies and Indians, bring in enough just to do that—only way to take care of things and don't think I'm kidding!"

He leaned closer to her. She was quiet now, puffing her cigarette, looking at him.

"They sure know how to, Jan, honey. They're just about World Champions, believe me, honey."

He threw his arms out—

"I just LOVE them!"

Pause.

Silence.

Applaud now?

He slumped back in his seat now. He puffed a cigarette and blew out a big cloud of smoke. He was mumbling—

". . . what peaches . . . *peaches* . . ."

And then. "They marry these creeps. Jesus! And in a few years they're just like them—They Become Like Them! Ain't it tragic?"

He lapsed into silence, other things on his mind now. He looked about the place. He looked all around the place. His gaze came to rest. He uttered a scoff. He said to her, "See that s.o.b.?"

She looked.

"He's a critic. Big Deal London Critic. Weekly. Makes, breaks plays—sometimes. Books, too—"

She gazed at the critic. A very young critic.

Jack laughed now. "You know, if that guy had brains, honest to God, they'd rattle. They really would rattle. Want to talk to him?"

She sighed, "I don't think so."

"A bastard. Real bastard."

Hands on the table, he was just before her, looking at her.

"I Hate The Bastards!"

She yawned, covered it. She said, "Jackie, I'm so tired. Better get back now. Really better—"

She started to rise.

He said, "Can I come with you?"

She sighed, she nodded.

She let him come with her . . .

21

Clarise Longhorn read her sister's letter.

Dear sister Linda's letter.

She wrote such good letters. They bubbled over with news, all sorts of news. This time it was Janet . . .

"Poor Janet!" Clarise sighed, aloud.

"Poor, poor Janet!" she added, gratuitously.

Feeling nothing within, however . . .

When Janet had been on top of her world, Clarise had been petrified with envy. Indeed, during that period, she had come down with a strange ailment, a sort of paralysis of her left arm and leg, very distressing, painful. The doctors, mystified, had not been able to do anything with it. Outwardly, like the rest of the clan, she had been thrilled, proud of Janet. Within, she only prayed it would come to an end. *Soon.* She longed for it—age, accident, what have you—so long as it *did* END. Clarise had almost given up hope, had indeed plunged into a nasty depression, when, miraculously, her wish had been granted. Ever since, she had thrived, her health restored, always welcoming any and all additional *little bits of news* about Janet . . .

Dear Janet.

Bits of news. She feasted on them. She had gained twenty pounds, no less, since *The End* on them . . .

Just this morning, over breakfast, she had said to her Roland, "Dear. I must go on a diet. That's final."

"That *sooooh?*" he rumbled, like an old volcano.

"Yes. I certainly must. If I keep this up, I'll soon be a real *Fat Mammy!*"

This was a very sore point with the Senator at the moment. He was a good Southerner and what was happening in the country, in the South, all the uppity nigguhs trying to get all the good nigguhs to demand their "rights," was getting him down, making life downright miserable for him. It was all the fault of the damn Federal government, "supreme" court and so on of course plus the pinkos. Red white-pinkos from the North, no decent folk involved in any of it, that was sure. *No Suh.* So, the very mention of that fine traditional word reserved for the American female nigguh set him boiling. To top it all, he had just been reading an item in the paper about the situation.

He muttered something, inaudibly.

"What, dear?" Clarise queried, somewhat peeved.

"These goddamn nigguhs," he rumbled, "goddamn, hon, look here, just in the next county they're trying to get four of them into the school! *White School!* What you think of that? Ever thought you'd ever see the day here, now? Didya, hon?"

"Shhh—" Clarise cautioned, noticing Mary, their maid, approaching with the coffee now.

Roland, looking up, spoke more quietly, "By God, we'll put a stopper on that now—"

Adding, "And how, now . . ."

"Coffee, ma'am?" Mary said, sweetly.

She was a pleasant, good-looking young Negress.

Well-developed.

The Senator looked at her.

He liked her.

Yes, really quite liked her.

She was a good nigguh, she gave no trouble . . .

And besides—

. . . What tits! b'Jesus, Those Tits! . . .

. . . Someday . . .

He quite trembled within, thinking of it.

"Some for me, too, Mary," he mumbled.

She smiled, nodded, and poured his coffee.

She left the room.

Clarise looked at him.

He drank his coffee.

Clarise said to him, "What were you looking at? I saw you. Don't you think I saw you?"

"What's that, deah?" he queried innocently.

"Don't pull that on me!" she bristled.

"What, deah?" he persisted.

She glared at him.

. . . by God we don't straighten things out soon some nigguh'll be gettin into huh . . .

"Now now, deah," he chided her, murmuring to her . . .

He reached out and patted her hand.

"Get hold-a-yourself, deah, there, deah . . ."

She did soon, and he darted off, all two hundred fifty pounds of him. He had to attend an early-morning session of his favorite committee. Then he had to attend some luncheon, and make a speech at that luncheon.

. . . goddamn luncheon . . .

Alone with her thoughts, after his departure, Clarise settled down. She mused, snugly . . .

—what does dear Lin think of it? My, my, she certainly seems pretty upset though. Maybe that's because Jan hasn't written though. That's probably it, I bet you dough. Ho Ho, dough. Sweet dough. Lovin dough! Ho ho. I hardly believe —what the dickens! dickens dickens and chickens. Who can

know it? Ever would know it? There's the depths of it. She seems upset. Is she upset? I hope Jan sees Ned. I must write her. Lin says: write her. Oh, I'll write her. Ned loves it there. Been a long time there. Long, long time there. Charming place. Really. When last was I—oh, two summers ago. Do hope she sees him. Oh, I must write her. Dear Ned. What a nice man. So at home over there. Has such a nice place. Say, charming place. Oh, quite charming place. When was I—oh, of course. Of course of course. Cigarettes. That Mary and cigarettes what can she—did you see him? God, did you see him . . . Poor Jan. Off again, all alone. Last time—when was that—oh, last time—oh, what a time. Down came the House of Cards, whole b'jingoed house of cards. Whoops! Humpty Dump. Put together. Whoops. Hmm. Hummm Hmm. Ha. Ha ha ha hmmm . . .

She was laughing, softly, quite carried away now.

"Did you call, ma'am?"

It was Mary.

"Where's the cigarettes?" Clarise asked, icily now . . .

—*I'll keep my eye on him . . .*

Laying aside *Time* magazine, stimulated, inspired and uplifted by his reading there, the Senator was thinking . . .

The nature of man, the absolute, final, distinguishing, primal essence of man is—*Morality*.

Man has a Moral Nature.

He alone lives according to Moral Principles.

Lacking these Principles, he is a—sub-man, a bad-man.

And when far gone, really far gone—a plain Animal.

That, after all, is at the core of us. Ain't it the truth now? Ain't we all animals now? That, after all, *is* the core of us. That—and shit—is the core of us.

But there's more to us. We are more. We are—

H.B.H.S.

Human Beings, *Homo Sapiens*.

Sapiens, by God, Sapiens.

Something new, completely new, under the sun. When all is said and done, when all the cards are counted, that's the thing with us, sure, sure as Hell with us: the State of our Soul, our Moral Soul.

Am I honest? And, am I faithful? Do I know right from wrong and do I defy temptation?

The Moral Nature of man is the basis of our whole society, our Civilization.

Somewhere, back there, I don't know where, who knows

where? An animal, maybe an ape, turned into a human being and received God's own gift of Morality, in short a Moral Nature. That's it in a nutshell. Yes, man, a nutshell.

That's the situation in the world today. We have a fundamentally Moral Society in this country of ours, we base our lives, our way of doing things, on Moral Principles, and we try to live by them, though God knows how frail the human kind can be, how strong the pull of temptation, how powerful the urge to return to our primal, animal state, which is always there, lurking, calling to us. Yes, man, calling to us. In the world there are two Principles, rising out of our fundamental Dilemma: (1) the Good (2) the Bad.

Now, Our society, our Nation, basically, on the whole, for the most part—In God we trust—is *Good*.

And theirs, on the other hand, *their* way of life, *their* civilization, is Bad.

Not only Bad, but False, utterly False. The whole setup is an arch betrayal of Man's soul, Moral Soul.

Since this is so, our duty is undoubtedly, yes, my friends, to be constantly on the alert, on guard against agents of their devil-world. These agents are everywhere, and they have only one goal: to subvert, to damage, and eventually to destroy *Our* way of life. They are clever, cunning, and all about us.

And most of them are disguised as *eggheads*. I said *eggheads*.

Tucked away in some corner of some university, or writing for some subversive paper or magazine, or acting, or painting, or some such thing. All "smart" boys, very "smart" boys. And we even have them over here from Europe, spending a year or so here, writing, or something, like that "smart" boy on that New York magazine, that troublemaker. But we have the goods on him. We've had our eyes on him since he first landed over here. Look at the people he associates with! My God, all subversive! Every one, a *known subversive!* The sort of people who want to destroy Our society—change it, they call it—yes, I'll say, I'll just say—change it! Well, a few months in our cooler here, if we can arrange it, might teach him, might help to teach him.

Too bad so many of them have no steady place of employment, where you can get at them, uproot them.

Damn writers, painters, actors, they're the ones.

College professors. There's my meat! Just put the finger on them once, and they've had it. More or less for life. Those college presidents, administrators, they're O.K. They help out, cooperate all they can, just give them the word, and they'll do the rest. Bend over backwards to do the rest! Just let a prof with the finger on him get a job anywhere! And let his so-called friends try to help him. We'll get them too! You bet we'll get them too!

The Good.

The Bad.

That's how it is, there's no getting away from it.

We are the Good.

And They're the Bad.

We have the responsibility of preserving, at all costs, the moral Fabric of Our Society, and, ultimately, the World's society.

On the alert, constantly, against subversives and agitators, trouble-making Red white-trash all over the place, especially the Jew-North.

They're all around.

We'll ferret them out, that's our job, that's my Committee's job, to ferret them out.

We'll see today what we can do with this foreign fella, this smart-alec British fella. By God we'll see, and how we'll see. The nerve, huh? Comes over here as a guest, making a good little pile out of it to boot, and holy po there he goes, writing subversive TV programs, signing his name to advertisements in newspapers criticizing the foreign activities of the Government and so on. Imagine, signing his name to something completely against what the President of the United States has been advocating in Public this whole past year! Imagine, eh? By God we'll show him! Make him wish he had kept his nose in his own little ol Island! Half of them are damn Reds anyhow there. *Labour*, they call it. Not all that sure about the other half either. First we'll find out who his friends are. Then, where the *gold* comes from . . .

Our Great Democracy, founded on the sacred Principles of our Founding Fathers, Liberty, Justice, for all, Declaration of Independence, Constitution, and all, must not Flounder, I repeat, *Flounder*, on the treacherous rocks of Internal Subversion as well as Foreign Interference no matter what or who it might be so help me God so long as I live that is my task my Committee's task and We Won't Flounder . . .

They succeeded in killing off that Great Patriot Joe, but by God we carry on, oh yes, we exist and carry on and will Do Our Duty so long as one Red Bandit exists and there are plenty of them all right alrighty we are infiltrated through and throughout with them, just so long as one single one exists with their cunning Infiltration Tactics, Fluoridation, Subterfuges, Disguises, Eating into Our Body Politic, Our Great Nation, This Gem, This Only Paradise on God's Own Earth,

Sweet Earth, I, Roland S. Longhorn, stand and defend it, always, now, forever, so long as I Live, So Help Me God, I SWEAR TO ALMIGHTY GOD. . . .

"I'll fix this British fella, I'll fix him good, suh—"

He muttered . . .

"Senator, sir—"

They had arrived. He hadn't even noticed they had arrived. Only Jimmy's voice now made that clear.

He maneuvered out of the car, with Jimmy's help.

"Ah—Right—Thank you, Jimmy—"

"Same time, Senator, sir?"

"Same time. Be prompt, Jimmy boy—"

"Yes, sir, Senator, sir."

He roared off to the parking lot.

"Horse Balls, sir, *Senator, sir . . .*"

He sang out, roaring along.

"Wasn't that rather odd?"

"I don't think so, Senator, no, I really don't—"

"You don't?"

"No. I don't."

"Young man, do you realize you are a guest in this country?"

"I do."

"Do you realize that what you appended your signature to directly contradicts the statement issued just the other day by the President of the United States, the statement stating clearly what a menace that island has become to the western hemisphere?"

"I realize that."

"You realize it, do you? Then why did you?"

"What?"

"Sign it!"

"I must say, Senator—*Longhorn*, is it?—I hadn't realized that in your country it was no longer possible to express an opinion contrary to one held by your highest popularly elected Official and, presumably, Chief Defender of your Constitution and Bill of Rights, including the Right of Free Speech."

There was a silence. Shuffling of papers. Feet. The Senator cleared his throat. He took a sip of water.

"Who are your friends?" he resumed.

"What do you mean?"

"Here—in this country—who are your friends—"

"I don't see why I should tell you that. I don't see at all that you have any right to ask that."

The Senator stared in astonishment.

He thumped the table.

"See here, young man, now look here—you know where you are? This is a *Committee* of the *United States Senate.* Do you understand that? We're not Members of Parliament, understand that. You'll answer the questions or face a Contempt charge. Is that clear to you? As easy as anything we'll slap a Contempt charge on you. You see that?"

The young man looked straight at him.

"Well, Senator, if it's going to make you feel any better, please do so. But before that, allow me to tell you—"

"Never mind, now, just answer my question! You're not here to *tell* us, or make speeches—just *answer the questions!*"

"—that, in my opinion, and, I must say, in the opinion of any intelligent foreign observer, this Committee, its *modus operandi,* its persecution and prying into the affairs of anyone and everyone, ruining careers, lives of many of them, is the height of stupidity, cruelty, and folly—a travesty of all your country supposedly stands for—a prize gift to the very "enemy," the very system, you're supposedly all against. Sir, I tell you, unequivocally, it and things like it have smothered your country. If their most cunning propaganda and intelligence specialists had devised it, they couldn't possibly have done better. They would all, I am sure, have received the highest awards, straight away. You warm the very heart and soul of friend Kosygin—*Mao*—"

Roland roared, "Enough! ENOUGH! Will you answer my questions?"

"No, sir, I will not!"

"We hold you in Contempt! Young man, do you hear? *We hold you in Contempt!* DISMISSED NOW! *Show him out now!*"

22

Morning.

Staring out at the morning, London, her London morning . . .

Olive bustled about her, cute in a new blue thing. All around her.

"Sweet."

"Isn't it?"

Jane held her hand.

"When shall we see you again? Do make it soon. On your way back! Are you going back? Oh, stay! Why don't you stay? Shall we come with you?"

Olive, "What fun!"

Laughter.

Some tears.

Tiny, dewdrop tears.

"Good-bye, dears—"

"Oh, dear—"

"My dears!"

"Dear Dear—"

White hands, waving . . .

So white—

Waving . . .

_____23

. . . *Her mother's hand, hanging out of the sleeve of a brown dress, groped for her* . . .

. . . *a voice whispered,* Chauviré . . . *Swan Lake* . . . *she saw her* . . . *she was filled with admiration for her* . . . "Yvette, développé" *she murmured to her* . . . *exquisite pas de deux* . . . *the Prince swayed her, gently, to and fro* . . . *he lifted her* . . . *higher* . . . *he held her* . . . *higher, higher* . . . *if she could fly* . . . *higher* . . . *a dizzy height* . . . *higher* . . . *She was flying* . . . *higher* . . .

She awoke, breathless, in her Paris hotel room. It was dark. She was alone. She was frightened. She didn't know where she was. She tried to come out of it. She knew she had to come out of it. She groped, hoping to find a light switch. She stopped and turned at the sound of something. Her small clock, ticking. The luminous numbers stared out at her. She reached out, desperately needing it to hold on to. She drew it to her. Just after 2 A.M. She saw that. She understood that. She tried once again to find a light switch, but could not. Still holding the clock she left the bed and went to a window now. The curtains were fluttering. White curtains, fluttering. Her heart calmed somewhat. She looked out. A few cars were passing. Some people were walking. She read a neon sign, not too far away. The dream weakened. Suddenly, it was clear. She knew where she was. She remembered. Softly, she was weeping. She looked out at the night, she heard its sounds, she sat down, weeping . . .

A letter from him.

She carried it around. In the afternoon, late afternoon, in a park, she read it . . .

—*let me hear from you*—

She held it, staring at it . . .

Jamestown. Pocahontas. She stands there, arms outstretched, leaning forward slightly, welcoming the sick, exhausted colonists, offering her aid to them . . .

She is beautiful.

Hands.
Hot hands.
Hot hands on her breasts now.
   oh
Explode.
Explode now.
Darling   my darling   darling

      NOW

Tomorrow.
      come sit in the park
      green park
      come
      now.

In the small club the band was playing a cha-cha. She felt

good, how she loved dancing the cha-cha. He danced so well. She held close to him now, her breasts pressed against him.

His name was Paul, he was a young man, a movie director. He told her all about his ideas, new ideas, for movies. She loved listening to him. She had met him earlier in the evening at a party, a very nice, French party. There had been dancers there. She had steered clear of them.

"You don't know what fun I'm having," she told him now.

"You're a marvelous partner, you dance beautifully," he murmured to her.

She smiled, she thanked him, "Wonderful rhythm, the cha-cha. I love the cha-cha."

They danced a long while . . .

At the table they sipped wine, smoked cigarettes, and talked about movies. *He* talked about movies. She listened. There was no way of stopping him, he would be capable of talking all night and all day about movies.

"Is material hard to come by?" she asked him.

He looked at her.

"That's just the problem!" he said at last. "You've hit on it, perfectly."

"How marvelous. Lucky!"

He looked again. He held it.

"You would think it wouldn't be—but it is, *supremely*. It's the biggest obstacle to overcome, absolutely."

She heard the band.

She loved it.

It was a mambo.

A fine timelessness . . .

She said to him, her face brushing his, "Do you want to make a film of me?"

"Wouldn't that be a marvelous film though?"

"Is that why you took me out?"

"Don't be silly now."

"Why did you take me out?"

"Come on, now . . ."

. . . *Hotel du Paris* . . .

The mambo.

Loving the mambo . . .

. . . *Monte Carlo* . . .
. . . music . . . movement . . . music and movement . . .
I was in my room. I heard the music. It was magic. I remem-
ber . . . I moved toward it. Ever, always, toward it . . . In
the dark I moved toward it . . . Back, back, touch time with
both hands . . . toward it . . .
What was he then . . .
The Frenchman, holding her, said to her,
"What are you thinking?"
Hardly a seed then . . .
"Nothing, nothing."
"I know you're thinking."
"Tell me."
"Shall I tell you?"
"You can't tell me."
"I wish you would."
She sighed.
"Your country's so sick."
He smiled.
"That's not what you're thinking."
She persisted. "Why it's worse now than ever. Didn't you
realize?"
"You don't trust me. That's why you won't tell me."
"Is it?"

He had a charming apartment. She sat in a cozy antique
sofa and looked at the collection of drawings, paintings, hung
all about her. A window looked out upon most of the city, it
seemed. A wide avenue. *There was the city . . .*

"Where did you learn French so well?" he asked her, near
to her.
She hesitated, then sat back. She sipped her drink. He had
made a lovely drink.
"Sir," she smiled at him, "I was brought up well."
"Yes—ah yes—I'd heard that."
He paused, sipped his drink.
"Was your family—so rich, then?"
A pause. She put her glass down.
"Stinking rich, then."
Another pause.

"It surprises me."

"Why?"

"I don't know. It surprises me."

She looked, she smiled.

"Your drink's a marvelous success, Paul."

"Thank you."

A pause.

"Can I have more?"

A longer pause.

"More?"

"My god, *more!*"

She kissed him.

His arms were about her, caressing her . . .

. . . *Late afternoon, her room, late autumn sun . . . she stood, sur les pointes, before the mirror, turning, watching herself in the mirror . . . The door opened. He was there. She saw him in the mirror . . . in the doorway . . . He stood in the doorway, watching her. She turned, slowly. She saw him. A slight movement, hands above her head, fingertips, touching . . . He entered, closed the door, gently . . . She barely heard the door . . . His eyes, upon her . . . She loved him. She was aware only of love for him . . . He had always watched her practice, from long back. Often, quietly, he stayed as long as she. When there was need for music he played the records for her . . . But he had stayed away. Now, for a long while, some months now, he had stayed away . . . she had missed him, waited for him . . . Relief, warmth now, all through her . . . She had been tired, doing poorly, pushing herself . . . New life . . . She was smiling at him. She felt tears forming . . . He watched her . . . She went into arabesque, extending herself slowly, beautifully . . . There was music . . . He had put a record on . . . Swan Lake . . . She danced, a long while, to it . . . he watched her . . .*

. . . Over. It was over. She stood still. Watching him. Perfectly still, a long while, watching . . . He was moving. She was aware of him, moving . . . She turned, sur les pointes, her arms two wings now, moving . . . Near her. He was near her . . . Now before her . . . Dark eyes, meeting hers . . . a long time, upon hers . . . The eyes, within her . . . They were within her . . . She felt him, loved, within her . . . her heart raced . . . white hands, her hands, moving . . . upon him, his face, gently, caressing it . . . His hands, moving . . . slowly . . . touching her . . . they were touching her

. . . she encouraged them . . . Hands, over her . . . His hands, gliding, over her . . . Hands on her young breasts, young warm breasts, loving them there . . . shoulders . . . she touched his hands on her shoulders . . . gliding, gently, with them . . . her back, her waist, her hips now . . . warm, trembling, heart pounding now . . . his hands on their own now, gliding, her thighs now . . . She held him to her, she felt him, his warmth, his maleness, against her . . . Her mouth, lips, parting, seeking . . . against his . . . a long time, wet, seeking . . . my body . . . he held her . . . white body . . . she was falling, taking him with her . . . "Carl" . . . upon her . . . "Carl" . . . she felt him, she was wild for him . . . "YES CARL" *. . . her garment slipping . . .*

"TAKE ME!" she screamed, tearing his back with her nails.

The Frenchman, uttering a short cry of pain, lunged into her . . . again, and again, deep into her . . .

Dawn.
In his arms.
She said to him, murmuring,
"Fine . . . so fine . . ."
And,
"I loathe you . . . *God how I loathe you . . . only . . .*"

. . . applause . . . wave after wave . . . no end to it . . . she held on to it . . . desperately now, she held on to it . . . yet, so tired . . . ever . . . tired . . . she wouldn't go out again . . . just couldn't go out again . . . Bernice near her, kissing her, happy, smiling at her . . . corps all about her . . . excited, fluttering, all about her, touching her, trying to touch her . . . the ovation went on . . . she had to go out again . . . Bernice, urging her out again . . . holding her hand, urging her, gently, out again . . . one more . . . she said . . . only once more . . . the corps *made way for her . . . curtain parting for her . . . great roaring . . . huge bouquets . . . she plucked a rose for her partner . . . she kissed it, smiling, handed it to him . . . she bowed low . . . deeply, gratefully . . .*

Big
so big
IT'S SO BIG

. . . with the waltz . . . carried by it . . . swooping, reaching ends, beginnings, everything . . . Time's end, knowing it . . . reaching out, touching it . . . entire corps with her now, swaying, about her, swift, dazzling . . . among them . . . leap . . . soar . . . a moment in time now . . . lovely white moment in time now . . .

I in myself for myself and what in place of dying DYING may interpose intertwine interweave intercede cannot hope in the gambit desperate gambit My Gambit to presume Assume proclivity with nativity in myself ever for myself nothingness beingness ravished beingness mortals balanced momentarily precariously OH GOD PRECARIOUSLY the precipice hurtling falling forever and ever falling and nothingness darkness and Nothingness Nothing NOTHINGNESS

ever . . .

In myself.

. . . Vevey . . . lovely Vevey . . . we were in Vevey . . . what happened in Vevey . . . God I loved Vevey

my

lovely

Vevey.

Isn't it

24

In a country house, not too far from Paris, she sat and talked with Madame Saint-Ange, an old patron of ballet, who could talk easily of Diaghilev, who had helped support Diaghilev . . .

And recipient of a note from Bernice, uring her to "inquire about" Janet.

A message had reached Janet. Such a sweet message. She couldn't resist it.

She sat and chattered with her, splendid old lady.

Somewhere, a violin echoed, someone had turned on some music. Tschaikovsky, Violin Concerto. She sat quietly now, listening to it . . .

"Do you like it?"

"Yes—I always have."

"It is magnificent . . ." she paused, she was smiling, "I'm so glad you came. I was terribly afraid you wouldn't come."

Janet returned the smile.

"The Opéra—your last time in Paris—it wasn't so long ago! I was there—I came to see you, afterwards—do you recall? Superb! *Superb evening,* dear Janet. You taught us all something. We thought we knew everything! My dear—"

She sat back, beaming at Janet.

"Paris was yours, that evening!"

The old woman leaned forward slightly, her voice was very quiet now. "I had no idea you were here. Who knew? You should have told me. My dear—I wish you had told me—"

She leaned closer. "I have slippers—" She paused, she spoke urgently now, "Couldn't you—just for me—*here*—in private—"

Janet looked at her. A long while, quietly, she looked at her.

At last a voice, not her own, yet hers, only,

"No, Madame."

The old woman sat back in her chair. Her head turned slightly to one side now. She was listening. She looked at Janet. The gaze was warm, yet unhappy, fully on Janet now.

She heard her breathing, they sat quietly, a long while.

The music ended. Janet went to her. She leaned over and kissed her. The old woman smiled, took her hand. It gripped

her firmly. She felt the warmth and strength in it. She was
surprised at the strength in it . . .

"Good-bye, Madame—"

The old woman spoke, murmuring something.

The voice was there, murmuring good-bye, something . . .
Janet left her.

<hr>

25

HOW NICE

. . . right foot . . . trembling . . . petits battements . . .

She looked at the clock.

*. . . in the hallway, main hallway, of her home: Titian, a
Delacroix, a Picasso, but no Cézanne, a Turner, Vlaminck, a
Constable, Latour, the Cézanne would be upstairs, her father
insisted it be upstairs . . .* Hamilton always makes fun of it
*. . . Degas, of course the Degas . . . she was in the hallway,
near the clock, she looked at the Degas . . . two dancers,
young girls, one sur les pointes, arms en attitude . . . the
other leaning toward her, left foot flat, turned out, arms à bas
port bras . . . white, diaphanous, knee-length skirts, black
neck bands, roses in the hair of one . . . lovely girls . . .
lovely young girls . . . the Vlaminck, thatched cottages, red
gash of road, golden fields on the left, an angry sky . . . She
stared at the angry sky . . .*

She closed the book.

*. . . her father, near her, said very clearly, softly, to her
. . . What do you think of it . . .*

my breasts
two treasures.

. . . What do you think of them . . .
lovely nippled treasures all men desire
. . . hands, how they love their hands on them . . .
fondle them
gently
. . . oh gently your hands gently lovely tips gently cup my breasts your hands so gently white breasts your . . .
WHAT DO YOU THINK OF THEM?

_____26

Jerry, a jazzman, American jazzman, trumpet and—some-times—only sometimes—alto sax man, held her close to him, and rolled truly with her, synchronizing his movements with her, marvelous, undulating movements, with her . . .
    soon
    soon will
    SOON WILL THE WORLD END.

In a booth in the club they sat, late, nearly dawn. They listened to a blues tune. Near each other, what remained of their drinks before them, cigarette smoke curling, and ris-ing . . .
He was saying, softly, "I'll tell you about it. Want me to tell you about it?"
Pause.
"Tell me about it."
"The lift."
"Yes."
"Trip to the moon."
"Yes."
"Out of yourself, right out of yourself. Yet, in with your-self, right there, in *close* with yourself."
"Yes."
"Get me?"
"I understand that."
"Sure, you understand that, sure sure you do—Jan, you understand that—"
"Go on, Jerry."
"More drinks?"

"Make mine the same—"

"Waiter!"

"He's gone, Jerry—"

"Bartender! Hey, Bartender—"

"Bartender!"

They got their drinks . . .

"There's life—there's death—This is Life. Jan, the beat, the melody, the lift, Jan—I want life—I prefer life—"

"Life!"

"Let's get outa here."

"Can we get out of here?"

"I know the way outa here—"

"You work here—"

"That's right, I work here—"

"You haven't played all night—"

"That's right, I haven't—"

"They'd probably like you to—"

"Would you like me to?"

"My god, I'd love you to—"

He stared at her. He turned to the three musicians, resting now, near the bandstand.

"Hey!"

"Hello, there!" one answered.

"Listen, get my horn out!"

"Oh, man, his horn out!"

Laughter, soft laughter, soon gone laughter . . .

He said to her, "I'm going to play now."

She said, "Where? Oh great. Terrific now—"

He said, "Here. Tonight. I'm going to play my first tune tonight. Now. They pay me. It's about time I played my first tune now."

"Terrific Now!"

"My horn's up there. That's where my horn is . . ."

He maneuvered himself to the bandstand. He spoke with the men. They started to play. He led them. It was a Blues tune. Good beat, good, solid blues tune. It rose, it fell, she loved it, coming through to her. He played well. He played so well. She closed her eyes, listening, the horn was alive now . . .

Dancing, by herself, slowly, her eyes still closed, remembering, the tune now, alive in her, soft slow beat, in her . . . dawn, moving in, watched her . . . the few still in the place, the players, Jerry, watching her . . .

. . . In her white car they had gone to the club, striking

*south on the highway, turning off when they reached the sign,
he had told her . . . He had wanted to take her there . . .
good dance music, jazz too . . . He led her onto the floor.
He danced with her, holding her close, so close to him . . .
He spoke to her, softly, tenderly . . . She moved, easily, with
him, part of him, at that moment, loving him . . . She told
him, whispering to him, I love you, Fred . . . Do you mean
that . . . Yes—Mean That . . .*

. . . swing Giselle . . .
    hurry
. . . now Giselle . . .

FLURRY

*. . . the window. She was so tired. Gray clouds moving.
Near them a few wisps of white, hovering. She sat back in
the chair, breathing heavily, sweating. She had finally mas-
tered the new ballet. And she was exhausted. She sat immobile,
watching the clouds. She heard, somewhere, far off, a piano.
Still playing. And, occasionally, Bernice's voice. Out there.
She was still out there, working . . .*

*. . . A great orchestra, surging, powerful, it lifted her to
ecstasy, she was fused with life, the very mystery of it revealed, suddenly, she danced beautifully, leaped, turned, mag-
nificently . . .*

"Jazz is everything, jazz is life," Jerry was mumbling, caressing her, lying next to her, under cool sheets, in the night,
warm Paris night under cool sheets . . .

"It's going to end, Jerry—"

"Sure, Jan."

"They're going to blow it up. *Come to me.* Bury yourself,
in me. Man the Beast. Incarnation of every evil in the Universe. He Was Chosen. *Chosen, Chosen.* Beast! Who invented
him? Was he invented? *Jerry—Was He?*"

"I didn't invent him—"

"Awful Beast—Worst Beast—"

"You're right, Jan—honey—"

"Why, Jerry?"

"Who cares? Just who cares? An accident. Terrible accident. Ridiculous. Huge joke of the Universe. Big ugly belly
laugh of the Universe. The moment. There's only the mo-

ment. I play. I know that. It's everything. I keep going. I wouldn't last—It's all there is—"

"I know that—"

"You knew that—"

"Yes—"

"*What happened?*"

"I don't know—"

"What happened?"

"Don't! I don't know!"

"Listen—"

"No! It's the night—This night—You play beautifully—"Only This Night—*darling*—so beautifully—*Jerry darling!*"

. . . *Vermeer* . . .

_____27

Letters . . .
    turn back the letters
    young fool
    Young Young Fool
    it died *long ago* torn out of me *Bernice*

SO LONG AGO

Out of the voice, for the voice, obeying the voice, heir progenitor to the voice, blackness parting, momentarily, recalling the voice. Out of time, for time, ever . . . *"yes . . . that's it . . . yes . . . turn . . . lovely . . . bend . . . now bend . . . lovely . . . pirouette . . . ah . . . lovely"* . . . In suspension, declined in embryo, malign darkness encroaching, but the voice through to her, guiding her, holding her, the whole of her . . .

. . . *slowly, tenderly, turn now, lift, barely touch now, unfold, yes, you are a flower, yes, unfold as a flower . . . now whirl . . . élancer . . . tour en l'air . . .*

. . . Autumn. They were driving somewhere. Golden autumn. Morning. She was sitting between her parents. She was eight. Carl was in front, beside the chauffeur. Her parents were talking. She caught snatches of words here and there. They were like snowflakes, falling, striking her, disappearing. Woods. The trees. In a few weeks, she knew, they would be all white. A few clouds in the sky, otherwise all blue. Carl was turning. He looked at her. She was smiling. She saw him. She was smiling at him . . .

. . . erect, tall, dignified. The woman Obviously had Dignity. Yet—under petticoats—sheer things—such things: Oh, master! Shorn of Dignity, save in the act of removing them . . .

REMOVE THEM

god oh God
removing them

Simple matter. Is not homo essentially an animal? Dearest. Oh, dearest! Sweet dearest. Dearest dearest. Can he—possibly hope to evade the animal? Well. And: the deadness. Within. Always deadness. Yearning for deadness. Veering, irrevocably, toward deadness. Is he not deadness? Matter. Alive and momentarily evading deadness. Matter. Monstrosity of matter. Alive matter, Terrified, terrifying, absurd MONSTROSITY OF MATTER *. . .*

the probe
the plunge
there
do you know
THERE
the matter

Essence of Matter.

. . . Her mother was there. Her mother was white-faced, shaking. Her father was near her. Her father reached out his

hand to her, touched her. He was trying to say something.
She heard her mother say something. The voice, not the
words, reached her . . .

_____28

oh pussy . . .

"Jerry—"
   "I hear you baby—"
   "Come with me—"
   "Where, baby—"
   "Who cares, Jerry? Do you have a passport?"
   "Sure! Hey what the hell you take me for? *No passport!*"
   Laughing, she hovered over the laughing, looking down,
holding him tight in the laughing . . .
   They were in the club.
   It was around midnight.
   The place was full of noise and people.
   The band was taking a break now.
   "I got a Beautiful Passport!"
   Camille, sitting next to them, said, "Do you like it here?"
   "Where?"
   Sweet gesture, so sweet feminine gesture, "Here!"
   "Oh yes—yes—I love it, yes—You know?"
   Where had she come from?
   "It has—Life—no?"
   Pause.
   "Yes."
   She must have come from—
   She asked Jerry,
   "Who is she, dear?"
   He peered at her.
   "Camille—"
   "I see."
   Pause.
   "She sings with us." Pause. "Sometimes."
   "Tonight, dear?"
   "Yeh, tonight. Over there's her friend Jacqueline—you see
her? Nice gal, Jacqueline—"
   "Shall we take them?"
   "Ah, I don't think so. What's the use? Am I supermouse?"
   "Might be fun—"
   "Glad you think so—"

"Let's go then—"
Camille, sweetly, "Are you going to live here?"
"Well—" sighing . . .
"Jerry lives here—"
"I know—"
"Don't you think you'd like to live here?"
"I—"
"Don't you, Jer-*ri!*"
"I sure do, hon—"
. . . *oh   hon* . . .
Eyelashes beat at him . . .
"Gotta go now—"
"Oh, *Jer*—"
"Work, now—"
"See you later, *Jer*-ri?" . . .
"Sure thing, hon—"
"Well, well, is the trip off?" Janet asked him, coyly.
"No, no, she's just a—pet—"
Camille flashed at him, "I resent that!"
"Time to work now!"
"Take her with us!"
"See you later—"
He was off. Smiling, making his way to the bandstand . . .
"I resent that!"
"And you should."
And, smiling at her,
"You are so pretty."
"And you, Janet—"
"Do you sing? Do you really sing?"
"Oh, I do! I go on soon—"
"Well, well, good—"
And
"You're ripe—lucscious—you are *Ripe*—"
"Oh, Janet—"
A blush?
"I do mean it."
"Are you going? Are you both going?"
"Oh, I don't know. We may do that. Would you come?
You can come. Have you a lover?"
She shrugged her shoulders.
"Jerry."
"I mean— *a lover*—"
"Jerry."
Sighing, "Well, I won't take him."
And
"Unless you come, that is."

"Oh, you take him. There are others. He's not the only. You get hurt with an only . . .

"Well, you come with us. Bring Jacqueline. Bring your others. We'll have fun."

Camille, sighing, sweetly.

"I can't leave Paris. Janet, dear. I just die when I leave Paris. I swear that."

"Why, that's romantic."

"Oh, I assure you—"

"I believe you."

They were giggling now, the two of them, together, high, but quiet, feminine giggling . . .

"Well, we shall leave you," said Janet, a while later.

They were quiet. The place was quiet, listening to Jerry. He was really playing. He was hitting high notes. Fantastically high notes. Then swooping, down, down, hugging low notes. The place came out of it. They applauded, went into an uproar. Camille was laughing, waving her arms, standing up now, shouting . . .

Janet thought: how pretty she is, seductive, full lips, warm brown eyes, fluffy brown hair, elegant girl, really. Long-limbed, full-breasted, full-lipped elegant girl. Go Jerry!

Camille to Janet.

"Oh, I sing now!"

She was off.

She made her way through the crowd to the platform. They knew her. They applauded her.

Beside Jerry up there.

Talking with Jerry.

. . . *quite a goddess, really . . . would you say . . .*

The tune started. A blues.

She sang well.

She really sang well . . .

. . . *her hair   autumn leaves   wouldn't it*

. . . *spectacular burst of music, suddenly, upon her—* Dance of the Hours—*from the wings she swept out, beautifully, easily, leaping now . . . turning . . .*

. . . *Sibelius . . . she was listening to Sibelius . . . she loved Sibelius . . .*

SO NICE

white breasts   my breasts
  under which   heart beats   all parts of me
  the languor   content to dissemble

Striking south on a tangent designed to preclude knowingness, hued solely in transience . . .

A lovely car. She drove it steadily, happily. A fast car. On open stretches she had pushed it close to its limits. Jerry was resting now.

A road sign.

Tours.

She said to him, "Shall we go there?"

He replied, drowsily, "Why not?"

She took the turning, quite excitedly, suddenly.

"What do you say we head straight for Nantes—then work our way down the coast—far as Bordeaux—then—inland—Toulouse—Carcassone—Perpignan—"

Pause.

"All right, hon."

"You're just a sleepyhead."

"All right, sure—I'm in favor—"

"I've been this way before! Long time ago. I was a little girl. Mother, Father—"

Pause.

"We had a lovely time."

Jerry mumbled, "Where did you wind up?"

She thought.

"Italy!" She paused. "We took a boat to Rome—we cruised all over the Mediterranean! It was great fun—"

"Fun."

"Shall we do that?"

"No boat—*God, not the boat*—"

"Seasick?"

"No—too damn slow—I'd go nuts—" He paused, mumbling . . . "Boat drives me nuts—"

In Tours, all was summer.
She had a good time.
Jerry was fretting.
He was missing his music.
His Paris . . .

Late one night, walking, arm in arm, they heard singing, and an accordion. A lively tavern, nearby.

"Jan hon—you're beautiful. I love you. How's that to say to you? Is it all right if I say it to you?"

She laughed, hugging him to her.

"You're a good man. You've got what I want. Don't be so low. Don't you like having what I want?"

A pause.

"I'm shocked."

"Are you? It's shocking!"

They were laughing . . .

"Are they enjoying themselves?"

He replied, "Let's ask them, huh?"

"Camille was terrific."

"Just terrific."

"She should have come with us."

"Funny gal."

"We couldn't—budge her!"

They came to a halt near the tavern. Much activity inside. Singing, music, no doubt dancing. The night was so warm. Raucous French voices.

In the tavern. Thick with smoke.

Jerry ordered.

Nice wine.

Somebody offered them seats at a table.

Somebody made an announcement. They couldn't catch what it was. It just couldn't be heard. But it was mad. Janet knew: *mad*. And it brought cheering. Thumping, banging of tables. Then music, a loud chorus, lively, surging, pulling . . . pulling . . .

"That does it!" she shouted to Jerry, laughing.

"Come on, hon—" He led her. Held her.

They were caught up in it. They joined in, giving the melody words of their own. The crowd, half-pushing-dancing, had them now. A buxom blonde caught hold of Jerry.

"Hey!" Janet called out.

She tried disengaging them.

She screamed with laughter.

She watched them disappear into the dance-mob.

She headed back to their table.

She drank some wine . . .

Someone fell into Jerry's chair.

Muscular young man.

He poured wine for himself. Then, noticing Janet, for her. She was staring at him. She was struck by him. Greek God. Was he a Greek God?

. . . San Francisco . . . five years ago . . . he was good . . . Don . . . my god he was good . . . Bernice . . . we were perfect . . . she said we were perfect . . .

He was looking at her. He smiled, broadly. He raised his glass. They drank . . .

. . . perfect . . .

He was saying something. She couldn't hear. The noise was terrific. The floor was swaying . . .

She sipped her wine.

Lovely red wine.

It made her feel good. She felt so good. Where was Jerry? She looked into the swamp-mob. There was no sign of him. Hussy blonde. He had been swallowed up . . .

She laughed, she said as much. She couldn't help herself, she yelled out as much. The young man was laughing. White teeth, laughing. More wine from the young god . . .

. . . the season had ended . . . great finale . . . Giselle . . . The ovations had thrilled her . . . Bernice kissed her . . . handsome young god . . . Bernice embraced them . . . Corps about them . . . all about them . . . rest . . . three weeks . . . absolute rest . . . unbelievable . . . great party . . . happy, wild . . . she hugged her young god . . . Bernice, near her . . . her arm around her . . . "Won't we show them in Paris? Won't we? . . . Dearest . . ."

With the young man, she was among the dance-mob. She was pressed against him. His arm tightly about her. His face against hers. His lips brushed her ear, he was murmuring in her ear. She was drowsy, yet hot, excited. She felt all excited. She felt him against her. She was dizzy. All was strange now, she didn't know where she was, what it was all about now. She was crushed against the young man, his wonderful body against hers. She was being swept along, carried away, somewhere. A darkness . . . She heard a door slam. She was sure: a door, slamming. A bright light. Swinging. Swinging bright light. She seemed to be in another room. The noise from the

dance floor was muffled. She was in another room. The door
had closed behind her . . . Slowly, she came to. She saw his
form, before her. The young god before her, holding her. She
stared at him. Her face was turned up to his. Her mouth was
partly open. He was upon that mouth, with his eagerly, fiercely
. . . She let him kiss her. She kissed him. Her arms went about
him. His tongue probed her, she loved it, probing her. His
hands glided over her, caressing her, fondling her. He was
undressing her . . . She felt her undergarments loosen, pull
away from her . . . She was falling backward . . . backward
. . . Her breasts were free, white breasts, free, his mouth
upon them, suckling, kissing them, wet mouth, rose nippled
breasts, in his mouth now . . . He was upon her. She felt
him upon her. His warm, hard phallus brushed her thighs,
was between her thighs, seeking her . . . He thrust himself
into her. She felt him lunge into her, loved him, lunging, into
her . . . She felt him ecstatic within her. She clung to him
fiercely, wet and ecstatic with him, screaming, with him . . .
He withdrew. She felt him withdrawing, touching her. She
touched him. Wet, hot phallus. She touched it. She was spinning, sighing . . . Hard floor . . . Her eyes were open. In the
swinging light she saw, vaguely, other forms. They were
across the room. There were four of them. There seemed to
be four of them. They became clearer. She stared at them.
They were four men. Not the young man. Four men. The
young man lay near her, asleep now. On the floor, beside her,
he lay asleep now. She was frightened. They were staring at
her. They were eager for her. *She didn't want them.* She tried
to cover herself, pull her dress over herself. She was on one
elbow, trying to rise now. Her breasts. She saw her breasts.
She was trying. She was so dizzy. She couldn't make it. She
screamed out. "JERRY!" They were upon her, laughing, half-
drunk, breathing heavily, holding her, caressing her, touching
her. Desperately, she struggled to free herself. She saw the
young man, still, near her. They were upon her, all over her.
She fought them. She could not stop them . . . She fell back.
A sigh and a shudder went through her. She closed her eyes,
she was limp. . . . *She felt them upon her, hungry, strong
animals, mauling her . . . they took her,* one by one . . . *she
let them all take her* . . .

   *now god   take my heart god   tear it out   hold it god   drip-
ping blood   my blood   my red blood   my god   living beating
heart   my heart   hurl   hurl it god   out   far out   oh god
black   unending cold*
   Cold universe   ever   forever

    my dear
    dear dear
    pir
    ouette

    nicely
    there now
    so nicely.

                    OH GOD

                *   *   *

————————————————————30

General Hawthorn, Lieutenant General Roscoe Hawthorn,
blinked. Was he seeing things? How could he be? He had
been a pilot for years, he was, as a matter of fact, still on
active flying status—how could he be? Roscoe really wondered: *Could* he be?

He concluded he couldn't be.

A high SAC man, the General was over here in these parts
on an inspection trip.

He inquired, "How long have you had *this?*"

The squadron commander, a colonel, answered hesitantly
—after a moment or two, having detected a slight note of
surprise and—possibly—disaffection—

"Six months, sir."

He answered, prayed and waited.

The General raised an eyebrow. He turned to a subordi-
nate, a brigadier general, who had accompanied him on this
trip. He said to him, "Did you know this?"

The man leaned forward, peered closely, looked at the colonel, then at the General.

"I'm afraid I didn't sir."

The General had flown in from the States just a few days
ago. He didn't particularly care for this inspection trip—he
didn't like the British very much, and liked even less the idea

of having bases on Their soil. But these decisions were, unfortunately, taken higher up, and there was nothing, absolutely nothing—for the moment—to be done about them. *For the moment*, a voice whispered within, distinctly, confidentially.

No, he didn't like it. Everything—*just like the British*—got fucked up. No matter how good something was, how smooth it worked anywhere else, once *here:* All Fucked Up.

This, for instance.

Here was a perfect example.

Just take a look at this, for instance.

"How did it get here?" he asked the colonel.

A pause.

"Well, sir," said the colonel, "we received them."

Another pause.

"You *received* them?"

Pause.

"They were sent over, sir."

God!

By God!

He turned to the brig general.

"Look into this. See that I get a complete report on this. *Complete*, you understand? *The whole matter*. This item shouldn't be near here. Not anywhere near here. *It's still in Development!*"

The item in question, highly ingenious and elaborate, was connected with the Squadron's principal mission: delivering The Weapon. (If and when ordered to do so.)

He turned to the colonel.

"Colonel, keep completely quiet about this. Completely. You understand me? *Completely!*"

"Yessir!"

"Dismantle all of them. Return all of them."

"Yessir!"

They stood there a few moments longer, the General muttering somewhat inaudibly, and then they moved on.

He couldn't get over it. He wasn't at all surprised, but—he just couldn't get over it.

By God! Sent over!

Miraculously enough, everything else was in pretty fair shape. The aircraft all lined and, ready to go, gleaming, their crews living, eating, sleeping just near them, airborne capability a matter of minutes, all set for their one-way trip—*anywhere* . . .

No, Roscoe did not at all like the idea of these bases on this soil. He had encountered one Briton too many. He had received, heard, one report too many—about The British. He knew them thoroughly. He disliked them and distrusted them —thoroughly.

Tits on a doorknob, he thought, suddenly.

By God, if I had my way—by God—

He was seized by the phantasy which mushroomed in him whenever he reached this stage in his feelings toward Britons: testing the Weapon—over London. With a wave of excitement he visualized the thing happening—the aircraft hovering high over London—the countdown—the release, the fall— *the detonation*—the disappearance of the city and a fifth of the island's population—*A fifth at least* . . .

He was smiling . . .

His mind, now, abruptly, turned to other matters. He saw a pretty WAF captain. She was standing near the desk in the Headquarters building. She reminded him immediately of Janet. He had received a letter from Cousin Roland just before coming over. It had, firstly, wished him a good trip. And, secondly, asked him to "do the whole family a favor" by "looking out" for Janet while over here and having a "little talk" with her, letting her know "we were all with her."

He hadn't liked the letter.

For one thing, he knew it had probably come to be written as a result of the machinations of his own wife Ellen and dear bitch Linda—and possibly Clarise. They always managed to gang up on poor old Rolly boy in this sort of way. It just reeked of it.

He was muttering, within— Where in hell will I see her? *Why* should I see her? I had them check that damn address in London—hell, she left there two weeks ago! What can I do about it?

He was shaking his head, and watching the WAF captain. She had walked to another desk. He kept his eyes, admiringly, on her.

. . . Nice little ass . . .

He really liked that round little ass . . .

Not a thing, Roscoe thought, what can I do about it?

He was glad.

He hadn't looked forward to seeing her.

He felt, he had always felt, she was the *oddball* of the family. The only oddball of an otherwise *mighty fine* family.

He paused a moment in his reverie, reflecting on that . . .

The WAF had returned to her desk. She had given him such a nice smile.

. . . my god what an ass . . .
Roscoe contemplated—somewhat agitated.

His wife Ellen—*"El"*—used to be mad about Janet. She raved about her to everybody. She had been her main topic of conversation, just about, when she was up there. When that movie about her had come out El had hit seventh heaven. She had taken her club *four times* to see it. She had sent reels of it to all affiliated clubs. Roscoe, tactfully, had put it to her, "Goddamn, El, you're a one-man publicity agency."

Yes, that business had bothered him.

But in the end, it came out all right.

She had come to her senses.

At last, at least, when the end came—

She had come to her senses.

Roscoe paused, reflecting again.

And now—What The Hell—

I should go trouping all over Europe for her?

He turned back to Ellen—

I could have sworn she had come to her senses!

Roscoe muttered, within again—I, Roscoe C. Hawthorn, the Security of the Nation square on my square shoulders—I should Just Do That?

. . . Christ . . .

. . . what an ass . . .

SHOULD I?

"Sir?"

The General, unwittingly, had become audible.

But he ignored the "sir", as was his prerogative when dealing with those for whom he felt the utmost contempt, i.e., his subordinates.

He went on thinking—

It's Clarice and Linda doing all the pushing. Clarice, that phony. Fat phony. Does El give a damn? Really a damn? Damn them! Harold. Sweet wonder boy Harold. Ho Harold. John Carlton. By God, you'd think he'd know better! That's always amazed me. Amused me. Highly amused me . . . Security, Nation, my shoulders . . . What if they really sic El on me?

. . . KEERIST THAT ASS . . .

"Bolthum!"

"Yessir?"

"Get me Washington."

"Yessir."

She was near a filing cabinet. He had watched her get up from her desk, walk to the cabinet. Her eyes, momentarily, had met his.

Ballerinas!

The General was getting ready for bed. He was tired. He had been through a pretty rough day . . . One bright spot, only one, in it. He would see, later on, what could be done with it . . . That conversation with Washington, to top it all off, turned out pretty horny. *Horny.* The Boss had been horny. Wanted him back soon as possible. Some report he had to present to some damn Congressional Committee or other. They had sprung it on him. They could never mind their damn business. No one could present a report like Roscoe! He wanted him back—soon.

Roscoe, muttering, opened his toilet kit and dug among its contents. He cursed a little, then found what he wanted: Baby Powder. Fresh, new, lovely can—of Baby Powder. He felt better, immediately. Indispensable. All else could go, but this— Indispensable! Where he went, it went with him. At home, he had a special drawer filled with it. Cans and cans of it. He needed it. He had— Troubles. *And by God, by golly God*, it helped him. It *sure helped* him . . . He loved the picture of the angelic little cherub on the sides of the can. He turned it around. He became unhappy. He didn't like this side. It read, very prominently, BABY POWDER. He turned the can again. This side bore the legend. NEW—NOW PREVENTS NAPPY RASH! But in much smaller letters. Hardly noticeable, *tiny* little letters. He smiled. He liked this side. This was the side. He kissed it . . .

------------------------------------31

Harold Hunter was on the phone to his sister Ellen. He had got through to her right away, oddly enough. She was rarely at home, and when she was her maid always answered, and the delay could be endless—almost. She took down all the details, reported them to Ellen, and then returned to say whether or not she was In. Brother or not, it didn't matter.

But there it was, Ellen's own sweet voice now, in his ear, cooing, cultivated, caressing, supremely assured—it sent shivers up and down his spine each time he first heard it.

There was a Woman!

What had she seen in that ass she was roped to? The uniform. *Must* have been the uniform. Long ago—

"How are you, *Howie?*"

He loved that, her pet name for him.

"Not too bad, El, really. Plodding along, as they say. Ha Ha. How are *you*, dear?"

"Oh, well—very well, Howie. We've been having a wonderful summer. The kids are sailing the boat to Florida. I'm not lonely though. Always a houseful. *How are you*, Howie dear? Linda? How is dear Linda? Have you heard from Jan? How is she?"

"Are you alone, El?"

"Alone?"

"I was just wondering—"

"Oh, Howie—*wondering!*"

"Well, you answered the phone, El—"

She tittered. "I see—I see what you mean, Howie—"

"Do you?"

"I was expecting a call, Howie!"

"I should have known."

"Oh, *Howie*—"

"El—"

A long pause.

"That's nice for the kids, El—is the crew with them? Or did they take it alone?"

"No, no—they're with them. It doesn't move without them! Oh, *Howie*, don't you know?"

"Sounds great. Really great, El."

"Wish you were young again."

"I'll say."

Another pause.

"Heard from Jan?"

"Well, actually, I'm glad you mentioned that—"

"Oh, Howie?"

"Yes—"

"Why, Howie?"

"I've sort of—lost track of her—"

Pause.

"The darling—honestly, she is a darling—she'll turn up, you'll see—"

"I'm worried about her."

"I have faith in her—"

"I wish she'd write—"

"Remember last time? She'll be all right. She's got so many friends over there, Howie. She probably doesn't have *time*—"

A pause.

"Did you say you were expecting a call, El?"

"Oh, that's all right—"

"Are you sure, El? I can talk to you any old time—"

"It's all right—I liked talking to my Howie *best of all*."

"You're a girl—you've always been such a girl—"

A pause.

"Well how's Lin?"

A longer pause.

"Oh, all right."

Brief pause,

"Is she in?"

"No, El. She went out for the day, somewhere."

"Thank her for the birthday card, will you? It was sweet of her. However does she remember, Howie? Do you remind her?"

"When is it, El?"

They had a titter.

"Well, I don't want to waste any more of your time, El—"

"I heard from Roscoe—"

"Oh?"

"He's still in England. Not for much longer, though."

"Oh?"

"It was just a little trip he went on, you know. Didn't you know?"

"No."

A long pause.

"Well, El, take care of yourself—"

"Oh, *don't go*—"

"Can't think of anything more to say, El—"

"What a shame. Don't worry too much, dear."

"I'll try."

"She'll turn up—bet you anything—I'll go and get her myself if she doesn't, Howie. You *know* I will."

"You're a great girl."

"It's the least I can do, isn't it, dear?"

"I think you're great."

"I have great faith in her—"

"You're *really sweet*, El—"

"She's great. She'll always be great, Howie dear. She's worth doing things for. I *always* said that. *Didn't* I, Howie?"

A pause.

"Howie, dear?"

"You're great, El."

"Come over to see us soon—"

"I'll fix something up—"

"Love to see you. How time flies!"

"Good-bye, El—"

"And *don't worry*—"

"Thank you, El—"
"Call me—*anytime*—"
"That's sweet of you, El—"
"Regards to *Lin*—"
"Bye bye—"
"*Bye—Howie—*"
"Bye, El—"
"*Bye Bye—*"
"*Bye—*"
"*Howie!*"

_____32

. . . *He was fourteen. He would stand for hours, immobile, at a window. She was terrified to go near him then. She hardly breathed. She was sure he was dead and would topple, at just the slightest touch. Afternoons . . . In the afternoons, usually . . . his room, the parlor downstairs . . . Once, she had found the courage to go up to him. She had stood near him. She had spoken, softly, gently to him. He neither moved nor answered. She reached out her arm. She wanted to touch him . . . Her mother was there . . . "What are you doing?" . . .*

. . . *Odile, beautiful, dangerous, in black, whirled across the ballroom and enchanted him, completely captivated him . . . she was Odette, he was sure of that . . . all illusion . . . she would win him, destroy him . . . the sorcerer would guide her . . . she obeyed him, completely . . . she would destroy Odette . . . separate, destroy the two . . . dazzling and brilliant, she circled the room, all eyes on her . . . the music raced on . . . a climax of amazing fouettes . . . now leaping, a wide circle, all about the ballroom, round him, and there . . . pirouette . . . sur les pointes . . . she had won him . . . she knew she had won him . . .*

. . . *Odette, outside, beat at the window, desperately . . .*
. . . *The Prince held Odile, spoke softly to her, caressed her . . . she smiled at him . . .*

. . . *Odette disappeared . . .*

On the white sands, under blue sky and brilliant sun, she lay with Jerry. She had driven down and across France, as planned. Suddenly, at Perpignan, she discarded the plan. She crossed into Spain. Memory urged her, revealing things on its own. Jerry came along. He didn't mind. They lay quietly, listening. *Surf sounds. Lulling surf sounds.* Groups of children sometimes, near the sea, romping. *He was with us.* Few people about. The beach was large, wide and long, touching the sea in a long, curving sweep, caressed by it, gently. *We ran on the beaches. They were so white. Pure white. We ran and played on the beaches. We lay in the sun on the beaches. Softly, softly surge. Gently. Touch. Caress the sea.* Janet had found an old friend. Nice, loving woman. Pure Spanish woman. She had put them up in her place by the sea. They had talked together, the three of them. Jerry liked her. They had a good time, talking together. And she left them alone now. Most of the day. *In a cove we lay. Softly, the sun lulling us, soft white sand, warm, gentle breeze feather-stroking us, by ourselves in the cove we lay.*

Jerry was saying things to her, softly, murmuring. Her face was near his, she smiled at him.

"I believe you," she whispered, caressing him, her hand on his face.

"That's right, believe me."

"I believe you—" she said, kissing him . . .

"We can stay here, Jan. What's to stop us?"

"Getting tired?"

"It's a nice place. It's Heaven. What's wrong with it?"

"Don't you miss Paris?"

He was quiet . . .

Three children, running in from the sea now, stopped near them. Janet waved and said some little things to them. They danced all about and giggled, and Janet and Jerry giggled. Then they turned and ran to the sea again . . .

_____33

Castanets, beating brilliantly, rapidly, exciting her. Heels clicking on concrete on the square just below . . .

They were on the terrace of a tavern in a small village. It wasn't far. They had walked there. In the perfect, lovely, moonlit evening they had walked there. She wore a white dress. Her hair was swept back, and up. She knew she was lovely. She felt lovely. She loved the dancing . . .

They drank good Spanish wine and watched the dancing, and, sometimes, the sky. Fantastic sky, pure, clear, million white lights now and more blinking at them. Warm night, enfolding them. The sounds of the surf, not too far off occasionally coming to them. The beat of the music quickened now. Guitars raced to keep up. Faster and faster now. The dancers, a dazzling couple, were whirling, beating the fantastic tempo now, even faster now. Ever faster, a frenzy now. The climax, at last, thrillingly, perfectly. He seized her, whirled, turned with her, she lay back as he held her, back, deep in his arms now . . .

Wild applause, table thumping, yelling. Janet joined in vigorously.

"Terrific!" she shouted to Jerry, who sat quietly.

"What's the matter?" she yelled.

He shrugged his shoulders.

Gradually, the noise died down.

He said, "It's phony."

"What?" She laughed.

"All phony. Honest!"

She leaned nearer to him

"You're very wrong. They mean it. It's in their blood, part of them, don't you see that? Don't you?"

Jerry stared at her. He filled his glass again. He emptied it in one long sip.

"As you say, pal," he murmured . . .

He was going back to Paris.

She saw that . . .

That was all right. What did it matter?

She decided that tomorrow, with or without him, she would move on . . .

_____34

She headed for Barcelona, without Jerry. He was at the end of things, he had to get back. He tried so hard to get her to come with him. He had to give it up, finally.

She was glad to be rid of him. Driving alone, across Spain,

she felt good. Near-empty roads. Deep warmth of sun and air. She loved Spain . . .

She had plenty of friends in Barcelona. It had been fun up on the coast, but now she was glad to be back in civilization.

She wrote him about it. A very brief note, one morning, early, gazing out from her room upon the long, beautiful avenue . . .

She read over the note, standing now, at the window. She smiled, wondering why she had written it . . . She would mail it. She decided that, she really would mail it . . . She thought of him receiving it. It excited her . . .

She went around with Joan, mainly. She was a smart girl, she got along so well with her. She was such fun. She knew all the places, day, night, any time.

She talked about the last time Janet had danced here.

"Giselle, Swan Lake—what was the other one?"

Janet tried veering away from it. Joan saw that. She said, "We loved you!" And dropped it.

She took Janet to fashion shows. She loved the fashion shows. She had forgotten how to!

But again and again she returned to her treasure, the unfinished, perhaps abandoned, Cathedral of the Sagrada Familia. She stood before it, loving it. It seemed to grow out of the earth. It overwhelmed her. The power and drama of it. Four steeples, primitive, powerful, alive, rising, rising, gripping her . . .

Why don't they finish it? she wanted to scream . . .

"Oh, Joan, look—"

Late day dress in white silk, bib necklace shaded from gray to white . . .

"Delightful, Jan—"

"Shall I?"

"You'll look divine!"

"What is that fellow's name?"

"Who, dear?"

"Last night—the Britisher—"

Joan laughed, "Oh, that one! Sir—oh—Lord howdeewhatsit—something—what was it? A one, isn't he?"

"Oh a one."

"That's Britannia."

Elegance on the beach in fringed toweling shirt, Dorville, exotic iris design in mauve, green, white . . .

"Nice idea," Janet said.

"Like it?"

"Oh yes—don't you?"

"Well—"

"Don't be bashful!"

"I'm deciding, honey."

Janet looked at her.

"Little Lord Mountajoy?"

Joan laughed. "Could be!"

*Strapless Italian silk dress, printed in jewel tones or rose,
amethyst and turquoise, gipsy earrings . . .*

Everyone sighed, fairly rapturously, now,

"Oh!" said Joan.

"I'll just say!"

"Wrap it up, dear dearest, wrap it all up—"

"Have you read Lorca?"

"Absolutely wond—" She halted, turned to Janet. *"Who?"*

"Lorca. Playwright. Poet."

"Here? They still have those here? Oh, honey, honest?"

Janet said, "You ought to, really."

She was reading three plays by him. Vittoria had loaned
them to her.

"You can borrow my—Vittoria's—copy."

"It's in Spanish?"

"Yes."

"Oh, I'm awfully slow with that. Got a dictionary?"

"You'll love them."

Joan lit a cigarette. She seemed interested now. A cloud of
smoke.

"Who gave them to you?"

"Vittoria."

"The darling! Isn't she a darling?"

"What does she see in *him*, though?"

"God alone knows! My God, *who* knows? These girls are
funny. Is it the heat? No matter how brainy they are—really
funny! Any Britisher sends them reeling, you notice—at first,
anyhow—oh, don't worry—give her time—just give her
time—"

*Emilio Pucci ballet-skirted cotton play suit, richly colored
in rose, tangerine, and white . . .*

"Sweet," Joan said.

"Oh, very."

"Is he coming tonight?"

"I don't know. Didn't she tell you?"

"Not one word."

"Oh, well."

Little drops of wonder . . . black silk dress in rich handle fabric . . . frille, silk gabardine—double gauze fitted bodice, skirt fullness flung to the back . . .

Polite applause.

"Would be nice. She's such fun."

"Do you like that?"

"Once a lifetime."

"Is she a Communist?"

"What-nist?"

Laughing, they were both laughing, they were having such fun laughing . . .

"Are you going back to the States, Joan?"

"My God, the States!"

And

"Oh, Jan, *the States!*"

Brown chiffon thing with underhem of clipped uncurled ostrich feathers . . .

oh   feathers

35

There was quite a gathering at Joan's place. It was set just outside the city, on a hill, and the view was magnificent. Barcelona lay spread out below, a vast, lovely panorama, and beyond, the sea . . .

Someone, in a sort of English, was saying to her,

"You like Señor Davis?"

"Davis?"

"Señor *Miles* Davis."

Where are you *now*, Jerry!

It was fabulous . . .

"Well, I—"

But a flock of people swept in, and upon them.

Vittoria was among them. Joan greeted them, kissing all of them. Laughter, happy laughter. Bubbling chatter . . . She pulled Vittoria to her. She smiled at her, and said to her,

"They're terrific, really! Thanks so much—so, so much!"

"Not at all! Finished?"

"One more, the last one—"

"It's the best. I think it's the best. Let me know which you think the best."

"Can I give it to Joan next?"

Peals of laughter, from the center of the room now. It was Lord Sir Whoever, entertaining as ever. Was that a belly dance?

Joan said, "Well, well, Vittoria, what have you done to him? What next, eh?"

"My dear—" Vittoria began, somewhat flustered.

"Who are your friends?" Janet asked her.

"Well, Janet— Look—this is José—"

"Hello, José!"

"Wait—I name them all—" She went around the circle. "Margarita, Dolores, Juan, Magdalena, Amelia, Federico—"

"Wonderful, wonderful, *hello all!* Aren't you *beautiful?* Oh, *so beautiful!*"

"Aren't they, though?"

"When will I be so young again? I envy you. It all disappeared on me—"

"Oh, Jan," Joan was saying . . .

José said, "You're very beautiful. We have all seen you—"

The smile disappeared, going off somewhere, yet holding her, in strict abeyance, remote from the moment, lone moment . . .

Vittoria sat beside her on a soft sofa. Some of the others joined her. More people arriving. Music. Quick, lively Spanish tunes. Guitars. Then, soft dance music. They were all dancing. Mostly all dancing. They moved across the floor. They were lovely people, dancing, moving across the floor . . .

Vittoria's voice, lulling her . . . Evening sun . . .

. . . *Madrid. It was Madrid. La Valse. Yes. She was certain of it. Rich, red curtains parting. Fleeting glimpse of gold-trimmed edges, drifting, drifting away. Coming in now, with the music. Momentarily lost in sudden burst of applause. And upon it, back, back upon it. Swooping, her partner lifting her, strong, lovely young man, lifting her. She was floating. She was aware of herself floating. Now, down, and beside him, now échappé, en arrière, tour en l'air, pas de bourée, dazzling, beautiful, all beautiful. Aware of this. Aware of all this . . .*

Joan said, "I see you got it!"

"Oh, yes."

"It's lovely. It's so lovely."

"See the back here?"

Vittoria touched her . . .

"What do they call you?"

She was dancing with one of them. He was quite nice. It had grown dark. Now, below, through the window, lights, acres and acres of light: *looking in on the sky, from above* . . .

"Miguel, *señorita*."

"That's a nice name."

From above . . .

"And so is yours—"

"Can you say it?"

"Janet!"

"Good! It's somewhat strange for Spanish tongues."

"Quite true," he laughed, "but I've been abroad."

"Oh?"

"We lived in London—"

"Lovely!"

"Oh? Not so lovely. Wet, too wet, I think. Do you think so?"

"You hit a bad year."

"Oh, several years."

"Yes—"

"Why yes?"

"How old are you?"

He looked at her.

"*Señorita*—"

"Won't you say 'Janet'?"

"Janet—"

"There—"

"Very young—"

"Won't you tell?"

"Perhaps I shouldn't tell—"

"Shall I guess?"

"If you wish—"

"No—you tell me."

"Twenty-four, Janet."

"A perfect age! You're very lucky—"

"Yes, Janet."

"What do you think of it?"

"It?"

"Everything." She laughed, adding, "The world—Spain—"

"No good, Janet."

"What? Not at all?"

"Hardly at all."

"Well, well."

"You dance so well. I thought only a Spanish girl could dance so well."

She was delighted.

And piqued.

But she liked him. She was quite attracted to him. He had a fine, slim body, white body. He had a nice face. He held her so well . . .

"How long will you stay, Janet?"

She said, "I don't know. I've not thought about it."

He smiled. "That's good."

His head against hers.

She murmured, "Are you studying?"

"I'm through studying."

"Oh."

He danced so well . . .

"Are you working?"

"Well . . ." He paused.

"Well," he went on, "my father—he has land—and more land—I help out there—sometimes—" He paused again. "It's very complicated. You see, to be blunt, I don't really work. I lead a strange life."

"Well, I believe you."

"I know you do."

And

"Who are you?"

"I'm just passing through."

"Where to?"

"It's not clear yet. Joan's my friend."

And

"Rome, eventually. Yes. I know that."

"Very nice."

"Yes?"

"You've just come then?"

"Oh, no—no, no—a few weeks ago—*you've* just come—"

. . . *love through the fence, love, sweet sweet love, through the fence,* amour, *gentil* . . . amour gentil, *through the fence* . . .

"Why are you smiling?" he asked.

"I was thinking."

It was a new number.

A cha-cha.

Oh—lovely cha-cha!

"Oh, I love this!" she said to him . . .

Joan said, "He's a nice boy."

"I think so. He leads a strange life."

"You be careful. I might tell you——"

"Oh, please, please don't tell me . . ."

Juan, a few others, danced with her. But they were dull. Miguel interested her . . . Soon, she was dancing only with Miguel . . .

The floor was very crowded. Joan had such a lovely place. On the terrace they were dancing. It was a wide, long terrace. It seemed suspended, and floating. It didn't seem part of things. They were drinking. Talking, and dancing. Such lovely people, talking, and dancing . . .

Around 2 A.M. there seemed to be more people than ever. In doing the cha-cha, everybody bumped into everybody else now. It was quite gay. Happy laughter, the house seemed filled with happy voices and laughter. Was that a shriek? She held on to him. She loved him. They called to her. She bumped into them. She felt so good, loving the cha-cha . . .

Vittoria, beside her, minus tweedie-pounder. It was Federico!

She said to Janet, "I see you've got him," and smiling.

"Who, now?"

"He's a smooth one. Watch out for him."

"For him?"

"I'm a smooth one."

"I love smooth ones——"

"She's jealous—Vittoria, you're jealous."

Vittoria whispered to her, *"He's political."*

"How thrilling!"

Vittoria, turning away, bubbled with laughter . . .

"Are you political?"

"I am political."

"How wonderful. Are you plotting to overthrow——"

"Ah, only plotting. It's so difficult."

"How exciting. How are you doing it?"

"——It's quite—flagitious——"

She looked up at him. She was laughing. She didn't know that one. But it was good. She knew, so good. He seemed so serious. A bit drunk—but so serious.

"Really?" she tried on him . . .

A new tempo. Hopping and jumping. People skipping happily, shouting and happy.

"My God!" she said, laughing. "The Charleston!"

"I don't think I—"

"Oh, come on!"

"I won't make it—"

Someone had hold of her. She was whirling around with someone. She had lost Miguel. She was laughing. Lost and laughing. The lights seemed dimmer. She tried to place the bobbing, smiling face before her. She saw Miguel suddenly, momentarily, far off, to the left. She reached out for him—

"Hey!"

"You're mine now—"

"Go way now—"

"Who are you?"

She looked at him. She knew him. She wondered how she knew him. He was American. She was delighted. Where had he crawled from? She tried to place him. Things were reeling, but she tried hard to place him. Was it—

"Who are you?"

"I know you—"

"I'm Shanty—".

Of course, of course, *Shanty!* She roared with laughter.

Miguel was nearby now. He was pushing the fellow off now. But he held his ground. Soon, the three of them found themselves jostled off the floor. Out the window, suddenly, she saw the Big Dipper.

. . . *God oh God dipper* . . .

. . . *Leap, fly to dipper, ride with it, ever, and ever, dipper* . . .

Shanty's horn-rimmed glasses. He seemed drunk. So intellectually drunk. She wasn't sure. Old suede jacket. Red shirt, open. He was bobbing up and down before her. He was talking to her. Miguel had hold of an arm. Miguel tugging the arm . . .

"It's all right, Miguel, let him go, Miguel."

"She knows me, Miguel!"

"Well, well, Janet—is he American, Janet?"

"Shanty, my God, *are* you American?"

"Forever, Janet."

"Stop bobbing, Shanty, *I'm getting seasick,* Shanty."

"Didn't I tell you, Miguel?"

"What, Shanty?"

And

"It *is* Shanty?"

"Goddamn, *Shanty.*"

"Don't *swear*, Shanty."

He studied her.

"What are you doing here?" he queried.

"Are you following me?" she asked.

"It's a party."

"A party?"

"Oh, Janet—" Miguel, near her.

"I really know him—"

"No, no, no! The country! The poor, goddamned country!"

"Shanty!" Janet cried.

"What country?"

"Who is he?"

"Miguel."

"Hi, Miguel. The goddamned country!"

"Give up London, Shanty?"

"Naw, I'm going *back* to London—"

"Is he going to London?" Miguel moved.

"Where's London?"

Shanty, before her, was winding up, she could tell, waving his arms, bobbing up, down, head up and down, glasses, up, *down* . . .

"Hey!" Janet yelled.

"Whatsamatter?" Shanty froze, completely immobile, open-mouthed, statue.

"If you don't stop that—stop that—if you don't—"

Shanty, shy, big grin, "Aw, I'm sorry, I get carried away, you know how it is, Janet—"

"Janet," Miguel, cooing.

Shanty got hold of himself.

He was getting set for takeoff now.

Janet said, "Shanty—"

"Yeh?"

"How did you get here?"

"Aw, for Christ's sake, Janet!"

Miguel said, "Come on, Janet, let's dance, Janet—"

Shanty wouldn't have it. There was the countdown. Janet waited. He launched himself.

"Jan, I last saw you in London, right?"

"So right."

"Well, I'm here now."

"My God, he's here now—" Miguel moaned.

"Look, Miguel—"

"Let me hear this, Miguel, please, Miguel—"

"Look, I'm here to—sort of—*look things over*. I'm traveling *all over Europe*. I'm gonna do some *articles*—big Sunday paper—London—"An American Sees Europe"—"An Ameri-

can in Europe"—got the pitch? I need background, real
background, information, there's a mine of information, you
gotta *find* the information—"

He was bobbing again. Janet grabbed him. He stopped it.

"This country's—*rotten.* Boy, what I've dug up! You knew
it was bad. Did you know it was *so* bad? Did you ever ask
yourself, '*How bad?*' "

He paused. He took a deep breath. He started bobbing.
Janet slipped against the wall. Miguel joined her.

"I'll tell you How Bad!"

Then, "No! you read my articles. About a month's time, I
guess. Where you staying? Where you gonna be staying? I'll
have them sent to you—"

"Yes—"

"Boy! What I'm finding out! Boy!"

And

"Boy oh Boy!"

Silence.

The Charleston raged on.

Occasionally, someone stumbled into them.

"I've been all over the place. All over!"

Miguel stared.

Janet sighed. "When did you get here, Shant?"

"Oh, Shant! I like that, Shant!"

And, "Yesterday. You're the first Yank I've run into. I
hear a Yank runs this place. I came here with Luis Rodriguez. You know Rodriguez? He was invited. He told me all
about her. Hey, is she in your stream, Jan? She fly *that* high,
Jan? Hell, I don't miss Yanks. I like London a lot. That's my
dish! Wow, what a place! What a place!"

And. "Spain, Portugal—*what tragedies!* Christ."

And, "You read the articles. I'm cracking them wide
open."

"That's good, Shant—"

"Look at all these people here—know them? Their families run the show, their families have all the dough. The rest
—*nada*—and—*silencio*—know that one, Jan?"

"Well, Shant—"

"Well, well, Shant—" Miguel echoed . . .

"Why did you come tonight, Shant?"

"To learn!"

"Have you learned?"

"Sure I've learned."

"Oh good, Shant—"

"Listen—" He came right up to her now. He held Miguel
off. "That fellow with you—*his father*—"

"Oh, Shant—"

"You ought to hear this—"

"*No*, really—"

She meant it.

Shanty retreated. He was hard hit. He stumbled a bit. Then faced her, hands in pocket.

"O.K., then—" he mumbled . . .

"My articles—" he added . . .

He started to shuffle away.

"Hey, listen!" Janet called out to him.

Head turned around, few yards away.

"Don't get lost now, *be careful*, I'm worried about you!" she said, quite sincerely . . .

Adding, "Write your articles when you're out of the country, remember that, please remember that! *Mental notes*, Shanty—"

Shanty stared at her a while, far off, looking like an owl.

Then, "I'll have copies sent to you. You tell me where, I'll have copies sent—"

He disappeared into the crowd, bounced and bumped around by the dancers . . . She caught glimpses of him later, here and there, waving his arms, bobbing, talking to someone . . . others listening, around him . . .

Miguel, "Quite through now?"

She held him, smiling at him, "Quite, quite, now . . ."

"Dance now? . . ."

Joan, "How are ya, honey?"

"Oh, fine, sweet—"

"Met Shanty, honey?"

"Say, he's a boy, Joanie—"

"We're saving him, honey—"

"Oh, God, look after him, Joanie—"

"Feeling all right, honey?"

"Oh, well, little bit—you know—*little bit*—"

"You stay a while, unpack and stay a *long* while, do you lots of good, honey—"

"That's nice of you, Joanie—"

"How's father, honey?"

"*Real* nice of you, *honey* . . ."

Groups now, settled here and there. Four A.M. Very few dancing now. Very soft, barely audible music. She heard the music . . . Guitar, clarinet, a bass . . . blues tune . . . nice

blues tune, slow, soft, blues tune . . . she hugged Miguel
. . . she clung close, to Miguel . . . one side of room some
sort of game, they were playing game, everybody seemed to
be kissing everybody . . . yellow dress . . . adorable yellow
dress, chiffon . . . she was kissing someone . . .

She couldn't find Joan. She looked high and low for Joan.
She had disappeared. They toured the house, saying good-bye
to all . . . Vittoria, hugging, kissing her, rubbing noses with
her . . . Federico . . .

Vittoria, holding her, looking at her, "Are you all right?"

"I'm all right—"

"Bless Lorca. Sweet Lorca. Are you all right, Miguel?
Look after him—"

"Coming with me tomorrow? I'm going to that monastery
—the cable car—I love the cable car—soars, and soars—it
soars—will you come?"

"I'll come."

And, "What time?"

"I'll call you—"

"Good-bye—*bye bye*—Miguel—little kiss good-bye—be
good, both—*so good—so—*"

"*So so—*"

"*Good-bye!*" . . .

Outside, on the terrace, Shanty still going strong.

Holding forth, waving, bobbing, small crowd around him,
early dawn light . . . occasionally—bursts of laughter, from
the crowd, from him . . . *Old Shanty* . . . She waved to him . . .

Down the hill, long, curving hill, Miguel driving . . . on
his shoulder . . . asleep on his shoulder . . .

Sweet fragrance . . . A garden. A house, white, looming
suddenly before her . . .

"Are you tied up tomorrow night?"

"No."

"See me tomorrow night."

"Yes . . ."

. . . *He spoke to her, but she was unable to hear. Standing
close, his lips moving, she, in that moment, could not hear.
She reached out to touch him. Her hand traveled a short dis-*

*tance, then stopped. Not on its own. But stopped. There, a
statue now, she stood, absolutely deprived of any meaning in
it. Staring, seeing, unhearing. A light, focusing on her, hurt
her . . . Words, forming within, struggling to emerge . . .
breaking out at last, stillborn . . . But the statue, stirring, returned to life. She moved slowly, sur les pointes, she turned,
she danced, slowly, round the room . . . The light was fading
. . . She halted . . . Now all was dark . . . Quiet, dark . . .
A figure grew out of the dark. White, dead figure, it stood at
the far end of the dark . . . She found her voice . . . The
scream, her voice, a part of the dark . . .*

"Honey—honey—"

Joan, beside her, held her, stroked her.

Slowly, the dream leaving, she saw her.

"All right—*all right now*—"

She smiled . . .

_____ 36

She had a good time next day. She loved Montserrat. The
cable car!

    if it snaps

Joan was with them. She had brought Shanty! She struck it
off well with Shanty. They laughed, and giggled together.
They talked on and on together.

She heard, "Few years there—oh, '33—'45 maybe—something was happening in the States, going good in the States.
Then it all ended. Now—holy cow!"

Joan, "What a mess!"

Shanty, "Hell of a mess! Not a chance, all a mess. What a
mess!"

Vittoria, "What's a mess?"

Janet, "Oh, Shanty—"

She looked forward to the evening, really. She had ar-
ranged to meet Miguel. She was intrigued by Miguel . . .

They were at his place. She had asked to meet his family.
She was curious. They were solid. Rich—and solid. But Janet
had fun talking with them. So polite. All polite. There was a
young sister. So white, and pretty, Miguel's sister. And one
brother, older . . .

Miguel took her to interesting places. That night, next, and many more nights. Little clubs, really. An unusual jazz, most unusual jazz. All very clandestine, so clandestine. They were all against the Government. They were biding their time. They hated the Church. Church and Government. Especially Government . . . So many jokes, stories. She laughed and laughed. She loved them . . .

"Miguel!" one of them shouted. It was hard to hear. The din was terrific . . .

He was saying, "We must do what we can."

A response, "What can we do?"

Groans.

Janet listened.

Miguel, "Listen—do you think there's no way? Do you think sitting and thinking and waiting is the way?"

Great cries of "NO!" mostly.

Someone, "Miguel, I love you, but it's impossible. They're on top of everything. Us. One night—they'll have us. And we don't even move! Imagine if we moved!"

"How can we live with that? Is that the thing, to live with that? Must we accept that? My God—I abhor that!"

Cheers, table-thumping. Cigarette smoke, floating, everywhere. Janet puffed . . .

A voice, "What do you propose?"

"Agitate."

More cheers. Some groans.

"At the roots. Get to the roots. Here—the factories. Shake the roots."

"They'll shake us."

"And so? We'll have *done* something!"

"Futile."

"Spain's soul is futile. Dark, fatal, futile."

"If you *think* so. If you let them *see* you think so. They want you to think so. That's their prime weapon. Did you know that?"

"I want no part of it."

Voices were drowning this. The man was in danger. He started to leave. They were restraining him.

Miguel shouted, "Let him go—let him go, if he likes!"

"He'll turn us all in!" voices shot back.

The man yelled, "Don't be stupid!"

And, "What do I care? Do I care about them? About you? You're all fools, *Spanish fools!* I want no part of you, any of you! What do I care? It's nothing to me. Spain is a stench, a powerful stench. It always has been—stupid, stupid, dead— cruel, base, ignorant—God deposited the worst of man's traits. eternally, in this place—nothing will come of it—nothing can come of it—you'll wind up in jail—worse—have you memories? Eyes? Let me go! Good night to all—Look out—"

And, "For what? I ask you—*For What?*"

Much noise, scuffling, but no great harm to the man, who finally made his way to the door and fell out, or was pushed out.

Janet was fascinated . . . the commotion . . .

Miguel, "All right, let's calm down now—quiet, quiet now! Shall we have *Quiet* now?"

There was some quiet now.

"Firstly, does anyone here wish to join him?"

Great chorus, "NO!" And hooting . . .

Miguel, "That's fine! All of one mind, eh? We must be one mind. How else? All right now—listen— Suggestions! Let's have suggestions!"

Someone was on his feet. The voice was powerful,

"Just as you said! Get down to the workers! Stir them, plant the seed in them, there—where else? Christ God, do you know where else? The middle-class? Those toadies? Their backs are smothered with it, from lying in it! How about the shopkeepers, fine scavengers, or lawyers, et cetera? How about the military? Shall we start on the military?"

Hoots of derisive laughter greeted that one.

He went on, "Or the clergy? How about the clergy?"

More laughter . . .

"The workers, only the workers—the only hope, one and only hope we have to topple the whole thing from the bottom—"

Someone yelled, "And the peasants?"

A shriek, "My God! The Peasants!"

Hysterical laughter . . .

A voice, "They're stones, man! They've had it! A long time ago they were *petrified*— Wake Up, *hombre!*"

"Petrified!"

A chorus of voices, "The workers! The workers!"

Janet was so excited. She watched Miguel. He was so serious. He calmed them. He was talking now, "The world looks at Spain, shakes its head and says, 'Hopeless.' We say, 'Who says so? We don't say so!' My foot, 'hopeless'!"

Much cheering, stamping of feet now . . .

"Committees! We'll appoint committees, work from committees. These will be—Action Committees!"

And they formed their committees. Janet insisted she be placed on a committee. Miguel protested. Janet would have none of that. She got her way . . .

"You can't cheat me!" she told him.

He threw up his hands, "All right then, but remember—"

"Pooh—remember!"

"We're Spanish!" he finished.

"I'm human!" she retorted.

He laughed, wrapped his arms about her, she joined him . . .

Where was Shanty? She wondered about Shanty . . .

Her committee would concentrate on factories. They would catch the men going to and from work, and at meal-breaks.

Other committees would visit their homes . . .

But where in the world was Shanty?

She told Joan nothing of her venture.

Vittoria guessed.

"What are you up to? *That Miguel!* Listen, why are you always with Miguel? He's a naughty one!"

"I gave Joan your Lorca."

"Janet—"

No answer.

"Janet—*what is it?*"

"What of it?"

"*I knew it!* Oh, he's silly! So silly! It's futile—Janet—*so futile!*"

Janet flashed, "You say so—they *want* you to say so!"

Vittoria was quite alarmed.

"God! What *are* you up to?"

Janet said nothing.

Vittoria stood still.

White, she turned finally and left . . .

Miguel, "Your country was very silly. We could have had the fellow and all his gang out, he was on his way out, the economy was dying."

Janet, "My country—"

Miguel, "Your country saved him. Aid, bases—you *needed* bases, *so sure* you *needed* bases—you saved him. Now, how much longer? Who knows how much longer? Damn the fools, cynical, callous fools!"

Janet, sighing, "All over the world, it seems, the wrong

people have power. *Always, everywhere,* WHY do the wrong people have power?"

Miguel, quickly, "The right ones have no taste for it . . ."

A few days later—operations in earnest.

Janet went with Miguel and a few others to a factory. They handed out leaflets during the lunch-break and asked the workers to attend a meeting a certain discreet distance from the plant. The leaflets urged them to attend. A matter of great importance . . .

A nice number turned up. Miguel addressed them. He spoke a long while, calmly at first, then urgently, ever more urgently, exhorting them. It was impressive. Janet thought it was most impressive . . .

There was little response though. Most were frightened or amazed or both. Others—listless, bored, shifting from one foot to the other, hawking, spitting. Some applause and cheering from an element which had not quite been with it . . .

Someone, near her, "Is this the lottery? So soon? The lottery?"

Many drifted away, before Miguel had finished.

She said to them, hoping to stop them, "Where are you going?"

They stared at her. They shrugged their shoulders.

"Ah, well, *señorita*—" sadly.

"They will just hang him—" apologetically.

"Or worse—*señorita*—"

Janet, most unhappy about it all.

And, noting their wretched condition: unhappier . . .

She went back. A few workers were about Miguel.

"But what can we do, specifically? What can we do?"

"Strike!" Miguel said.

"My God! That's Forbidden!"

"We've had our taste of it!"

Miguel was dismayed. In his talk he had explained it all. Why should they say this?

He reiterated, "The power is all in your hands. Think of that. You're not aware of it. Think—if all were aware of it! What could stop you? What? You're too afraid. Too intimidated. They have cut the guts out of you. You have let them. Why? Is that a Man? Is that how a Man lives? *Why have you let them?"*

Joan, that evening:

"Good God! Good holy God! What's this I hear?"

Janet sighed.

"Miguel?"

"*You!* And Miguel! *That Miguel!*"

"Oh, Joan—"

"Don't start on me now! I like it here. They'll have us out in four minutes—if we're lucky! My God, Jan, honey, a kick is a kick— But—"

"No kick—"

"My God!"

"It's—"

"No! Not me! Think where you are. You don't say '*Boo*' here."

And, "*That Miguel!*"

That night, late, she and Miguel were arrested. They had just stepped out of her car, near his place. They had been to a meeting. A group of plainclothes toughs surrounded them and took them off. At the police station, they found a good many friends . . .

They were taken to separate rooms and interrogated, most of the night . . .

Joan learned about it very quickly.

She swung into action. She got through to a friend in Madrid—the Ambassador. He was not the sort of man who generally did much for—*anyone*—but—Joan's herd, *Janet's*—

He was quite helpful.

She was released, turned over to Joan and Vittoria, who kissed her, lectured her, and bundled her off in a car to the French border. She would board a train there.

"How awful!" she told them.

"You'll thank us—someday—" Joan said to her.

"What about that poor boy? What will become of him? They're brutes— *Brutes,* you know! What will you do for him?"

"Oh, Jan, what can I do? He's made his bed—"

"It's awful!" Janet sobbed now.

Vittoria, holding her, "Perhaps his family—I'll do what I can—"

They fell silent, save for Janet's soft sobbing . . .

She boarded her train. Her ticket was for Milan.

"We'll see you again. Soon! I'm coming to Italy!" Joan cheered her.

"I'll bring Vittoria—" she added.

Vittoria smiled. She tried hard to smile.

Janet just stared.

"Good-by—" Vittoria was saying, waving, crying, *white face crying* . . .

_____37

Hamilton Upwind was settling down for the evening. This was Friday, his *special evening*. He was a little disgruntled, a little out of spirits this evening, though. His young brother Raymond—"Ray Ray"—had borrowed the new sports car yesterday and wrapped it around the nearest telephone pole. Hamilton cursed himself for having loaned it to him. The car was a total wreck. Ray Ray had escaped without a scratch, "as usual," Hamilton mumbled. He had ordered a new one. It would arrive tomorrow. "And you keep your sweet ass out of it," he had told the young lad. "I'm going to get hold of something else for you to kill yourself in, old sport." Ray Ray was entering the movie room now. Hamilton was settling in, getting things ready for tonight's feature. Yes, it was Movie Night. Each Friday night, for three or four hours, they watched movies—medical movies. Sometimes, a few friends dropped in or were invited in, but not often. This was a treat Hamilton liked to indulge himself in all alone, of course with Ray Ray . . . They lived together in this rather large, sprawling, highly intriguing *maison moderne,* as Hamilton put it, "away from things yet right in on things," and they got along very well. In any event, tolerably well . . . RR was in his late twenties and a rather shy boy. In some respects, one might even say, a somewhat—*immature* boy. For instance, the teddy bear. He could not be parted from it. Wherever he went, whatever he did, there too the teddy bear. Just now, for example, he had it tucked under his arm, tenderly, resting there, for all the world an animate object or append-age, part and parcel of him. Hamilton, over the years, had grown used to it. There were other little eccentricities mani-fested by the boy to which he had also grown used . . . But tonight, in truth, he was really somewhat unhappy with him . . . disgusted with him. After all, hadn't he demolished his new car? Hadn't he, in fact, demolished, at last count, his *six* pre-vious cars? No, no, thought Hamilton, shaking his head, it was too much, just too much . . . he simply would not let him drive again—*not my buggies,* at any rate.

"How ya doin', Ham?" said the boy, sheepishly.

"Oh, O.K., champ, how're you?" Hamilton responded, quietly . . . going on with his work.

"Uh—not too bad," said the boy.

Silence.

"What we gonna see, Ham?" asked the boy, edging nearer, shifting his bear to the other arm now.

Hamilton said nothing for a minute or so. He was inwardly debating whether to bawl the lad out or not. Finally, he voted against it: What good would it do? He sighed, he resigned himself: He's just a kid . . . not a *bad* kid . . . really . . .

"What we gonna see, Ham?" asked the lad again.

Hamilton was about ready now. He flashed a few shots for focus on his screen.

"What would you like to see?"

The lad shrugged his shoulders.

"Heck, I don't care, Ham, anything you put on is O.K. with me."

"Well, just sit down, then," he said, without looking at him.

In fact the boy did, carefully edging into one of the soft theatre chairs, of which there were about fifty . . . settling himself and teddy very comfortably, expectantly . . .

Hamilton really hadn't quite decided yet which film to show.

He wasn't in too good a mood, what with one thing and another—this morning, *for instance,* he had been rather rattled to discover, on entering a patient's abdomen, that his preoperative diagnosis had been entirely wrong—and so he didn't want anything too dull; on the other hand, nothing too exciting. He wanted something—*something*—he didn't know quite what he wanted. He brooded over his film library. Ray Ray sat in his seat, patiently waiting . . .

"Let me know when to hit the lights, Ham, ol buddy, willya . . ."

Perhaps—"Surgical Treatment of Carotid Body Sensitivity in Man"—the lad would like that . . .

Or—"Surgical Approach to the Sternoclavicular and Acromioclavicular Joint . . ."

No, perhaps—"Repair of Retro-Urethral Fistula . . ." He had reacted peculiarly to that one . . .

"Intra-Abdominal Closure, Descending Colon Colostomy . . ."

Tedious . . .

"Simple Anterior Closure of Transverse Colostomy . . ."

Poor technique, really . . .

"Aneurysm: Quadruple Ligation and Excision of the Femoral Vessels, lower third: Areterovenous Fistula . . ."

Imagine, image that—total wreck . . . how he escaped, how he always escapes . . .

"Partial Neurorrhaphy of the Sciatic Nerve in the Buttock . . ."

You would think . . .

"Operative Procedure for Total Urinary Incontinence . . ."

Oh, Christ, he's just a kid . . .

"Ineramaxillary Loop Wiring in Treatment of Jaw Fractures . . ."

They heard from their girl today, oh, man, that girl! Wonder how in hell Harold got that black eye? He looks sore all over . . . Ol Lin been on him again? Hee Hee, ol Lin, she sure can raise Hell . . .

"Hey, Ham—" came the lad's voice, slightly worried . . .

"O.K., O.K., champ . . ." Hamilton responded, searching a bit nosily now—he just *couldn't* make up his—

"Got it!" he called, suddenly . . .

"Guillotine Amputation of the Lower Extremity."

He took it out of its case.

He turned it over and over.

He was content now.

He placed it on the projector.

He was set.

He sat back, relaxed, happy.

He lit a cigarette. He smiled . . .

"Hit the lights, champ . . ."

. . . in color too . . .

"O.K., Ham," the lad said brightly.

There were clicking, whirring sounds. Darkness.

"Roll'um, Ham . . ." the boy said, settling down.

He stroked his teddy bear . . .

That night, sleeping peacefully, Hamilton dreamed of his ex-wife. She was all right, Hamilton always said, an elegant piece of Radcliffe minx—but—she had got into that habit of going to bed with RR. That ended it. He was just a kid, after all, *what the hell.* Yes, Hamilton had found her just once too often in bed with RR . . . In his dream, now, he saw her fine, long, white limbs beside him, she was sighing to him, she smelled like red roses and was sighing to him, she murnured to him, he tried to catch what she was murmuring to him . . . *"honey . . . so much of me . . . look . . . just ook how much there is of me . . ."*

Morning came and, after opening his eyes, he lay in bed awhile, as was his custom, contemplating. Possibly even— meditating . . . The voice in his head, soon in gear, purred along . . .

—Ham boy, you are operating this morning, what the hell are you doing in bed? You are removing one gall bladder from one old female geyser this very morning—so why the hell don't you get up? Get up! What the hell now. Handsome. Ain't you handsome? You are quite handsome. You have always been handsome. Why, at Harvard—ho ho, Harvard!— who was better off for it? All they do is have it in for us doctors. Yesterday I heard about this article in some monthly rag—what the hell was it—*pinko rag*—anyhow, the guy was bitching and moaning, spewing out ream after ream of "statistics" showing how we "fleece" the public, how we are "incompetent," how many sponges and so forth are "left in patients"—the bastard—how many "unnecessary" operations are performed and so on—*RR sure liked that last night, didn't he?*—how many "wrong limbs" are knocked off, et cetera—sickening! Sponges! O.K., once or twice I've slipped up, that's easy to do with the kind of half-ass nurses these days, could I help it? It could happen to anybody, mister. *You* take my job! *Take It.* Just one day, walawer. They brought this guy in for an amputation. Wrong arm. O.K., could I help it? *He wasn't even my patient!* Joe said to me, the night before, Look I'm tied up as hell, wanta do it? O.K.; he's a pal, I do it. Did he tell me? He never told me! Everybody there thought it was the right arm. He was Joe's patient. Did Joe ever tell me? Oh, brother! It was all down in the chart. I asked the nurse, she told me, yes sir, the *right* arm. So? The right arm. Malpractice insurance, God bless it! Hell, the ungrateful vermin would have my last sock! I always count the sponges. There was that rubber glove once. How could I help that? I took it off, I placed it on the tray, I asked my assistant to sew up, *he* sewed up, few days later the patient was dying, we opened up, there was the glove, could I help that? *He* sewed her up! Damn glove must have JUMPED in there! Oh, boy, what a life. Bitch, bitch, bitch, that's all they can do. Would they like my job? I'd like to see them have my job. Why in hell did I ever become a doctor? I should sit on my behind like Harold, *ol Harold*. What a laugh! Come on,

they're waiting. One gall bladder, bite the dust. What else is
in there? What else will we find? There's the treat! You never
know. Ha, ol Harold! What time will the car be there? Hell,
they'll bring it. Better get the kid out of the way. What a
laugh. They're looking all over the place for her now. That
letter was strictly from—*nowhere!* And written—weeks ago!
The great ballerina, running all around Europe. What a
laugh! Better shave, hurry up and shave, what a pain. *Diago-
nal line, transverse . . .* I'll take that little honey for a run
tonight. What a peach! Yeehee, what a peach! Wonder how
Roland—ol fat-butt Roland's—getting along? Getting much
these days? He sure can pick 'um, sure likes the young ones!
and darkies—I know! Last time down there—man, the old
bastard! HA! What a life, oh, man, just what a life. Take a
shot this morning, just small shot. Stuff's really good. Come
on, Upwind, move now. *Interventricular septum.* Where
would she be now? Where would the little gal be now? There
was a case now, and a nice little piece now! What a gal, huh?
Coccyx, Cock coccyx. Serratus anterior, Pectoralis major,
Rectus abdominis—the one, oh, the one, *Uppy ol buddy,* my
sweet little ol buddy . . . Ballet! How I laughed! *She* liked it,
I think RR liked it, but how I laughed! Each time I went, I
just laughed! She was a gal though! Trim little ship though!
They dragged me. She was the thing then. Dear family. Anything for dear little family. You know me. Honest to God, I
laughed and laughed. What could they see in it? 'Course, I
couldn't let out right there in the theatre—but inside, God,
inside! I nearly died! That was real agony, man. Next time
I went, I loaded up good. I shot in two doses. Man, *I was
floating!* She was a honey though, in those frilly costumes—
what a honey! Upwind, she was a honey, and you a prize
fool! You could have—my God, man— Right Under Your
Nose, Man! Do they make them like that nowadays? Hoppity
hop, hop hop, all over the stage, arms waving, feet flying,
jumping—man, she could jump though! And all those other
cute gals too though. They had some real beauts there.
BEEUTS! And what for though? In aid of what though? Those
legs— They ever gonna find her though? The glove though.
Was I to know? Stupid broad of a nurse there supposed to
keep track. I put the thing on a tray. Was I to know? My job
is to operate, not count things. Did I do the sewing? Donno-
van, that jerk. A howl! They tried to sue the pants off me,
hell, they would have busted me! Smart little ol lawyers those
insurance people have though. 'Course John Carlton helped a
lot though. *Mastectomy, transverse radical incision, left to
right.* Could I help it? Didn't the damn pathologist make out

the report? Was I to know? What a life! Oh, those jerks, those holy jerks! Funniest thing though is when they twirl around, right in the air, and beat their feet. *That* must be hard as hell to do. I tried it once and nearly broke my god-damn neck. What shrewd little outfits they wear though. That's what the hell women ought to wear all the time! I'd love it! Up went the leg, forward the head, right around they'd turn, and around, and you couldn't see one hair on their sweet happy twats—*not one teeny sign of their twats!* I know, *I Had Binoculars!* I tried like hell. God knows I tried. Those damn pants are shrewd, shrewd as hell, PERFECT. What can you see? Nothing! Christ, *I even brought the high-powered hunting ones* once. NOTHING. I'd have loved—Janet —*that gal*—HELL, Upwind, WHAT THE HELL. Get going, man, they'll go berserk up there soon. The ol bladder's probably fallen out on its own by now, pal. CHRIST, those bastards! Attacking, eating away at the very foundation of American Medicine! The nerve! *The Bastards!* THE SOCIALIST BASTARDS!

—what the hell should I charge the old bat . . .

"How ya doin, Ham?"

Ray Ray was there.

"O.K., pal."

"Busy today, Ham?"

"Yeh, little bit, ol pal."

"Huh—wanted to talk with ya bout somethin', Ham—"

"Yeh, Ray?"

"Yeh. Uh, when we gonna get our Shelter, Ham? Everybody's gettin' theirs these days. What we waitin' for, Ham?"

"Well—have to look into that, I guess."

"Cause I mean better not to wait too long, y'know, just about everybody's got theirs by now—"

Hamilton eyed him.

"O.K., buddy, just leave it to me, huh?"

"Get the guns too, Ham."

"What guns, pal?"

The lad looked surprised.

"The guy on TV, Ham, the priest guy. He says not a bad idea to have one or two in the Shelter. In case anybody tries monkeying around, like breakin' in. Ya gotta have the guns, Ham, don't forget. Get some quick-firing jobs, Ham."

Hamilton mused over this.

Meanwhile, the lad held out the teddy bear.

"Whaddaya think, Ham—gettin' better?"

Hamilton examined a foot.

"Coming along pretty well, now, ol buddy."

"That's good, Ham. He was hollerin' quite a lot last night, guess you heard, din't ya?" He paused, smiling fondly at Teddy, "Better get him a gun too, ya know. All the hands you could have firing in there the better, Ham."

Hamilton nodded, he was about set to go now.

"O.K., champ. Well, see you later—"

"Yeh, O.K., Ham—I probly won't do much today. Just kinda take it easy. I'm pretty tired, Ham." He paused— "Hey, ya don't wanta give him another shot, do ya? Ya could if ya want, Ham. What the heck, we can take it, don't worry about that, Ham—"

Hamilton, departing, thought about that . . .

38

John Carlton was disgusted.

Utterly, absolutely disgusted.

And dumbfounded.

Acquitted!

The damn fools had *acquitted* the man!

The very word was ice in his ear.

No culprit who came before John Carlton was ever acquitted.

True enough there had been one or two cases where the jury had deadlocked and new trials were necessary.

But we got them, second time around! We sure got them!

John Carlton liked sailing. In fact, he spent most of his free time at the shore, the Cape, and this is where he planned to go, for a few weeks, when this trial was over. He would return just in time to catch the finale in the gas house. Now, his plans were blown all to hell and back again. He couldn't possibly do it. What fun would it be? This catastrophe— He would probably drown himself! "By God, I'd drown myself!" he said aloud.

What had gone wrong?

What in hell's bells had gone wrong?

He didn't know what to do. He was really beside himself. He nursed a wild plan to charge the jury with fraud and corruption, or failing that, *non compito*, throw the trial out and start all over. But he discarded this, and an alternative plan, not quite verbal, which saw him tracking down members of the jury, one by one, and putting a quick end to their miserable existences. He discarded the plans, in truth, because he was paralyzed with shock, incredulity. When he finally came back to himself, it was too late to do anything.

Besides, he had problems.

His fourteen-year-old, Handy, had been caught again!

This time, things looked bleak. No mere marijuana—*heroin!*

And his wife blamed it all on to him, per usual.

God oh sweet God! he said to himself, gnashing within at the bad things . . . *to get rid of that Bitch, the Bitch, Bitch, Bitch Bitch . . .* He saw the chamber . . .

He resolved: he would really look into it, *getting rid of her . . .*

He read his mail before going down to see what could be done about his little offspring.

There was no hurry, this one would take *some time,* all right . . .

Letter from Roland. One from Roscoe (*somewhere in Spain now, inspecting his damn bases*) and one from his broker. Roland was going on and on about his hard life. He mentioned he had put the word to Roscoe about Janet, as John Carlton had requested. Roscoe's answer—one of the very few times he had ever heard from That fellow—was polite enough, and brief, but gave no information or comfort, indeed stated quite openly that he doubted there was really anything much he could do on the matter, not to expect *"miracles"!*

"Ha!" muttered John Carlton, "miracles! The lad said miracles!" And, "By God, one of those little Health Bombs ought to go off while he's touring those places. That would be his miracle, that sure would, wouldn't it!"

He had breakfast, alone, and then sat down and wrote a long letter, a tender letter, to Janet. He addressed it to her last known point of departure, as per the kindness of dear mother Linda. He told her so many things, he quite lost himself, all his troubles receded. He was in another world. He told her how much he loved her, and wound up with a heart-rending plea to look after herself, and bring herself, fresh, new, back again, to *start all over again . . .*

He meant it.

That was how he put it, meaning it.

As for Roscoe, he dispatched a curt note, thanking him for his message and telling him to take his staff, his bases his bombers, his own self, and head down the smoky road to Innermost Hell, as fast as possible, preferably by special reverse rocket . . .

Then, leaving Roland's letter for the time being, he went off to see about Handy . . .

———————————————————— 39

The Senator was disgusted. Details of the "Spanish affair" had started trickling in to him yesterday morning. Since, they had become a flood, a very embarrassing flood. His opponents and enemies were already making hay out of it. John Flowal, outspoken and fearless columnist, was right on top of things, gleefully firing home hearty salvos into poor Roland's exposed, ample hindquarters.

SENATOR'S NIECE IN THE RED IN SPAIN
A Bug in the Old Back Yard
And so on.
But the Senator was not one to take such a thing quietly. He had already devised a masterstroke of counter-strategy which would turn the tables effectively on all of them. Soon, he would put it into operation. To begin with, he would subpoena Flowal for a little session before his Committee. Secondly, he would find Janet . . .

He was very worried about her. What, really, had she been up to? Was there a shred of truth in it? This terrified him. The slightest shred could mean ruin for him. He was bitter. The irony of it!

He had to find her, bring her home quickly, quietly. It had to look normal. Otherwise, it would only mean more ammunition for Flowal and company.

He could not really believe the reports were true. Janet was a funny girl, true, ballet, all that—but— An Agitator! Roland laughed, then sweated— *A Subversive?* He was weak, cold, things were fading—

But he caught himself, and soon was guffawing, "Ho Ho— Our Janet?— Ho Ho Ho— *Janet?*—"

He nearly guffawed it all out of himself.
But not quite.
Friend Flowal bastard and Company.
To begin with, a letter—
Nice, long letter to her . . .

In bed that night, lying beside his dear wife, the Senator dreamed an intriguing dream:

He had arrived home unexpectedly and found Mary alone. Employing all his charms, he managed to entice her onto the floor with him where he proceeded to undress her. She seemed happy about it. He gaped at her, burned for her, and was soon petting her, fondling her. He was in seventh heaven with her. She was under him now, whimpering a bit, hot as hell, just dying for him. He quivered and plunged himself into her, murmuring passionately to her, "Don't worry none, gal, I'm Uncle Roland, *nice lil ol Uncle Roland*, whoa there, there there, what a gal, little ol luscious gal, here you go, *whoa ho,* All For You, *Oho,* my gal, *What A Gal . . ."*

"Roland!"

The voice, in his dream, somehow seemed detached from the dream—

"Oh, gal!—"

His own voice, bizarrely, likewise—

"WAKE UP, WILL YOU!"

Now he surfaced, abruptly, pulled by the voice—

A light as well, blinding him—

Clarise screeched, "Look at you! LOOK AT THE STATE OF YOU! Get Up From There! Get! You're Not Fit To Sleep Here! *My sheets!* Look at You! Tomorrow that black bitch goes—first thing I see her—OUT SHE GOES! *Uncle Roland*— Get Up Now! Get! GET NOW!"

"Clarise honey—" the Senator mumbled, moaning.

"OUT NOW!"

She screeched at him.

"I was only—*only dreaming of you,* honey—"

The Senator, whimpering, tried now.

"The Spare Bed! Get Now! *That's* the Only Place For *You* Now!"

"Look At You!"

He stood there.

"GET NOW!"

He stumbled, shuffled, out of the room, all of him.

In the hallway, heading for the spare room, he heard her voice—

"TUB OF LARD! We'll Just See About You! Have A Good Sleep, *Uncle Roland*—WON'T YOU?"

. . . he came to her . . .

On the train, in her compartment, alone, enveloped by night, she lay, she listened . . .
The train was flying . . .

. . . a martyr, he always came to her . . .

the stab . . . *oh my God* . . . feeling the stab . . . *My God* . . . deep, deep stab . . . *You My God* . . .

. . . for her . . .

The mountains.
Uncle John's place.
Summer mountains . . .

. . . seventeen . . .

. . . my blood . . . moonlight . . . caressed white breasts . . . blood depths . . . My Breasts . . .
. . . she drew him close, tenderly, under cool sheets, so tenderly . . .

"How are you?"

. . . whirl, Princess . . . her heart, wild now . . . *ever whirl, Princess . . .* she was flying . . .

OUR BLOOD

. . . I held you close, I loved you. You knew I loved you. Did you love me? I felt you loved me. Summer nights, lingering, holding us . . . Dark warm lips of the summer night, loving us . . .

The train rolled on . . .

─────────────────────────────41

In early morning light, Genoa, curving gracefully, touching the sea, and embraced by the sea . . .

She would get off at Genoa, she would certainly get off. She would get to Milan, yes, *later*—and perhaps Venice. But now there were things to do here, people to see . . .

Sylvia . . .

She smiled, feeling good thinking of Sylvia. She gazed at the sky. It grew ever brighter, and soon, she knew, would be brilliant. Blue, incredibly blue, brilliant . . .

She looked at the sea. It was green, then blue, ever-changing before her eyes . . .

Things to do. Spain. Where was Spain? *Painful* . . .

She was having some breakfast. Just a bit of breakfast. She was dressed. She thought of Spain. *More than painful* . . . She turned to the light. White, light, summer frock. Lovely, tanned, in her white frock. Loving herself in her frock . . . *Hateful* . . .

Genoa bustled as ever. She contacted Sylvia. She would be there—unless she was on one of her tours! In which case, the nearest place would be Argentina. *Oh Argentina!* She smiled, Sylvia answered. So thrilled to hear from her. She would come get her.

Janet waited in the station for her. She would come. And would it still be the pink car? Janet loved the pink car, she looked for it . . .

She felt so good, she felt home again. The long train ride, the sleep, they seemed to have shaken things off, heavy, oppressive things. Perfectly, wonderfully home again, Italy, her favorite place, treasure place. She murmured the words aloud, *treasure place* . . .

She watched people passing. She loved them. She followed their conversation, became part of it . . .

. . . The sun upon her, warming her, she had her face in the sun. She closed her eyes in the sun, her arms on the chair, her feet swinging, not anywhere near the floor. Her father's voice coming to her, his voice, there, in the sun . . . Lovely waterfall, white, sparkling now, in the sun . . . Mozart, Sonata in G Major . . . they listened to the music, he talked to her about it . . . Andante Favori . . . She listened to the voice, she adored the voice . . . Etude Symphonique . . . She was laughing now, softly, what had he said, she tried to understand what he had said . . . she saw the waterfall, she asked him again to explain what he had said . . . Ballade four in F Minor . . . listening . . . Granados . . . The water, rolling over the boulders . . . lovely, loving sun . . . his voice in the sun . . .

How would Sylvia be?

So lively, pretty, wonderful Sylvia, just how would she be . . .

She wanted Janet to live here, she just couldn't understand why she didn't live here. *Last time—*

She should live here. Janet told herself that now, she *really should* live here.

You could talk about anything, everything, you could name your places—

Where *was* there a place like this?

She smiled, *there wasn't,* she watched four young ladies, *just wasn't* . . .

She heard them.

She envied them, born to speak such a language . . . Their language. Smart young ladies. Wonderful Italian young ladies . . .

"Signorina—"

She couldn't help saying. She really was so pretty. Light blue dress. She faced Janet. Somewhat puzzled look on her face. But friendly. Well-formed *signorina,* perhaps twenty. Her hair was long.

"Ha chiamato?" sweetly.

"Si—Scusa! Solamente perché—because—you see—I haven't been here in years—you understand that—years—I'm American—well, somewhat American! *Un po Americana!* I adore it here. Forgive me. Won't you forgive me?"

Young lady smiling.

"Of course. My goodness!"

Smiling.

"Will you be staying long?"

"I don't know. I did want to get to Milan. I'm waiting for a friend. She's picking me up soon. Milan! Ah, Piccolo Teatro—"

"Oh, you know it?"

"Yes!"

"I've seen them once—"

"Do you like it?"

"I adore it!"

"Marvelous! Aren't they? *Just marvelous.*"

Young lady lingering, smiling, lingering . . .

Janet, "Look, now—"

"Yes?"

"Would you like to see them again?"

Hesitation.

Soon gone though . . .

"I'd love to!"

Janet, happy, smiling, "Give me your address—and name! I promise I'll be contacting you. You'll see if I won't be contacting you! You'll go with me."

"Why—how very nice of you— Thank you, *signora*—"

"*Signorina*—"

So softly though, she didn't hear it . . .

She gave her name and address.

Janet wrote it down, tucked it away in her bag.

They stood awhile, just looking at one another, smiling. The sun was so brilliant. They were in the shade of the station though. A puff of wind rustled her dress. The young lady's blue dress, rustling. They laughed.

"Are you from here?" Janet asked.

"Oh yes. I was born here. We lived in Turin for a while. But—mostly here. Papa works for the municipality. He—surveys things." She mimicked now, "A very important functionary, you understand, now—"

They were both laughing. *Signora*. Marna's legs. *Oh, Signora!* Long-limbed, beautiful. *Janet Signora.* Well-formed Marna, lovely, brown-eyed lovely. *Ah my.* Exquisite Marna. *Limbs flowing into her hips . . .*

"Wonderful!"

More laughter . . .

Silence.

"Do you work here?"

"I'm at the University."

. . . Exquisite hips . . .

"How wonderful!"

"I love it!"

"Marvelous!"

A pause.

"So you have been to Italy before, *Signora?*"

She let it go.

"*And* before! I love it. Marna, I simply love it! My home, really. I look upon it just as my home."

Smiling, lovely young Marna there.

"I think you have probably traveled a *good bit* of the world, signora—"

"Oh—here and there—no doubt of it—"

"I thought so—"

"What compares? Can anything possibly compare? *Our* Italy—Marna—"

She checked herself. She was aware of veering toward maudlin. She didn't want maudlin. She was intoxicated, really, she wanted to tell Marna—but—no maudlin. *She didn't want maudlin* . . .

"Why don't you live here, *Signora?*"

Janet, sighing, looked into her brown eyes.

"I've been busy. Oh, terribly busy. But now—not so busy. I shall seriously think of doing that—"

"One should try to live where one feels most at home— How long is life? *Ah, Signora—*"

Janet, smiling, was so happy with her. Shaft of sunlight, suddenly finding its way to her.

"Do call me Janet—"

Pause. Marna did so.

"That's so nice, thank you—"

Another pause, she knew she would go—

"Will you excuse me, Janet? I shall really be late—I do look forward to hearing from you. You will let me hear from you?"

"You *will* hear from me—"

"I look forward to it—well, good-bye then— Thank you so much, thank you—Janet—"

"Good-bye, dear—"

"*Ciao,* Janet—"

Two old friends, sisters, mother and daughter . . . parting . . . Janet watched her. Sweet figure disappearing into the crowd, swallowed up by the crowd. Brilliant sun now . . .

Sylvia, at last. But not too late. Janet loved her, so thrilled to see her. Pretty, *chic,* all *chic,* as usual. Dark hair, swept up, elegant. *How elegant!* There was the car. *Blue!* Convertible. American. Lovely car. They kissed and bubbled and chattered all over in greeting. So fond of one another. They had always been so fond of one another . . .

"Where have you come from? What a surprise! Delightful

really! Always surprise me. Haven't you always? Promise. *Always—*"

Janet laughed, "You darling. Absolute, dear, dearest darling!"

She kissed her, again and again, on the cheek.

She hugged her . . .

"Did I keep you waiting?"

"No! Of course not . . ."

"I came fast as I could—I was in bed—not bad, really—"

"You did splendidly! Really—"

"Never warn me—I'll never get here! You *won't ever* warn me—will you?"

Janet, "How are things?"

Sylvia, "Ah, *well*—so so—"

Laughing, the two of them, hugging, laughing . . .

Sylvia drove the long blue car through the city. Everyone made way for her. Whistles, shouts as they made way for her. They passed through densely packed areas. Dilapidated buildings, ancient buildings. Rows and rows of them. She didn't like it. She stared, she *didn't* like it. What could she do about it? Here was Sylvia. She chatted with Sylvia. The weather was so lovely. Divine, and lovely. Sylvia chatted on and on. Behind her dark glasses, a pair now for Janet. Lovely voice thrilling her, lovely language enchanting her.

Out of the city. They wound their way out of the city. Now, in the open, heading for her place. Out in the country, but not far from Genoa. Janet loved the sun. Smell of the sun. She smelled land and sun. She was so relaxed now, at home, she adored Sylvia. They had practically, after all, *grown up* together! *How many* summers? She thought of the summers . . . How *could* she have neglected her? How long?

"My dear, *dolce mia*— Will you dance again?"

At last.

In the silence.

Seeking, silence, all in the silence . . .

Sylvia, turning to her, looking at her, heard now, "I don't think so," at last, "I'm afraid I don't think so."

Sylvia, sighing, "What a pity, great pity . . ."

The car, surging, power-packed car surging, effortlessly pulling, climbing and pulling . . .

"How is your father?"

"Oh! Very well." Sylvia's sweet mouth, laughing, "Wonderful, wonderful. Do you know, he's off now—Paris. Mother's quite furious. He didn't tell her! What a lad. However, she's gone to Venice. She said that will serve him. Besides, there was something there she had to see. You know Mamma when she *has to* see! Imagine those two? How old are they? Ah, Jan, Janet, dear Janet!"

She loved her . . .

Simply—adored her . . .

"I do adore ballet costumes. Really, adore them. We should all wear them, all the time—men, women—specially women! Wouldn't it be marvelous? So simply marvelous? Who would resist us? Who could resist you? *No one resisted you!* Oh, you!" Sylvia told her . . .

A silence.

"I met a very sweet young lady at the station."

"*Oh Oh? Tell me!*"

Janet told her.

"Well, well, you have adventures! May I tell you some of mine? I have had some, you know that? Ah—well—some day. I've had a few!"

They were laughing, gaily, quite abandoned now, sailing along in the bright sun, under blue sky, speeding now, through fine, wide, open country, farmlands. White farmhouses, here, there, and somewhere. Looking back, she saw the city, white, retreating ever . . .

42

"We were all so *shocked,* though."

On a loggia at Sylvia's place, overlooking acres of olive groves, stretching over the rolling land as far as she could see, touching even the edge of the sea . . .

Sylvia.

They were sipping iced drinks. They were so relaxed, so casual: Sylvia, her cousin Tosca, Pietro—her brother—two or three others, some Princess, a blond, elegant French girl, who listened and listened, occasionally smiling, nodding, saying something—her Italian had such a cute accent . . .

"*Whatever happened?*"

Sylvia, looking directly at her, saying it only for her. The others listened. Waited.

Janet smiled, briefly. She was embarrassed. She wanted to flee from it . . .

Shrugging a shoulder, "What's the difference? I'm too old anyway. Want me to tell you how old I am? I lasted long enough anyway . . ."

And silence.

Only the silence . . .

Ice cubes tinkling in glasses. Some movement in chairs. Sylvia sipping her drink, Sylvia quiet and eyes still upon Janet, now turning, slowly away from Janet . . .

The Princess, to Sylvia, "Who's coming tonight?"

She did not answer. She sipped her drink.

"I say, *Sylvia*—" cooed the Princess.

They were laughing, all of them, laughing . . .

It was wonderful! So many old friends—and new ones. Sweet young things, *chic—foulard shirtwaister, relaxed and simple*. Adorable! Nice young men. Soft-spoken, charming young men. Time, and time, with her, pressing in on her . . .

. . . *dark road, late at night, by herself. Silence, and all in silence. Warm summer night. What was the night?* . . .

"Darling!"

She was sweet. Sylvia—caressing her, leading her into the room. A hum of voices in the room.

"Are you enjoying yourself? Yes? I'm so glad. You seemed low. I wanted to perk you up! Have I? Are you really going to Milan?"

. . . *they had found him* . . .

"Yes, dear," smiling at her, touching her.

"Mia cara. Mia bella cara . . ." Sylvia, murmuring to her . . . A letter . . .

Where was the letter?

Sylvia, "I was coming over to see you—but then—there were so many rumors. I should have come. It was naughty of me not to come. I started to write a number of times. It wouldn't do. What could I say? I'm *so* glad you've come . . ."

By themselves, sitting in a corner, Sylvia's arms over her chair, Sylvia's lovely arms . . . *exquisite in chiffon*. Black chiffon . . .

"It's nothing. Don't think of it. I'm so glad to be here."

"Mia cara. Do you remember?"

Janet, watching the others now, "I remember." Turning to Sylvia, smiling . . .

Lovely eyelids. Her eyelids.

Sylvia, "London?"

"I believe it was London."

"I'm sure of it."

And

"*Swan Lake.* It was *Swan Lake!*"

"I love your dress."

"Oh, thank you. Just a little thing."

"It suits you."

"I love yours! We must get some things while you're here. That was always such fun. Remember the time we took Mamma?"

"Oh, indeed."

"She knew the answers, all the answers."

"*Didn't* she!"

Large punch bowl. Group of handsome young people. Near the punch bowl.

"When, then?"

"Oh, my goodness!"

She was laughing, and Sylvia pressed on with it.

But they were all about Sylvia now, calling out greetings to her. And Janet too.

Janet was happy. She laughed and kissed them all. They were really so good-looking. Bronzed, healthy. Her heart beat quickly. They were adorable . . .

Delightful. Sylvia's white lounge filled with cha-cha. Everybody was dancing the cha-cha.

. . . *silence . . . sadness . . . in silence is sadness . . .*

"Gino!"

Not in—*years!* And here. Sylvia, leading him to her.

"What do you think?" So pleased with herself, smiling at Janet.

"I can't believe it!"

"How are you, Janet?"

"Wonderful, Gino! My, my, oh, Gino!"

"Give me a big kiss—"

She did.

"And a hug—"

She did.

Sylvia tapped them.

"I've had too much!"

"So soon?"

"*Ummmmmm—*"

"Wonderful, absolutely wonderful!"

She loved him kissing her.

Then, "Well—what are you doing?"

"Nothing."

Gino stared at her, "Come, now—"

"I assure you! Absolutely—nothing! Oh—reading a book here and there—s' etching—dabbling in painting, here and again—really, *nothing!*"

Sylvia sighed, "Isn't it dreadful? Would you believe it?"

Gino, "But dreadful."

And silence. They heard the cha-cha.

. . . *femininity exquisite my femininity* . . .

Now, Sylvia, murmuring to her.

"I'll come to your room tonight. You'll tell me all. Won't you? Do tell me all—"

. . . *in the knowing* . . .

"Dance with me."

In Gino's arms. The cha-cha . . .

"I *love* the cha-cha!"

Sylvia, dazzling, lovely in chiffon, smiling, happily smiling, casually waving, watching her, turning now to others, surrounding her . . .

"Well, Gino—"

He laughed for her.

"Well, well, Janet!"

"You've been busy?"

"Oh—so so."

"How's it going?"

"We try, we try."

"Don't give up."

"We won't. No fear."

"Did you know I'd be here?"

"Who knew? My dear, count on Sylvia. Naughty Sylvia. And so nice—*you*, I mean—*cara*—are you glad?"

"I'm glad—" almost coyly . . .

"Are you happy?"

"Oh, now—" pausing, hoping to form the words, touching the words, "very happy—"

"So am I."

"Gino. You've hardly changed. Only hardly."

He laughed, and hugged her close.

"And you?"

"And Sylvia—that angel!"

"We do love her. We have terrific times. She keeps us all happy—we poor—"

"*Poor* poor—"

Laughing softly, holding close, dancing . . .

. . . *oh my cha-cha* . . .

. . . *warm heart, beating warm heart . . . my heart* . . .

Gino, "You lovely—"

The music stopped for a while. Ripples of laughter, voices, everyone talking at once, it seemed, but softly, so casually.

She saw the Princess and Tosca. The Princess, a long cigarette holder. Tosca, sipping her drink . . .

A small group around Janet. Marcello came toward her.

"Stay a long time, *cara*."

"Long long time."

"You know we love you—"

"I love you."

Sandra, cooing to her, she loved her hair, "Stay here. De-
cide that tonight. O.K.?"

"*O Kay*," someone—Marcello—mimicked her.

"Let her have one of your places, Sylvia," Arturo, in form.
"Go on, give her one—"

Laughter, soft . . .

Glasses clinking . . .

"Two—" Sylvia, murmuring, drinking . . .

"One would do." Janet smiled at her.

"*Choose . . .*"

Sylvia, taking her by the hand . . .

They sat in comfortable sofas. She felt so good. Lovely
and good. Gino next to her. They sipped their drinks. They
talked and danced. The moon came out, its light filled the
room. The large French windows had been thrown open.
Lovely evening. Sounds of the evening. She listened at times
to the sounds of the evening. Sylvia and her brother. Pietro
was a charming young fellow. They said he wrote plays.
Janet watched them. Now a young thing, all in orange, a
lovely orange, joined them. Pietro went off with her. The
music. A tango.

Gino, "You know what's needed in Italy?"

"Oh—what's needed in Italy?"

They giggled. Both of them, gently, giggling . . .

At last, "Capital investment! Much, much capital investment. Industry. Expansion. The central problem is: *grinding
poverty*."

Pause.

"Here?"

Sylvia, beside them.

His moment was over.

Janet cuddled up to him.

"You don't mind?"

"Should I mind?"

Sylvia in someone's arms. Sylvia dancing. Lovely and
dancing. She recognized him. Giorgio.

Gino, "You're so lovely, *cara*. Soft, warm, and lovely—"

"Who said that—"

"Where did you get that dress?"

"I don't know. Paris?"

Strapless evening thing, pale blue, her breasts rising, soft, white swells of her breasts rising . . .

"I love Paris . . ."

He murmured . . .

"I love your dress . . ."

"I love you—"

They were walking in the grounds of the place. It was not yet dawn. From the house came the music. Laughter, music. Looking back, the lights of the house . . .

"Mia bella," Gino, murmuring.

She sighed, she was in his arms.

He kissed her—

Marvelously . . .

"Sylvia!"

She was awakened by her. It was morning, but she hadn't been sleeping long.

"Do I disturb you?" she heard her, near her.

"Not really. Have they all gone?"

"Oh—I don't quite know. Some will turn up—here, there. Giorgio. The Princess. Yvonne—oh, who knows—I'm sure of Yvonne, I've just seen her—"

Pause. She smiled at Sylvia. Then covered a little yawn.

"The Princess fell in the pool," Sylvia told her.

"Heavens!"

"She's all right. Pietro pulled her out."

"Dear Pietro."

"Dear lad, our Pietro."

Janet moved in the bed, slightly.

"How did she fell in the pool?"

"Someone pushed her."

"Really!"

"She's asleep now. Lovely, fast asleep now."

"Is he with her?"

They laughed. Janet wore a nightdress. Her breasts rose, as she moved, partly out of her nightdress. Sylvia sat on her bed. She stroked her.

"Cara—"

Janet held her hand. She smiled at her.

"A sad smile, *mia cara—*"

She stroked her face, gently, tenderly. Her neck. She found

her breasts, she fondled, caressed her breasts. Silk-soft hands, a long while, gently caressing her breasts . . .

"How are you?" she murmured.

Morning light in the room.

Half-drawn curtains, her arm about Sylvia, whimpering now, softly, to Sylvia, little cries, soft, infantile cries, to Sylvia . . .

"Mia cara . . . there now . . . *cara* . . ."

"And what happened then?"

"It ended. Suddenly, all ended . . ."

In the cry, holding close to her . . .

"Was there someone?" so gently.

"No one. I feel there was no one . . ." A pause. A moment. "I fell. It ended . . ."

"You fell—"

"It ended . . ."

A silence.

"My dearest—" Sylvia, stroking her . . .

"Tonight, Gino took me—"

"A good man, *un buon uomo,* dearest—"

"He went deep, so deep, dearest—"

"Is he in you?"

"I feel him—in me—"

"Still in you?"

Murmuring . . .

"I can't sleep, *cara*—"

"Won't you tell me?"

"I don't *know*—"

"How was Spain?"

"Very sad, really. A young man is in jail now. They'll harm him, I know—"

"A friend of yours?"

"It's political."

"Oh, Janet." She paused, she sighed. "I'm so sorry though. A nice young man?"

"Very nice. Really."

"I'm so sorry. Really . . ."

She sighed again.

"What a mess. One great mess. Holy mess. And there's Italy. My Italy . . ."

She looked at Janet. She touched her face. "We wait. What do we await? Ah, *cara* . . ."

"Will they blow it up?"

"I think they will. I think we may see it."

"I don't want to—"

"Ah, well—"

Silent, a moment. Both in the moment. Looking at one another, there in the moment. Then, softly, laughing, soft, feminine laughter, holding close in their laughter . . .

"Dolce, mia cara—" she said, sighing, at last, so tired.

"We'll stay here all day, Janet dear, I'm so tired, are you tired?"

Caressing her, falling toward sleep now, murmuring . . .

"So tired . . ."

. . . she was reading. She seemed to hear her own voice reading . . . adagio: *the ballerina, in* adagio, *displays her beauty in slow, unfolding movements and sustained graceful poses, for the principle quality of* adagio *is—control . . .*

. . . Bernice . . . I've been thinking about Death and Transfiguration. *Would it work out? Do you think we can work it out? Do you . . .*

"Wonderful!"

"Tonight?"

"Yes, tonight!"

"Just wonderful, wonderful!"

She looked forward to it. All settled then. They would run down tonight, a carful of them, Sylvia's lovely car full of them, along the coast, between Forte del Marmi and Viareggio—the *Bussola!* Wonderful place! And Carosone was there. She had heard some marvelous records by him. What a thrill! Would be *fun* . . .

She longed for evening . . .

Her yellow dress. Beautiful, she knew, in her yellow dress. Caught up just beneath her breasts, slightly to the right, precious clasp, and two flowing strips of chiffon. They had several tables, and Sylvia found many more of her friends in the place. She seemed to be going from table to table. Cigarette in her long, elegant holder, she moved, it seemed, from table to table.

Pietro, "My sister never sits still. *Sorella!*"

Janet, "Oh, Pietro—a wonderful sister."

Pietro, "Yes, wonderful—but look at her!"

Janet, "I think you're jealous. That's your trouble. You're
jealous."

He went off with Tosca, tanned, lovely in white, Tosca.
She watched them. They were dancing. They looked so
lovely, dancing. She felt good, watching them dancing.

The Carosone music delighted her. She danced with everyone to it.

"Divine!"

"He's from Naples."

"Who said so?"

"The music."

Chella La—ah, *Chella La!*

"Wonderful! Sylvia—come here—*Sylvia*—"

"What is it? My darling—what—"

"Have them play it again—"

"Which?"

"*Chella La*—do—please—"

"You like, *eh?*" She was smiling . . .

"I love! Eh . . ."

They did. They played it again. And again. She was delighted. The irresistible rhythm of it. The drive, yet sadness,
of it. The tune lingered in her. The tune found itself within
her. They were drinking champagne. She clinked glasses with
the Princess and Gino. Oh, handsome Gino. Smiling Gino.
Bubbling stuff thrilling her. Music and bubbling stuff thrilling
her.

"Take him home with us. Oh, oh, take him—"

"But the poor fellow works here."

"Sylvia! Hire him. Can't we hire him?"

"We have his records—"

"Oh, Sylvia, I know that—"

"Come on, *cara*—"

"*Vieni—vengo!*"

Dancing with Gino.

Serenatella Sciue'Sciue'.

"Wonderful—isn't it wonderful—"

Laughing and happy, everyone so happy . . .

"You're wonderful—"

"How wonderful?"

"Stay in Italy, *wonderful*—"

"With *you*, wonderful?"

"Yes, won—"

"Oh, Gino—a proposal from Gino! *Sylvia*—"

"Stop that—now don't make fun of that—"

"Oh, Gino . . ."

Dancing, dancing, with Gino . . .

Piccolissima Serenata . . .

The hours . . . near her . . .

"Take him home with us . . ."

"La Contessa—"

Ah la contessa . . .

"*—Mi ricordo—*"

"*Roma!*"

"*Cara . . . In Roma*—Yes! *Bella* . . . Yes, my dear—"

"How are you?"

La Contessa. Upright, white-haired, bejeweled, bespectacled (elegantly), near her . . .

She kissed her.

"*Bella!*"

She turned to Pietro. She called him.

"Yes, *my Contessa?*"

"*Devil!*"

"Oh—*my Contessa—*"

"What did you promise me last time? Do you recall what you promised last time?"

"My—"

"*Devil!* Dance with me!"

Sylvia, turning to Janet, "She adores him—"

Contessa, "You mustn't hide this young angel of yours, Naughty Sylvia—You *are* a Naughty One, Sylvia!"

"*Contessa—*"

"Look at us, Sylvia!"

"Enchanting, Contessa!"

"When's the wedding, Contessa?" Arturo, drawling.

"That's uncalled for, young scoundrel!" she threw at him.

"Ah, well, who calls for . . ." he said now.

She looked at him . . .

Music!

Yvonne—all French now. Where is her Italian?

She cuddled Marcello. Cute, brown-haired Marcello.

Lazarella . . .

Oh, she loved *Lazarella!*

Again and again, *Lazarella* . . .

Marvelous evening!

Best, one of the *very best*—of evenings.

They got back to Sylvia's next morning. Janet knew little about that. Someone carried her. When she woke up, late in the day, she found herself in a large, comfy bed. They were snug in the bed—she, Sylvia—and Gino! she laughed. She had to laugh. *Gino!* They never heard her . . .

She lay there. There was the music. *Chella La*—it would not leave her . . . Lovely tune, *never leave her* . . .

Sylvia awakened.

Across Gino, she smiled at her, sleepily. She murmured to her.

"*Ciao*—"

"*Cara*—"

"Let's go down to Grosseto—there's a little town there, near there, up on a hill. It's a thousand years old. At least that. I want to see it."

"Have you seen it?"

"*Montemerano*. I've seen it."

"All right. Tomorrow. Next day. Whenever you say."

"Just the two of us—"

"Of course—the two of us."

"It's something to see—up on that hill—"

"I don't know it—"

"On top of that hill—"

"I should know it—"

"We'll go—"

"I want to know it—"

<hr>

43

One morning, on a sunny balcony, just outside her room, she wrote him. She didn't say much. She missed him, was thinking of him . . . had he written? Never mind, she said, you haven't time, how could you have written . . . She told him of Italy. A few lines, all about Italy . . .

Sylvia kept her busy. They did get to Grosseto. *Montemerano!* She had loved it. Sylvia raved, she simply had loved it! Occasionally, horseback riding. It was fair fun. Then, her place on the shore—delightful beach, exciting runs in her boat, water-skis! Such fun on the skis . . . Shopping, walking about, enjoying Genoa. She hadn't forgotten Marna. One day, soon, she would contact Marna. Lovely Marna! In the evenings there was always a houseful of people. They walked in from all over. Or they went somewhere. Elegant places. Delightful people. Sylvia gave such nice dinner-parties. Her parents hadn't come back yet. Sylvia led an active life. She even had a husband—somewhere! She had lost track of him . . .

"I must go to Milan," Janet told her one day, as they drove along.

Sylvia said something, she didn't quite catch it . . .

That evening, as they were looking at slides Pietro was showing, she told her again.

Sylvia answered, "Oh? Milan, eh?"

She just didn't like it!

"Yes," said Janet, "I really must—I want to—"

Sylvia looked at her, "All right then." She paused. "When?"

Someone said. "Look at that one! Isn't he handsome on that one! Where was that one?"

Pietro, lazily, "Aix-en-Provence, the Festival."

Janet told her, "Oh—Friday morning." She paused. "All right?"

Sylvia, still looking at her, gave a slight shrug—

"All right."

Janet, "I must call her."

Sylvia wondered.

Janet explained: "The young dear at the station—*La Stazione!* I told her." She was smiling. "Didn't I tell you?"

Sylvia nodded, remembering.

"I promised I would. I must call her now."

She went to do so.

Sylvia showed the slides now, Pietro had tired. He lay near his Tosca. She stroked him, brown-haired Tosca, and murmured to him. There was a small audience this evening. The Princess, Arturo, Marcello, Sandra, Yvonne—one or two others . . .

Janet was back soon.

Nude Negress. On the screen flashed a magnificent, full-breasted, curvaceous Negress.

Murmurings, approval, all round—more from the men, though.

"Now that's nice! That's what I like!" Gino was there . . .

Giorgio was quite animated, "Those black ones, yes, yes, ah, the black ones—"

Janet smiled, she liked it.

"Where did you get that one?" the Princess.

"What? Want to take lessons?" A languorous male voice, Arturo's.

Laughter, softly, circling them . . .

Sylvia, "Argentina."

"Ah, Argentina," Pietro, sighing. Tosca tapped him. She leaned and kissed him.

Arturo, "Aha, Giorgio—have you had a black one?"

The Princess, "I'm not good enough?"

Arturo, "My dear—*My dear*—we all know you're good enough—"

Again, laughter, somewhat louder, longer now . . .

Sylvia tried to change the picture.

Protests from all quarters.

"Her sister's the next one!"

It appeased them.

"Ah, well—let's see her," Marcello.

She appeared.

She was lovelier—softer, exquisite. Wonderful milk-chocolate color.

Sighs, murmurings, stirring . . .

"Where is she? My God—Sylvia—My passport!"

"Giorgio! Sit down—you're blocking the view, man!"

"Man!"

"Che mare! A far bagn in quel mare!"

To bathe in that sea . . .

"Sit down, Giorgio!"

"Oh, sit down. You'd drown, man! Do sit down. What can I see?" Marcello.

Bella! Bella bella bella! Bellissima!"

They moved him, finally. He sat next to Gino. He said to him, though all could hear, "Have you had one?—I say— Have you really had one?"

Gino assured him.

"How was it? Tell me, how was it?"

"Go to Paris—" He paused. "What's wrong with your Princess? She's almost black. Look at her. Isn't she?"

Soft laughter, delighted . . .

Sighs—

"Black cunt—" Arturo . . .

"Sweet cunt—" Gino . . .

"Whose cunt?" Sandra . . .

More laughter . . . softly . . .

Sylvia, changing the picture . . .

Arturo, "Janet—"

Arturo, in her arms, caressed her, said to her,

"Life is a swindle."

She said nothing, accepting that, moving closer to him, so her breasts brushed him. He fondled them—

"Colossal, awful swindle."

Silence. He kissed her breasts. In the silence, his lips over her breasts, her nipples tingled . . .

"What do we get out of it? What in hell do we get out of it? The years pass, Janet. *Mia bella*. Janet. We get old, ugly. Stinking, dried up, ugly—I don't want to be ugly!"

"There now—"

"Janet—"

"You're lovely—"

"I've wanted you—"

"Oh, now—"

"Bella donna, exquisite, you flew, *you were another world—"*

"Shhh—"

"Un Altro Mondo!"

"There now—"

"Swindle! Nothing—"

"Hush now—"

She stroked him, she gave him her breast. He embraced her, held her close . . .

She murmured to him, a finger curling his hair, "Did you like the Negress tonight?"

"I did indeed."

"Have you often been with Negresses?"

"Not often."

"How are they, *caro?"*

"Animals. You go into a hot, savage animal—"

"Lovely—"

"Amore—"

"Bello—amore—"

He kissed her, deeply . . .

She sighed, in his arms . . .

He was in her . . .

She whispered, *"Find me one—"*

He sighed, "Certainly—"

"I need one—"

"Of course—certainly—"

"So long since I've had one—"

"Certainly—"

"Nice, big, black one—"

He smiled, he touched her nose—

"I'll find you one . . ."

and,

"Just one . . ."

Quiet party. A quiet little party. Just a—get-together. Gino was there. He had brought this *Literator*. American, female *Literator*. He had run into her—somewhere. That was his world. Partly his world. He had brought her. She was *well-known*. Novels. Janet tried to think of her novels. It seemed, somewhere, oh, way back there—she had *read* one of her novels. Dim, dim was the memory. *Had she?* Janet watched her, listened to her. Such an accent!

"My deah—"

"Let's speak Italian—"

Literator, obliquely at her—

"You don't dance anymore, *do you?*"

"No I don't."

She turned to Gino.

"Ah, well—" in Italian now, "you were saying?"

"Well, you see—" he began, "Lawrence—"

"Pooh!" she poohed.

Silence.

"Filth! Don't mention him!" she went on.

More silence.

"Ah, well—*Chatterley*—" Gino.

"Precisely!" she thrust in—"Precisely, precisely! Pure filth! I wrote an article on that. *Read my article on that.*"

Great pause.

Gino, "Ah—well—the work is admired—"

"Ha Yes!" Literator—"Of course! *Yes!* The Devil's own work—*Corrupting!*"

Awkward pause.

The group about her.

Smoking, sipping drinks, quietly, only tinkling of ice in glasses . . .

Sylvia, crossing to Janet, smiling, murmuring to Janet . . .

"Ah—well—" Gino.

"Well?"

"I like it."

Literator, stony.

"What do you mean—*Like it?*"

Shrugging his shoulders, slightly, sighing—

"Like it."

Sandra, "I like it."

Laughter, brief burst, popping out—perhaps Tosca.

Sylvia, "I really like it."

Literator, staring.

Petrified staring . . .

Gino, kindly, "Don't you like it?" A pause. "Wouldn't you —*sometimes*—my dear—"

Sylvia, "Once in a while?"
Gino, "Once a night?"
Mountain.
Trembling—
Gino, *Now?*
"Monsters!"
Erupting—
"MONSTERS! MONSTERS!"
Glass smashed, smithereens . . . Literator, storming out . . .

Gino, petting Janet, sighing.
"Ah, well—"
Janet, smiling,
"Well well—"
Sylvia, looking on—
Sighing . . .

. . . *late day   darling   straight tunic   in chiffon   printed
chiffon   weighted   with   bead   over   fitted   sheaths   enchanting
they swing as you* . . .

. . . *walk darling* . . .

_____44

. . . *le jeune homme . . . la morte* . . .

. . . *She watched the leaves. When they fell they seemed to
be parts of her. Falling from her. She stared at them. The
great tree near the lake had lost nearly all its leaves. Great,
bare arms, suddenly exposed, gaunt, reaching this way, that
. . . A breeze caught some leaves drifting to the ground. It
spun them, lifted them . . . The breeze died. They fell,
silently* . . .

Milano!

They talked, and laughed, all the way to Milano. Four of them—Janet, Marna, Sylvia, Sandra. Sylvia's lovely car, up hills, down, flying away on the stretches . . .

Sandra, "That Giorgio. Oh, that Giorgio!"

"Spoiled," Sylvia.

"Thoroughly," Janet.

"What does he mean to you?" Sylvia.

Sandra, "But nothing! Absolutely! I swear it—"

"No need to swear it— We never swear it—"

Laughter, rippling, through all of them.

Late summer day, brilliant . . .

Marna, "Superb car, Janet—"

"You're lovely, Marna—"

"Isn't she—" Sylvia.

"Love at first sight!" Janet.

Laughing, near Marna, now both of them, laughing, hair blowing, fluffing, the wind, about them . . .

Marna, "Exhilarating! That would describe it. Absolutely—"

Janet, *"Exhilarating!"*

And laughing . . .

All of them, happy, laughing . . .

At the Piccolo Teatro it was wonderful. They laughed and laughed, tears rolled down their cheeks, Janet's sides hurt, she hadn't laughed so in years. From beginning to end—she was helpless with laughter. It was difficult enough trying to keep up with the dialogue. Incredibly swift dialogue!

Marna was thrilled.

She gave Janet a big hug.

Lovely big hug . . .

Then, a good meal. Wonderful place, Janet knew it well. She and Sylvia had stayed quite a little spell in Milan, *once* . . .

Sandra, "Wasn't she lovely? Too, too lovely! A peach!"

"Just a peach!" Sylvia.

Excellent wine.

Happy.

The city around them. Swirling—

"Janet—"

"Cara—"

"How can I thank you?"

She was a bit woozy. Marna lovely, woozy.

"Mia cara!"

Janet touched her face, lovely, smooth, young lovely face . . .

She murmured to her, "We'll stay here a few days, eh? Can you stay a few days? *Mia bella.* One of Sylvia's friends has invited us—wonderful place—"

"I must get back—"

"Oh dear!"

"My classes—"

She turned to Sylvia.

"Marna can't stay."

Protest. Sighs. Appeals.

"Not a few days?" Sandra cooed.

Sylvia, "One day?"

Janet, "One tiny day?"

Marna, finally, "Well—"

A pause, they waited.

"One tiny day—" she yielded.

They cheered her. They all drank a toast, cheering her . . .

She stayed a week with them. She fell in love! Claude, a nice young Frenchman. He had come to a terrific record session Adile threw one night. She was Sylvia's friend, at whose place they were staying. Fascinating place! An architect with real talent had played with it. That's how she said it. Janet had loved the session. Adile had stacks of wonderful *old* records. Harry James, Marterie . . . *There* were dance bands! *Milano.*

She looked up her friends. At the Caprice she found quite a few. Ah, the cha-cha! She could dance it all night, the chaaa-cha . . . They took Marna with them. They got her a *sweet* dress, a blue thing, pale blue, she was exquisite in it. Her Claude danced the cha-cha. Janet danced with him. Delightful, handsome young man, he had a flat on Ile Saint-Louis, together they cha-chaaed. He had just come to Italy, he brought her up-to-date on things, this and that, in Paris . . .

"Sylvia—"

"*Cara?*"

"Let's dance the cha-cha—"

"You and I?"

"The cha-cha."

"Ah well—"
They danced the cha-cha . . .

—————————————————45

One day, after Milano, suddenly, she told Sylvia she must go
to Rome. She wanted to get to Rome. Sylvia was very unhappy. She told Sandra, and the two of them launched a
major campaign to keep her from going. She wouldn't be
swayed. Finally, they insisted on coming with her. But she
objected, sadly. She explained to them: She wanted to be
alone, she had always wanted to go to Rome, just once, *all
alone*. Would they let her? *Please? Per piacere* . . .

At last, they let her.

"Do take care of yourself," Sylvia entreated.

"And come back. You won't stay all that long, will you?
You'll write? There's so much to do!" Sandra.

Janet, smiling, "I'll write. *I promise*."

She went for a walk that night, with Sylvia. They walked
arm in arm, slowly.

"Are you—going back?" asked Sylvia, quietly.

She replied, "I don't know. I don't. Honestly."

"Don't go back."

A pause. Sylvia's arm slipped about her.

"We love you. *Honestly* . . ."

So quietly . . .

—————————————————46

The sun in Rome, drifting into her room, stirring her. She
listened, and watched. She sought its source. She wanted to
touch its source. Trailing. Crossing. Effort only in crossing.
Concealed, ever, crossing . . . *Brisés volés*. Be its source . . .
Her lovely bed. She loved her bed. Black iron bedstead, exquisitely formed, delicate lace patterns, interweaving, sweet

bedstead. White wall. Touching the white wall. Lovely
against it . . .

She thought of him. She would write him. *You would love
Milan. I'm in Rome now* . . .

She lay, quietly, in early-morning sunlight . . .

*. . . Time. Hold time. I hold time. No time. Nothing but
time. In time. Speak. Stupid time. Scream. Scream To Time.
Kiss. Enfold . . .* DESTROY TIME . . .

She heard her breathing.

She lay, barely breathing . . .

Rome, golden city. She adored Rome. She felt wonderful,
free, alive now, in Rome. She walked that day, and next,
about Rome. The sun held her, caressed her. The sun loved
her. She knew the sun loved her . . .

Via Veneto. Slowly, lovingly, swinging her white bag.
Trinitá dei Monti. She lingered before the beautiful stairway.
Her father, the stairway . . . *Chiostro di S. Paolo.* She stood
in the cloister, looking out through the exquisite arches of it,
a long while . . . Visitors came and went, they turned, went
. . . Exquisite cloister, she wished he were there with her,
suddenly . . . She closed her eyes, she saw him . . .

. . . we stare, starkly

She ate that night in a small restaurant, outside, near
Piazza del Popolo. Alone, slowly, she ate. She looked out on
the Piazza. Cars, people. They moved all about . . .

She smoked a cigarette. She sat, afterwards, a long while.
She sipped coffee, she smoked cigarettes . . .

*. . . She reached her hand out for him. She was falling,
away, falling . . . A strong chord of music caught her, held
her. She was turning, slowly,* sur les pointes, *the music guiding her . . . He watched her. He stood, immobile, silent . . .
watching her. Voices. Soft laughter. Sweet, feminine
laughter . . .*

She sat in the Foro, overlooking the ruins of the Temple of
Saturn. She was reading. Pirandello. He had told her once to
read Pirandello. Late afternoon . . .

Eyes upon her. She felt eyes upon her. She looked up. A
man was there. He was smiling at her.

"*Signorina—scusate—é occupata?*"
She stared at him.
"*Vatene.*"
He moved back.
"*Scusate. Signorina* . . ."
He left her.

She rode around Rome. One evening, in a little horse-
drawn carriage, she rode all about Rome. She looked out, remembering Rome . . . They were near the *Open Gate*. They
passed it, slowly . . .

. . . *he came to her. She held him close . . . The moment.
Transfix the moment. Movement. Abrupt shadows falling
away, moments . . . absolve the moment . . . a martyr, he
held the moment . . .*

She looked no one up. She walked around, she stayed in
her hotel, she was on her own. She wrote him. Once again,
briefly, sweetly, she wrote him . . .

"Ah, Janet—"
Signor Armandi. She smiled, so pleased to see him. Wonderful old gentleman. Gentle, solid. That was it, that came
through to her. *Gentle, yet solid.* She had met him at dinner
last evening. There had been a mix-up over tables, she had
found herself sitting across from him. She didn't mind. He
had wanted to excuse himself, but she wouldn't have it. She
had immediately liked him. And they hit it off well, at once.
They had talked all through dinner. She was amazed at him.
White-haired, an old gentleman—yet, what a grip on life! She
felt it, she was intensely aware of it. And warm. He was so
warm. Wonderfully. There was a strength in it . . .
"Good morning," she said to him.
She had come down from her room. She had finished
breakfast. She was going out. Simple, light green frock. So
comfortable. He was in the main lounge. He had seen her.
He had risen and bowed to her, a very small bow, more a
slight movement of head than a bow, really. And smiling.
"How are you?" There, the smile. Soft white hair. Her
eyes on his white hair.
So good to see him.

She wanted to pet him. Suddenly, she wished she could reach out and pet him.

"Very well—and you? I was just going out—"

"Ah—don't let me keep you—"

"Not at all, *Signore!*"

Pause. Lingering.

"Can I invite you?"

He said, "Well—thank you—that would be very nice indeed—thank you—"

"If we tire of walking we can take one of those horse and carriage things—what do you think?"

"Excellent, then! But I'll walk quite a way."

She was smiling. So glad. Smiling . . .

Rome, in the sun, glistening. Slowly, the carriage wound its way around. Easy fall of the horse's hoofs. She felt the rhythm of it. She told him of the rhythm of it. He heard it. He smiled, and nodded his head to it . . .

"Are you on holiday, *Signore?*" she asked him.

"No. Not really."

She looked about. Now, looming, the old Coliseum. Before her. It appeared, suddenly, before her. She was uneasy at it. A line of school-children passed by . . .

He said, "I have a place down near Naples—on Capri. I live there. Sometimes, I come up to Rome. I always stay at the hotel."

Pause.

"It's so nice."

"Indeed." He paused, looking at her. "It's not your first time there?"

"Oh, no."

"I thought not."

In sunlight. Silence, baring itself in the sunlight . . .

"Sometimes I stay a week. Sometimes two. Then I go back. I don't travel very much anymore." Pause. "When I was young—"

He fell silent. He looked at her. He had turned and was looking at her.

She said, feeling strange, "You still seem young."

So quietly.

"Ah, I'm not though." He smiled. "You mustn't be too polite to me. I'm ancient. Really."

She protested.

They laughed softly, both of them . . .

"You ought to come down there," he said, after a while.

She was surprised.

And delighted.

"Capri?"

"My place on Capri."

She thought about this. She knew what she was going to say, but—she thought about this . . .

"I think I'd like that!" she said.

He was pleased, she saw that.

He said to her, "Good. I'm leaving day after tomorrow. Care to come with me?"

She said yes, smiling. He was looking at her, only looking now, not smiling.

She knew it was there—somewhere—the smile . . .

───────────────────────── 47

The view took her breath away.

From the main terrace, where she was sitting, she saw, to the east, Vesuvius, and its plume of smoke; to the west, a pearly shadow, Ischia; and between, in the distance, Naples, Sorrento; and below, far below, a shimmering sea . . .

They had arrived a few hours ago, just this morning. She had strolled down to the terrace with him. Coffee was brought to them.

She said to him, "It's beautiful, the whole thing's too beautiful. *Bellezza!*"

There, the smile. She held the smile . . .

"That's good to hear. I'm only happy, really, when I'm here. This is home. Yes. That's so."

"I love your home! It's—perfect!"

She was enchanted.

In passing, "I designed the house myself." And, "What do you think of it?"

"*Incantevole!* Absolutely, enchanting!"

He went on, "I had in mind a sort of—gesture. A loving gesture, reaching up, and out, not aggressively, but in gratitude, affection. Have I succeeded? Sometimes I feel I've succeeded. Do you think I've succeeded?"

She marveled. He was waiting. He was looking at her and waiting. She held his question, close, within her. A white dot, far out, a ship, moved closer, ever closer. She watched it move closer . . .

"I think you have, *Signore*. Yes, I feel that. I do feel that—"

"Perhaps an odd thing to have in mind when planning a house?" He paused. "Well, there it was, guiding me."

"You've succeeded," she murmured to him . . .

Now in silence. The sun upon her. Warm in the sun in silence. The sea, blue one moment, far below, then shimmering, clear, limpid and silent . . .

Looking at him. She was strangely affected by him. There was the sun and the sea in him. Long life in him. She was aware of these in him. Depth. She respected the depth in him. She was aware, suddenly, of a certain awe of him . . .

"How long have you lived here?"

She was asking him, looking away from him, toward the mainland. Her heart was beating quickly.

"Oh, many years. My people have always had a place here. I've been here—oh—let's say, Janet—*many* years. My people come and go—but I'm permanent."

"Is this their place too, then?"

"No no—only mine. They're over there—"

He extended his arm to her right, along the coastline. A pink roof, far off, on a white building, buried in green . . .

She smiled. She saw him.

She felt him draw close to the smiling . . .

_____48

She was reading. He had a wonderful library, and she was reading. Maupassant. How she loved Maupassant! On the terrace, where she spent a good part of her day now, she would read, and often get through a book in a day. He had something, it seemed, in his library, by everyone . . . Deledda. She had read Deledda yesterday, plunging deep into her world. Part of that world. *The Stolen Child.* Marvelous. Within the abductor. Knowing him. So well . . .

She wrote him one brief letter, telling him. Enchanted isle. *How I love this enchanted isle* . . .

Mail, forwarded from somewhere, from her family.

She threw it out . . .

. . . indifference of life. Death. Awareness of death. Help-less, insignificant, stupid, utterly stupid, before death. Con-demned to death. At conception, already condemned to death. All death. Longing. Terror, yet longing, for death. My body. One instant, now even, this, all, irrevocably, gone . . . Precious life. Precarious, flimsy . . .

. . . STUPID LIFE *. . .*

She loved it here. So peaceful and calm. She would go for walks about the island. She would stop and look out a long time at the sea. The sunsets. Astonishing sunsets. Great, cop-per-orange ball settling, slowly, setting. Eternally clear sky. It seemed. Sometimes, whispering wisps of cloud, hovering on the horizon. Quiet, warmth, the mystery of it, aware of the mystery of it. Dusk. Early dusk . . . She clung to it, happy and sad in it, speaking, within, to it. Longing, seeking, want-ing it. She would wait until darkness came in. Then, she headed back to the villa. There he would be. White-haired old gentleman. Old. Would be. *Old*. She smiled at that . . .

She smiled at the thought of that. There. Eyes upon her, smiling at her. She would wash, and change. They would have dinner. She felt so fresh, and they would have dinner. Amelia, his cook, was a marvel. Every evening it seemed—something new, something different, delicious. Always deli-cious! He spoke of her. Now, tonight, he spoke of her . . .

"Amelia's a treasure. She's been with us—oh—twenty years."

She looked at him.

She waited.

She tried,

"Is she from the island?"

"No. *Roma*." He paused. "We found her in Roma."

She waited . . .

"She and my wife were great friends."

He paused.

"She's very good."

She listened . . .

"My wife died ten years ago."

There, evening, only a breath of wind, drifting from one

end of the terrace to the other, and sea sounds, far-off sea
sounds, murmuring, sure she could hear the sea sounds.
Lights from ships, blinking, hovering, persisting. The mainland. Lights of the mainland . . .

Maria, a maid, stood near the table. She was showing him
a bottle of wine. He held it close to the table lamp. He nodded his head, smiling, turning to her, speaking softly to her.

"Fine, Maria."

"Shall I bring two, *Signore?*"

He turned to Janet.

"Can we take two?"

She smiled.

"Let's try to take two."

He turned to Maria.

"Bring two."

They were laughing. The three of them now, in the warm,
gentle night, laughing.

*. . . a quivering passed through the corps. It trembled. She
stood among them. It moved, round and round her. White,
lovely figures moving around her, gliding, turning. She was
en arabesque, she whipped herself about now, quickly, turning, pirouetting beautifully . . . The Prince, near her. He
touched her. She leaned back, falling, ever falling, he caught
her, held her, she fluttered her leg, développé now, slowly,
beautifully . . .*

*. . . in Venice, Casino del Lido . . . she remembered . . .
she loved Casino del Lido . . .*

In the moonlight, a swirl of smoke. Vesuvius. Before her,
there in the moonlight, Vesuvius.

*. . . leap, dear . . . land like a feather . . . my dear . . . a
feather . . .*

"Signore—"

He was near her, his face in profile in the dim light. He
was sitting quietly, looking across the bay. The night.

He looked into the night. He turned to her . . .

She was going to say something. She thought she was going to say something . . . But only a smile. And she offered a cigarette . . .

Quietly, "Ah no, thank you, Janet . . ."

She lit one up for herself.

She pulled long on it, she let the smoke come into her, drift through her, she loved the smoke coming into her, she was lulled by the smoke, in her . . .

"Look—there—that pattern of stars, *Signore*—"

He nodded his head.

He told her the name of it.

She said, suddenly, "It's impossible—all—isn't it, really? Who would believe it? Would you believe it?"

He was listening, turning once, slightly, to her, only listening . . .

She went on, "The distance! They don't even measure it in miles! *Time*. How *long* it *takes to reach us*. They say millions of years! Imagine? What are we? That star—see it—its light possibly started out toward us *some millions of years ago!* Imagine that! Try conceiving that! My God, sit here . . . conceive that . . ."

Quiet.

She stared at the sky.

All quiet . . .

"Who are you distant from?"

She heard it. Cigarette, on its way to her lips, checked. She turned to him. He wasn't looking at her . . .

Cigarette, her hand, before her. Smoke rising, curling, before her . . .

Cigarette to her lips, slowly . . . She puffed the cigarette. The smoke hovered, drifted, drifted away, slowly . . . She pulled again, she blew the smoke out . . . it billowed. She watched it, caught by the night, billowing . . .

"*Signore*—" she said, quietly.

He turned to her. He was looking at her. In the night, she saw him, looking at her . . .

Breathlessly, controlling her breathlessness, quietly,

"*Do you know me?*"

On her.

The eyes, before her, on her . . .

"You're Janet."

Softly . . .

She faltered.

He waited. He was looking, and waiting.

She turned away, slowly . . .

Coffee. He was sipping coffee. Maria had brought some.

Soft breeze. Fragrance of oleanders. Time was the fragrance. In time, the fragrance. Back, back. The crater. Her eyes on the crater . . .

"When did you last dance, Janet?"

She fell from the crater.

"You knew—" a whisper.

Quiet.

"All the time, *you knew*. Somehow, I was sure you knew—"

He sat quietly, sipping his coffee, sometimes looking at her, waiting. Listening, waiting . . .

He said, finally, gently, "When was it?"

She said, looking fully at him, "Does it matter?"

"When was it?" he said, urging her . . .

She said nothing. She looked away. She wanted to say something. Words clung to her, within her. They would not emerge from her. They started to come, but they died. They stopped, and died . . . But some struggled. They kept up the struggle. She helped them. She sought to help them. She stirred. A whisper. Softly, just a whisper, still looking away from him, but near him, aware of being so near him—

"When did you last see me?"

"In Rome."

A pause.

"Three years ago."

"Giselle—"

"You were magnificent."

"I remember—"

"I'd never seen anything like it."

"I *remember*—"

. . . *remember . . . circle . . . round and around the circle, within the circle, turning, swiftly . . . the melody . . . part of the melody . . . Giselle . . . the melody . . . Giselle . . . you are the melody . . .*

She heard him,

"You're not very old."

Laughing, suddenly, aware of her laughing, seeking to stop her laughing . . .

"Not really—" finally.

"Ulanova, I believe, is in her fifties!" he said.

Now both, softly, laughing . . .

Silence.

Both, silent . . . .

"You're not much over thirty. Are you more than thirty?"
Smiling. "A bit more than thirty."
He nodded.
Gentle, barely perceptible nod there . . .

She said, putting her cigarette out, "You're thinking that's
all there was to my life, and now there's nothing at all to my
life. That's what you're thinking." She paused, looked at him,
"And—why did I make this trip—"
He was looking at her.
He said nothing . . .

She walked in the night. Blue night, warm night, warm
blue night, held and caressed by the night. She walked, hear-
ing the sounds of night, letting them come into her, hold her.
within her . . .
  On the terrace.
  Alone, she was standing there.
  She saw the bay. She looked far across the bay. Moonlight.
Full moon, strong, lovely, upon her, the night . . .

  . . . *she*, Armida, *moved into* arabesque . . . Rinaldo, *gently, swayed her arm up and down . . . the music . . . her
lovely music . . . she, the music . . . He turned her round
. . . arabesque allongée . . . He swayed her to and fro . . .
raised her from the ground . . . three small lifts . . . his arm
about her . . . slowly, he turned her . . . right leg sweeping
the air . . . rond de jambe en l'air . . . the music quickened
. . . He tried to kiss her . . . she bent her head out of his
reach . . . Kiss would be fatal . . . They would die . . . He
tried again, bending over her . . .*

  She lay in bed. He had put her in such a pretty room. Pale
green room. Moonlight filled the room. It fell across her bed,
upon her. She looked at the moon. She was sad, longing.
aware of loss, something within her, lost . . . But she was
peaceful. She felt such peace now. Just now . . . *Stay a long
time . . . ask him . . . so nice . . . perhaps forever . . . can
I . . .*

She lay there, thinking of him, looking forward to seeing him, being with him, near him, once again, tomorrow . . .

She dozed off.

. . . *He was there, he was a young man. Handsome blue costume. She was in white . . . brisés volés . . . She moved away from him, quickly, pas de bourée . . . He watched her . . . His arms were raised now, slightly . . . awaiting her . . . She circled him, sur les pointes . . . round, round and round . . . circling him . . .*

_____49

OH NICE

. . . *foundation. First, my dear, velvet finish flowing base, oh, Orlane's creme Vestale, yes, golden beige (Oh beige), dotted on sparingly, smoothed evenly, all over. There. Don't forget eyelids! My dear . . . then, beige-rose rouge, highlight the eyes (oh eyes), contour the face . . . Eye color! Double take, soft blue pencil for line, close to lashes, yes, oh perfect, just . . . Veronese shadow for wing of color . . . Powder . . . darling . . . Lightly, patted into, not just onto . . . Now . . . now here: two shades of powder, light over dark. Darling! Déese No. 4 over Beige Patna . . . Mascara, vert, deep deep green . . . apply twice . . . finely . . . Eyebrows: feather stroke with dark brown pencil. Now lips (oh lips) . . . bow shape, extend lower lip beyond its own limit . . . Rose Amour stick . . .*
    Oh beauty!
    She lay there . . .
    Morning sun, kissing her.
    She smiled, musing at Beauty . . .

Delightful place. Really. The garden was out of a fairy tale. Ever changing design of *alées pergolas*, low hedges. The house itself was enchanting, standing there looking out onto shaded courtyards and garden. A path. She was walking along the path. Intricate design of white pebbles. It led her past a bed of large-leaved farfugiums. *Oh Farfugiums!* Terraces. Each a garden in itself! Some shaded with pergolas . . .

Vines, wisteria interwinding themselves with jasmine and bougainvillaea. Others open to the sun, and here sun-loving plants, thriving . . . brilliant carpet . . .

He smiled.

"Ah, well, is it good?"

They were on the main terrace. They were having some breakfast. Just a tiny breakfast.

She stretched, laughing, back in her chair, bending back in the chair. She loved it. She loved the feel of her stretching . . .

. . . *a cat purrs, pretty pussy cat purrs. oh purrs* . . .

"Oh, it's good!" She yawned, demurely. She was still waking up . . . "Don't you think it is good?"

"Very good."

He sipped coffee. He looked across the bay.

He said, "Did you go for a walk last night?"

"I did."

"And this morning?"

"I Did!" Sprightly.

"Wonderful. Was it wonderful?"

"So wonderful. *Magic!*"

Smiling. She was sure he was smiling. She wanted so much: the smiling . . .

"Once," she said, "when I was young, when we came here —*first* came here," she paused. "My father brought me. I was just a little girl. I asked him, 'Have we come to Heaven?' I asked him! You're smiling? Why are you smiling?"

"Am I smiling?"

"You *are* smiling," she said, quietly . . .

He only looked at her.

She said, "It *is* magic. It seems to be magic. Where is the world? I've forgotten the world."

A pause. She looked away.

"Horrid world . . ."

They were quiet. They finished coffee and were sitting there, quietly . . .

She was in a dream. She had closed her eyes, momentarily, and was in a dream. The sun touched her, warmed her and lulled her. Her breasts were warm. She was aware of their warmth. She loved them. She saw her breasts . . . A voice. Out of the dream came a voice. Through to the dream—the voice . . .

"What do you remember?"

His voice.

Her eyes opened.

She was flustered, vaguely, a moment, and smiled at him. She felt a slight blush at him . . . She had heard the words, had understood them. Within, they alighted. They rose again, hovered. She trembled a bit. Just a bit . . .

"It hurts to remember."

"You don't dance at all now?"

"No."

"No practice at all now?"

"No."

He sighed. He seemed to sigh now . . . soft breeze now, about them, taking up, drifting . . . about them . . .

. . . orange night, long night. Round night. She had the round night. Hold of the round night. She had grasped firm hold of it. It throbbed. In her hands, under her hands, hot night, velvety . . . Round and hard. She had hold of it. It throbbed. Huge. And growing. She was swinging. She was swinging and holding. More violently, swinging, but holding on, trying to hold on, to it . . . She was falling. It was following her. Moving with her, in on her, toward her. She landed. The shock hurt her. She fell back. It was before her, large, larger . . . It obscured all else. It would crush her. She screamed. She fell, suddenly, far, the ground opening, she fell, screaming . . .

He was nowhere. She searched the terraces. She descended the hill and searched all the terraces. She trembled, skipping quickly over the white-pebbled pathways . . .

_____50

One day, she said to him, suddenly, looking away from him,

"Who are you?"

"You know that," he replied, calmly.

"Yes, yes—but—"

She turned to him.

"Do tell me!"

He only looked at her, long, quietly. White hair. The white hair. She turned away. Quickly. She started sobbing. Tears spilled out of her, urgently. They had leaped up, suddenly, like fire, within her. She could not hold them. They washed over her . . .

A long while . . .

He watched her.

He sat quietly, watching her . . .

The sun, brilliantly, scattering itself in its white flight, lost in its flight, touching her . . . *Light. Blue sky, so blue, cling to me, render me, reach down, touch me, and hold me gently, lift me, tenderly . . . hold me . . .*

He was there. Quietly. Looking away now, then turning to her, again, watching her, eyes upon her, tenderly, she felt them, upon her. She wanted them, she wanted to be in them, part of them, she wanted to have them, within her, take them within her, deep, deep within her . . .

. . . The baseball was flying right out of the park. Right out of the park. It had been hit so hard, so well, it was flying right out of the park. Someone was with her. Someone, beside her, had come here with her. A great roaring. Screaming and shouting and roaring. Long, long roaring. Crowd, all about, huge crowd, roaring. How had she come here? She tried to think how, why she had come here . . . He was with her. Beside her. He was sitting, mutely, looking straight ahead. Only. Pain. Within her. Tiny at first, then growing, spreading, all through her. She wanted to scream. She touched him. In all the roaring. She reached over and touched him. She turned his face. She held it. The eyes stared into her. The eyes, burying themselves in her, took hold of her, complete hold of her, within her . . . She screamed. Long, loud, fiercely . . .

"You're very wealthy, aren't you?"

He asked that. She sat, not moving, half smiling, surprised at his asking that. Evening. They were indoors, in his long parlor, lovely long parlor. One wall, facing the sea, was a window. She could see all. The night, the bay, all before her . . . In the room, a grand piano, to one side. Soft lights and furniture. Lovely, light grayish furniture. She loved the furniture. Her chair was so comfortable. She had sunk snugly into it. She felt so good in it . . . She saw the night. The mainland. Flickering lights of the mainland. Ships. Bobbing lights of ships, moving, persistently moving. His voice caressing her. Aware of his voice, there, caressing her . . . Yet startling her. Never failing to startle her. Her heart quickened, each time he spoke. She heard it . . .

She said, "My family is wealthy."

A pause. He was looking at her. She turned, slowly, catching him looking at her. She said, casually,

"I earned a good bit, you know—"

"Yes."

She smiled, faintly . . .

She turned away, to the window again, finally . . .

He said, "Shall I put something on the phonograph?"

"Please."

She did not turn. She looked long out the window.

"A nice quartet—is that all right, Janet?"

"Yes," she said . . .

She heard the music. It drifted to her.

She murmured, "It's Beethoven. Isn't it Beethoven?"

"Yes."

She heard him . . .

It was lovely. It was the night, and entered her. With the night, entering her. There, alive, in her. She loved it, within her . . .

In the soft light, she turned to him. He was sitting back, quietly, listening. The white hair. She loved the white hair . . .

"Watch the sea, Janet. The moon will appear. Shortly. It works wonders there," he said now . . .

. . . *white night* . . .

She watched the sea.

. . . *my night* . . .

There, the sea . . .

"Does it happen ofter, Janet?"

She heard now.

"What, *signore?*"

She turned now.

"A wealthy girl takes up ballet—" he answered, pausing now, "I mean, seriously—professionally, ultimately—"

She didn't answer. She didn't like the question. She didn't at all like the question. *Why had he asked the question?*

She didn't answer.

She heard the quartet. Lovely, living quartet. Tender, true depths. *Blood depths.* She was aware of its blood depths . . .

"Forgive me if I upset you. I was only curious to know how you got started," the voice, tenderly . . .

She said, still somewhat piqued, "I don't remember."

"It just happened?"

Was he teasing?

She looked.

She didn't think he was teasing.

She ventured, "I think so. Yes. My father—" She paused. "My father loved music. I remember this piece. We—"

She halted. Abruptly. *What was she saying? What for?* She withdrew, to herself. In herself . . .

"Did you dance for him? Did you dance this for him?" he said now.

She sat. Staring at him.

She said, she heard herself say,

"In the music room—"

"How old were you?"

"I remember now—"

"You danced to it?"

"I tried to dance to it—"

"How old were you?"

"Very young—"

"Ten?"

"Younger—I'm sure—quite sure—"

"You danced to it—"

"I tried to dance to it—"

Waiting.

In the silence.

She seemed to be waiting. Aware of him, waiting . . .

The quartet was ending. He was listening, head slightly inclined to it . . . She was suddenly upset, angry at the quartet . . .

"That was very young," he said.

"That's how I started."

He looked at her.

"Don't you love this?"

"I love it—"

Quietly . . .

He was looking at her. Was he laughing at her? She felt he was laughing at her, she could see no sign, but she felt, somewhere, he was laughing at her . . .

Another record had dropped in place. Mozart. Lovely quartet. She closed her eyes. She loved it . . .

Nothing now, only the music . . . content with the music . . .

"When did you start lessons—serious lessons?"

That, the voice.

She opened her eyes. *Kind voice.* So pleased with the voice. She loved the voice . . .

"Oh—ten—eleven—yes, eleven."

"In New York?"

"Partly. Paris. London too—"

Silence.

"You know Europe well—"

"Oh, very well! Second home, really—"

Looking at her.

"I've spent as much time here as there—" She laughed, she felt gay, suddenly, "Do you know *there?*" She paused, watching him. "I was just a little girl, you know, the first time I came—" She paused again. "I have tons of friends here!"

Of the silence.

She sat, snug in the silence, looking at him . . . She turned, finally, she looked long at the night. The bay . . .

"Signore—"

She said, suddenly,

"Do you think I'm lovely?"

Without turning, coyly.

She heard him,

"You're very lovely."

So good.

Warm, all curled up, snug, smiling . . .

Snug and curled up, smiling . . .

"I know I'm lovely . . ."

In her castle, here.

Castle overlooking the bay, Vesuvius, Solaro . . . *all* . . . Here.

He said to her, "You speak beautifully. *As you danced.* Very beautifully—"

She fell back. The words fell on her, and she fell back.

She looked at him . . .

The music surged now, toward a crescendo.

There, the four instruments, blending . . .

Words. She found words.

So quietly, "Which do you like?"

He was smiling, looking at her.

He said to her, "Will you think me old-fashioned?"

She watched him. She listened now, watching him.

"An old romantic?" He paused, he moved in his chair. "Well, never mind, I'll tell you—*Swan Lake—Sylphides—Giselle—Sleeping Beauty—*" He paused again. "Shall I go on?"

Silent now. Serious and silent now. He leaned forward. He placed his hands together, the tips of his fingers touching.

"It's all there. Movement, and beauty, *life*, all there. Do you agree with me?"

She stared. In the silence, staring . . .

Her voice. She heard it.

"Everything. *There*. Dreams are there . . ."

"I knew immediately who you were."

He said quietly, "There was a modern one—I can see it— *poème dansé*—*Angel*—*Dark Angel*—what was it, Janet?"

. . . in the park, young lovers. She watched the lovers. She closed her eyes . . . drifting . . . years dissolving, drifting . . . she danced with him. Flowing, poignant pas de deux . . . Her eyes opened, she stared, momentarily . . . She drifted to sleep . . . gray angel . . . death in the wings of the angel . . .

"*L'Ange Gris*," she said.

"I remember."

Eyes, upon her. Aware of his eyes upon her . . .

"Capri is an old island," she said, suddenly.

Another record was playing. She said to him, "Dvorák—" She loved the wonderful quartet by Dvorák.

He nodded.

She said, murmuring, "Strange island—"

"Why so?" he asked her.

"Always thought so," she answered. "Once—"

Halting, abruptly, listening . . .

She saw him listening.

Quartet's themes, struggling, hovering . . .

. . . en bourée . . . skip softly to him . . . by the sea . . . love with a love that was more than love, Anabel Lee . . . soar, leap . . . love, my love . . . struck while alone by the sea . . . lie beside me . . . die . . . by the sea . . .

"Janet—"

51

Sunrise.

She stood, looking out at it.

She stretched.

On tiptoes . . .

She felt good. Alive, good . . .

A letter from him, written some time ago, had found its way here.

She kissed the letter . . .

Sunrise upon her, kissing her, and the island. She saw the island. Luxuriant growth of the island. She saw the sea, aflame . . .

. . . *tell him* . . .

She would tell him . . .

Out of the sunrise, a waltz. For her, a flower . . . suddenly, lovingly opening . . . *she, the flower* . . . She fell back, alarmed, and—thrilled . . .

In the middle of her room she was swaying, moving . . . *the surge, the beat of the waltz* . . .

Turning . . .

. . . *I love him* . . .

Over, abruptly.

She lay on her bed, sobbing, softly, into her pillow.

She saw, she clung to her pillow . . .

Skirt and blouse. She slipped into her skirt. She changed her mind. She took off her skirt. Shorts. Nice pair of shorts, today. *Oh, shorts.* Lovely legs, in shorts. Today . . . Her hair, back, and up. She looked at her hair. *Oh lovely hair.* Loving her hair . . . Slippers. White, comfortable . . . She looked at her face. In the sunrise, her face. She loved her face. Smiling, now, at her face. Eyebrows. Light brown eyebrows . . . *brown, lovely eyes, mine* . . . She saw her eyes

. . . alive eyes, mine . . . She adored her eyes . . . *he loves my eyes . . . looks into my eyes . . .* there, *my eyes . . .* Her nose. She touched her nose. Lips. Warm, full lips. White teeth, smiling . . . She blew a kiss at her face . . .

A sound.

Disturbed by the sound, she looked out. Overhead, an aircraft was flying. In the sunlight, ever brighter now, she saw the plane, glistening. *Where?* Perhaps Naples. *Is he on it?* She smiled. She watched the plane, a long time . . . She saw it disappear, finally, in the horizon . . .

She was on her balcony. She let the sun come into her, she felt it, so good, within her. She turned to the sun. She looked about. She could see practically the whole of the island. There, to the left, a cluster of white houses, pink roofs. Before her, a road, winding, climbing. Falling away, thick clusters of luxuriant growth, and, the sea . . .

Caves. Sea running into the caves . . .

There was no one about. She could see no one about . . .

She wanted to walk. She left her room and went downstairs. Lovely, marble floor. Light, ever so light green hallway. Paintings. She stopped to look at the paintings. A Picasso. Wonderful Picasso. She turned her head this way, and that. She smiled. She looked away. She was smiling . . .

On the terrace, a young maid was working. Not Maria. *Anna.* Sweeping, arranging things. Janet walked over to her. The girl, white-skinned, dark-haired, smiled at her.

"*Buon giorno, signora—*"

. . . Signora . . .

"*Buon giorno.*"

"Do you wish to sit here? I won't be a minute."

"No, no, I'm just walking."

She moved to the low wall. She looked out at Vesuvius. The sea. Alight, all alight.

"*Bellezza!*" she sighed, to the girl.

She stopped working, turned, looked, smiled at her.

"*Si, signora—*"

The path wound down the hill. Round and around, down the hill. She walked on it easily. She came to the foot of the hill. The sun was warm. She loved the sun. She felt so warm and good in the sun. Small road now. A group of children were playing in a field alongside the hill. They were running, running, and shouting. Sounds of firing. They ran to the hill and scattered. There was a whistle. Janet watched the war game. She smiled. They would be from the village. From her room she could see the village. At night, the lights, slowly, went out in the village. Early-morning warfare. She had wondered about the village. A little girl was beside her. She hadn't noticed her. She stood, near the roadside, just beside her. She was holding a yellow flower in one hand, and the hand was against her chest. She seemed so forlorn. She wore a tan little dress. Janet smiled at her. She reached out and touched her face, tenderly, caressed her face.

"And who are you?"

Chi sei?

The little girl was shy. She would not talk.

"Well, what do you call your flower? Have you a name for your pretty flower?"

The little girl, now, seemed to smile. She held out the flower. She said, "You smell it, *signora*, would you like to smell it?"

Heaven scent.

"How wonderful! And what do you call it? What would you call it?"

The little girl lowered her head. Her hand remained outstretched.

"I don't know, *signora*. I just found it."

"Ah, well—where did you find it? Will you show me just where you found it?"

"Over there."

Janet looked where the hand swept. Across the field, near a rock face, a whole mass of them waved, brilliant, yellow, dancing in sunlight. She hadn't seen them. They must have been there. She hadn't—

She started to walk away. Suddenly, she turned and started to walk away. She couldn't stay. The little girl followed. Now, beside her. Slowly, walking, beside her.

. . . *tell me of flowers can you tell me of flowers* . . .

The little girl.

"What's your name, *carina?*"

"Albina. *Mi chiamo* Albina."

"Ah, lovely, Albina . . ."

They were approaching the village. Shouts behind them. The warriors returning. She looked back and saw them. Albina was holding her hand now. The flower still in the other.

"Where do you live? In the village?"

"Yes."

"Shall I take you?"

"Oh, not yet! Mamma sent me out to play. I must play. My brother will get shouted at if he goes home without me.

Then he shouts at me. When Mamma's not around he shouts at me. He must watch me. He's back there now."

"I see."

Smiling . . .

The warriors, behind them, pressing hard upon them . . .

"*Ecco Agosto!*" The little girl shouted.

The platoon pulled up before them. Agosto, possibly ten years old, stepped forward.

"What are you doing?" he said to her.

And to Janet, "Excuse me, *signora—*"

"Nothing, Agosto," said Albina.

"You were supposed to wait for us—why didn't you wait for us? Back there—"

"We were walking. *Signora* and I were walking—"

"Why should you bother the lady? Excuse her, *signora—*"

"Why, Agosto, I asked her to walk with me!"

He was puzzled.

"See! I haven't bothered her—"

"Of course she hasn't." Janet added, "I may have bothered her, though!"

And, "Well, shall we all walk? I was going for a long walk. Would you all like to walk?"

Consultations, scraping of feet . . . announcement.

"Well, *signora*, we would love to—but—not now—you see that hill, *signora?* We have to retake it. We left many wounded there. Perhaps tomorrow?"

"I want to go with her! Let me go with her!" Albina pleaded.

More discussion.

Agosto, "All right, you go with her. But you must stop off and tell Mamma. Be sure you tell Mamma."

"I'll tell Mamma!"

"We'll tell Mamma," Janet assured him . . .

"*Ciao, signora . . . Arrivederla . . .*"

Good-byes, all round. She watched them return to the hill . . .

Walking, white sunlight, along the road, they were walking. Occasionally, a cart passed them. Donkey. Sweet donkey . . .

They came to Albina's house. They saw Mamma. With her, near her, another daughter, perhaps sixteen, slender, bust in full bloom, fully aware of her bust in bloom . . .

All right, all right, said the mother, it is all right. But a drink. A little drink! *Biscotti?* Have some nice *biscotti!*

Mamma asked, "Where are you staying?"

"Just up there—" Janet said.

"Signor Armandi's villa?"

"Yes."

"Bel posto! Magnificent! A good man. *Un signore."* She paused. Her voice dropped. "His wife passed away not too long ago—how long ago? Oh, they had gone to France. She passed away. In Paris. One morning, *una mattina,* they found her dead in bed. *In letto, morta.* So sad. So very sad. She was so good. *Una vera donna.* A real woman . . ." She sighed, long, before her. Tears. She crossed herself . . .

Out of the village. Sirocco. A hill. Lovely and hot, oh so hot! The little girl beside her, clutching her flower. They passed a church.

. . . in a church, this was the church, was this the church, monks chanting, voices rising, lingering, lingering, falling, she heard the chanting, the lovely, sad chanting. Candles, flickering, white lady, oh my white lady . . . lady . . .

Other flowers. Pretty blue flowers. Janet, delighted, picked them. She held them. She laughed with the little girl and kissed them. The little girl kissed them . . .

They sat on top of a hill. The sun caressed them on top of the hill. Out there the sea.

. . . Satin sea . . .

Round, all around, island washed by the sea. Deep caves receiving the sea . . .

"Albina—"

"Signora?"

"What do you wish for?"

"Most for?"

"Most of all for—"

A second.

Only—

"To fly! Like an angel! High, over all, to look down like an angel, keep Mommy and Daddy alive, like an angel . . ."

"White angel?"

"White, *so* white, all white angel—"

Smiling, beaming, Albina . . .

. . . my angel . . .

"Your mother would miss you—"

"Oh, I'd still be here!"

"As an angel?"

Janet hugged her, took her in her arms and hugged her . . .

52

She got back in the evening. She had stayed at Albina's house for supper. Mamma had insisted. There was no refusing. A great honor. Mamma told her, *a Very great honor*. She *Must* stay. She did. Magnificent supper. Wine. Wonderful table. She ate and ate, happy, laughing. The whole family. Lovable Poppa. Everyone doted on Poppa. She stared at the older daughter. Truly lovely. Janet thought, *presenza—what fine presence* . . . Agosto, and two older brothers. One, so handsome! In his twenties, soon to be married, *so handsome!* . . .

She got back. The older sister, Agosto, one of the brothers, walked most of the way back with her. They waved and waved near the villa, saying good-bye, *arrivederla* . . .

She went to her room and changed. Through the window, last of the day. Orange fragrance. Her balcony. Leaning, looking out. Music, drifting. Warm night. From somewhere —mandolins, guitars. Somewhere. The rhythm. She came alive to the rhythm. She swayed within, at the rhythm. She was part of the rhythm . . . *be the rhythm* . . .

Pretty frock, soft frock, pale blue.

Bra 'n' brief . . .

oh brief

Signore Armandi, on the terrace-*salon*, was sitting, reading. He had a pipe. She had not seen the pipe. He was puffing the pipe. She smelled the pipe, she loved the smell of his pipe . . . He was listening. She knew he was listening. There, yet, the music . . . She surprised him . . .

"*Buona sera*—"

"Ah! *Buona sera*—"

He was smiling. He held his pipe and was smiling.

"Should I apologize?"

"Apologize?"

"I should, really—"

"Why apologize?"

She sighed, she sat down. She looked at him.

"I've had a lovely day. I've walked and walked, all day—"

"Tired?"

"Not really."

"Hungry?"

"I've eaten. In the village—Signora—*Malda*? Mother of a little girl I walked with—"

"Yes—"

"She insisted!"

"Are you glad she insisted?"

"Delighted! My, she can cook!" She paused. "Almost like our Amelia!"

He smiled. He puffed his pipe.

"Ah, well—Amelia—" He paused. "Oh, they can cook, all right! In fact—well, I'll tell you—Amelia learned quite a lot here."

"I love this island—"

She looked about.

"Where is the music? Can you hear the music?"

"I don't know. Perhaps that place over there. That villa. I don't really know—can you tell?"

Janet, laughing, "Wonderful. Really!"

"Will you have some coffee?"

"I'd love some coffee!"

Moonlight, about them, on the terrace, all about them . . . Maria brought some coffee.

Janet smoked. She puffed, long, on her cigarette.

She said to him, after a while, quietly.

"Your wife died in Paris."

He answered, not turning his head, "Yes."

"They told me . . ."

He puffed his pipe. She watched him. He sat quietly, looking across the bay . . . She closed her eyes a moment, sipping her coffee. Lovely coffee . . .

"*L'Opéra. Chauviere. Swan Lake* . . ."

She heard him.

"*Signore*—"

He turned to her. "But yours matched it. I'll tell you— should I tell you? *Surpassed it.*" He paused. "Yes. Surpassed it."

She was pleased, yet within, trembling . . .

She started to say, "You—"

And heard say, "We saw you there."

She was looking at him.

Silence.

The music had stopped, momentarily. She hoped: *momentarily* . . .

Whirring. Night sounds . . .

Soft movement about her. Night air, in movement, about her.

"Exquisite!" he said. "So difficult! I imagine—extremely difficult. The twin roles. Such contrast! The strain must be terrible. Such beauty. Out of the strain, *beauty* . . ."

She sat quietly.

He went on, "Once, in New York, Oh, years ago—" he paused, "how many years ago? Oh, a splendid thing—*Orpheus*—yes, I recall—" He paused again. "It's all before me. The Furies. That final scene—"

. . . in the wings, Bernice beckoned her . . . She swerved, glided, toward her . . .

Her voice, "That night—"

. . . she, Eurydice, *moved close to him . . . he tried to hold her . . . she slid to the floor, his arms reached desperately for her . . . He abandoned all patience . . . She was beside him . . . her face close to his . . . he tore the mask from his face . . . Silence . . . Absolute . . . She fell against him . . .*

The music—

She longed for the music. She waited, it should begin . . . *why not begin . . . Now. Begin* . . . A tune tugged at her. She knew the tune. She closed her eyes and heard it. *Chella La*. She loved the tune. Its rhythm beat within her, lovingly. She was the rhythm . . .

Her eyes opened. He was there. Pipe on the table now. A shadow drifted across the terrace. Momentarily, it separated her from the moonlight. She felt the moment. She was aware, hurt, in the moment . . .

"Did you like doing it?"

. . . doing it . . .

"Very difficult doing it. The theme got hold of you, such a hold of you, it got inside and hurt you." She paused, looking fully at him, "It was dangerous doing it. I can't say I *liked*—" she paused again, "doing it."

"Do you remember?"

"Yes. I remember—"

"The actual steps, the choreography?"

"Everything—*of course*—I remember."

Only remembering . . .

They sat quietly, sipping coffee.
She saw the moon, lighting the sea . . .
He, the night, held the night.
For her . . .

He said to her, she heard him say to her, "Your eyes are the loveliest. You know that. Your eyes, the drama—"

She heard, she turned to him . . . She saw him.

Eyes, seeing . . .

"Have you ever married, Janet?"

Gently.

Silent, staring at him.

Murmuring, finally,

"No, signore—"

Only staring at him . . .

He said, "You've covered a good bit of Europe on this trip. Have you seen your old friends, Janet?"

She was laughing, suddenly, within, wildly, hysterically . . .

Containing the laughing.

Quietly, somehow, "Most of my friends—"

He said, "You didn't stay long with them?"

"No—not too long—"

Looking at her.

An old friend, calmly, sitting there looking at her . . .

She turned.

She felt him, looking at her . . .

Now, casually,

"Who are you running from, Janet?"

So casually. Hitting her, falling into her, hurting her. She felt it, within, hurting her. Hanging on. She was dizzy. She felt she would fall. She knew, in a moment, she would fall . . .

Her voice, *"No one—"*

She would not go on . . .

She could not.

On the terrace, in her chair, she held to the night, tight, tight . . .

She whispered . . .

She fell from the chair, whispering.

. . . *The theatre was empty. Slowly, across the stage, three or four dancers drifted. Near darkness. They had rehearsed since morning. Now, at last, perfect. All perfect. They were leaving . . . Quiet, darkness. She stood, alone in the theatre, in darkness. She started to leave. She moved toward the exit . . . A whisper. She turned, startled. There was no one. She started to move again. She reached the exit. Again, the whisper. She halted, frightened. She stood a moment. She wanted to open the door and rush out. But she could not. She turned, she found herself turning, slowly. Down the aisle. She walked slowly. She stopped, halfway down the aisle. She looked up, a loud thumping, violent, in her . . . He was there, a white figure, stark, alone, on the stage, carved out of the darkness. He looked down at her. One hand was outstretched. Dead. White hand. Dead. All of him. Death, in the hand, all of him . . . She turned, she walked swiftly. The thumping, louder. She moved up the aisle, toward the door, swiftly. She would reach it soon, moving swiftly . . . She didn't. She was before him. She found herself there, before him . . . Her hand moving. She shuddered, she tried to stop the hand, moving . . . "Carl" . . . her voice . . . "Carl" . . . she clung to her voice . . . Cold. He was ice cold. The coldness came to her. The coldness, relentlessly, moving all through her . . .*

Awake, abruptly, cool sheets, aware of cool sheets, her heart thumping, violently . . . Awake now, breathing quickly, aware of night, knowing the night, in bed, not knowing where in bed, wondering where and how she had come to bed . . .

"There now—"

A voice, calmly.

Knowing the voice . . .

Calming.

54

Where was time?

Desperately, she sought time . . .

She was awake. Listening. Far off, on the sea somewhere, a ship's signal. She heard the signal. A soft breeze, drifting into the room, stirred the curtains. She saw the curtains. Swaying curtains. In the moonlight, gently swaying white curtains . . .

. . . white dress . . . white mist of my white dress . . .

He lifted her, beautifully . . . she turned, sensuously, he lifted her again, her arms extended . . .

She saw the curtains. She watched them. Her breathing. Softly. Aware of her breathing. She lay, listening to it . . .

. . . Marble. White marble. She touched the white marble . . .

She closed her eyes.

. . . Her father held her. She was a little girl and her father held her . . .

Timelessness, flickering, in and out, ticking . . .

She fell asleep.

. . . She, the Firebird, danced alone on a dark stage, only one light on her, enclosing her, following her . . . dazzling Firebird, white legs, arms . . . sur les pointes . . . she extended one leg and whipped the air in brilliant turns . . . A harp, far off, melancholy . . . melody, flowing, lullaby . . . she was still now . . . Mysterious forest, quiet, at peace now . . . move . . . birdlike movements . . . move now . . . across the stage . . . dance . . . fluidly . . . beautifully . . . feet trembling . . . Firebird, fly now . . . glittering Firebird . . . now . . .

55

Twilight. Day still warm, lovely and warm, she sat with him and talked with him. The sun, slowly, sank, and disappeared. The red glow. Red-orange glow. Changing. Ever-changing . . . She watched the changing . . .

She was sipping a drink. She loved her drink.

On the terrace-*salon*, looking out at twilight, over the bay, they were quiet now. She heard a melody. She was remembering a melody. A cha-cha melody.

. . . Cha cha cha, I love the cha-cha . . . tell him and what would he make of it . . . dance the cha-cha . . . move with the cha-cha . . . lovely . . . warm rush of the cha-cha . . .

"I love the cha cha,"

She said to him, watching him.

It had popped out of her.

She had let it.

He hadn't moved. He was lighting his pipe, puffing, puffing. Flickering yellow light, shaking out the yellow light . . .

"Oh, I love your pipe! Lovely smell of your pipe!"

There, faint smile, surely, a smile.

She smiled.

He said, "Where did you dance the cha-cha?"

"My goodness! Where *didn't* I? Even in England—imagine?"

Mount Solaro . . .

"Ah, well, England . . ."

He was smiling.

She saw Solaro . . .

"Do you like England?"

He said, "Bit cold in England."

"So many English—"

"Would you rather there were fewer of them?"

"Oh, well—no, no!" She laughed, softly . . .

And silence. He was looking away now, slightly sighing, she saw him sighing.

He said, "I don't mind the English. They're not so bad as made out to be! I've often been there. Their company is superb. So short a time, and yet—"

She said, "Superb—"

"Yes, yes, superb."

He said, "The Swedes are the ones."

"You don't like the Swedes?"

"I don't much like the Swedes. Did you dance in Stockholm?"

Catching her . . .

"Only once in Stockholm—"

"When was it?"

Now, looking at her . . .

"Four—five years ago—"

"What was it?"

"I don't—wait a minute—*Sleeping Beauty*—yes, that was one—"

"The waltz—"

"Yes—"

"Magic waltz."

"Oh, yes . . ."

"Did it feel that way? To you, while doing it, did it feel that way?"

A pause.

"Yes . . ." And, "That way . . ."

The moment.

Holding the moment . . .

She was looking away. Far away. Quite dark. It had grown
quite dark. Dark . . .

   . . . *a thundering, startling her . . . she turned, realizing,*
quickly . . . Révérence . . . *deeply . . . the ovation rolled,*
around her, engulfing her . . . rising, rising with her . . .
flowers . . . great bouquets . . . smiling . . .

   . . . *white princess . . . white lovely princess . . . turn*
. . . *princess . . .*

"That was in Stockholm—"

The voice, abruptly.

She turned to it.

"We toured all Scandinavia. I loved Copenhagen. I loved
the Danes. Keep the Swedes!"

She was laughing . . .

"Have you been there?"

She was asking him.

"Copenhagen?" He shrugged, slightly. "Once or twice—"

She settled deep in her chair.

"What do you think?"

"I agree with you."

Silence . . .

   . . . *oh comity . . .*

Thraldom, arcane, relinquish, only . . .

Approach: comity.

   . . . *my comity . . .*

56

He went somewhere one day. He excused himself and went
somewhere. She was sad to see him go. He would be back by
night, or, the latest, next morning. He had assured her. But
she was sad. Who would she talk with? She loved talking
with him. Since she had come, every day, for so long, she
had talked with him . . .

She took the sun, a while, sitting on the terrace-*salon*.
Looking out, happy and sad, feeling a loss, knowing the loss.
In her blood, sadness, flowing, and gladness, trying to fuse,
hurting her . . .

A jazz horn. A good jazz horn. Jerry.

Dear Sylvia.

She would see Sylvia. Definitely, again . . . Sylvia . . .
Here, perhaps, on this island . . .

My island . . .

She was wandering through the house. The servants were all off now. He had asked her, would she want them to stay around today? It would be all right. No, *signore*. Very well, then, we'll give them the time off. Shall we give them the day off? Do, yes, the whole day off . . .
Mia Isola
Lovely rooms. So many lovely rooms. Interesting rooms. Each, different, yet, somehow, forming a perfect whole, lovely whole. Here, his library, and study. Again, the long *salon*-parlor. Wall window, curtains half drawn. Anna would have half drawn them. A sitting room, a tiny, cozy sitting room. A bedroom. Whose had that been? He had children somewhere. She knew he had children somewhere. Piano. She sat at the piano, she touched the keys, played with the piano. Hallway, and dining room, French doors. She lingered before the French doors. Paintings. There were some wonderful paintings. She stood before the paintings. There were two Degas . . .

Wandering, in the garden, a breeze touching her, tenderly. Upon her, the sunlight, her face to the sunlight . . . She sat in the garden now, under a wide-leafed tree. The sun came through diffused by it, but finding her, tiny streaks finding her. Her face to it, her face upturned to it . . .
. . . Her mother, "Don't go too far with them, don't take them too far." Into the car, both of them. They were going, they were being taken for a little run. New, shiny, open car. Chauffeur talking to them. Carl looked at her. Just a little run. Perfect day. The hills, rising, before them . . . "It's all right, dear, let them be, dear," her father. "Just shut up, can you do that, shut up, Harold," her mother. She heard the voice, telling him that . . . The car moved. Roaring. Soon along the long stretches, reaching into the hills now, wind rushing, warm sun, touching them now . . .
Fragments, swirling, around and about her . . .

She wrote him.
She said,
—*Here, it's not part of Earth. Not at all part of Earth. A long time. What time? When is time? Tell me of time. We*

*have no time. I don't count days here. I can say, I will say, I
wish you were here . . .*

She read. It was Zola. In the library she had found wonderful Zola . . .

_____ 57

Evening. Warm, blue evening. He was back. She was so glad
he was back. They had a lovely dinner together. Amelia came
out and smiled at them, they thanked her, congratulated her.
Delightful taste of the wine, lingering . . .

"Did you have a nice day, Janet?"

"Very nice. I read a good deal."

"Did you walk anywhere?"

"No, just here. I love it around here."

They had coffee. They were on the terrace. He lit his
pipe . . .

She saw the moon. A few puffy clouds scudded across the
moon. *Reach out, touch the moon.* Reach out and stroke the
moon. She saw him. He sat quietly, puffing his pipe. She
loved him puffing his pipe. But she sat expectantly. He would
ask something. Suddenly, startling her, he would soon ask her
something. She feared this, but wanted this. She seemed to
want this . . .

. . . If he would . . .

*. . . He doesn't have to. I don't mind if he doesn't. He
doesn't have to. I love it here. This is a place. This is peace.
I'm not on Earth. No, not part of Earth . . .*

"What do you think of this place?"

Had he asked that? She tried to think when he had asked
that.

"Why, I love it, just love it." And "Shall I stay here forever?"

"That's all right, if you wish."

A moment, then laughing, both, softly laughing. Then
quiet. Rolling and touching the night. Reach the night. She
sipped her coffee. Within, the warmth and good flavor of
coffee . . .

"Did you go far today?" she asked.

"No, not very far. No, Janet."

He wouldn't tell her.

She was hurt that he wouldn't tell her . . .

"I wrote a letter," she told him.

She waited.

She said to him, "A young man."

"That's fine now."

"Is it, now?"

He held his pipe. He turned away a moment and held his pipe.

"He loves you?"

She sighed, "I think he loves me. He tells me that he loves me. What can it mean, he loves me? Why should he love me?"

A silence.

Adrift in the silence . . .

"I don't believe that. It's absurd to believe that," she said at last.

"Have you been loved, Janet?"

She didn't answer. Within, a hard core held her. It had hold of her, and held her . . .

"Have you had lovers, Janet?"

Her voice, finally, "Had I the time, *signore?*"

. . . *pick a little tot up, play with him, so many games, little tot, pick right up and turn over, hold and over, again, over, whoopsedo, over . . .*

"You haven't danced for some time, Janet—"

She thought that one over. She was a long time, thinking it over.

She said finally, flatly, "No lovers."

"What a pity."

And looking at her.

"Shall I believe that?"

Calmly, friendly, still looking at her.

"You must believe that. My whole life was work. I was nothing but work. What was time? When there was time, I slept. And how I loved sleep! Exhaustion brought sleep—"

"And when you stopped dancing?"

"*I didn't stop dancing!*" It flew out of her. She couldn't stop, she saw him. "Does that make sense to you? *Out there* —yes— *It Ended*—I know—the steps, the movements— *They Ended*—"

She stopped now, catching hold of herself, her breath now. Near her, just across from her, looking at her . . .

"I understand that."

Blue evening, soundless now, warm, about them, enclosing them, timeless, indifferent, passing by them . . .

"The young man may love you," he said now.

. . . my body . . .

"Fred couldn't love me, couldn't possibly love me. He'll forget me. I came away so he would forget me. It won't take him long to forget me—"

A pause.

"You write to him."

"Yes. I write to him."

"Why do you write to him?"

"I don't know why I write to him."

"Does he write you?"

"He did write me."

"When did he last write you?"

"Some time—*it's been some time now*—"

"A part of you knows."

"Hopes—"

"That part of you."

"I don't know . . ."

Again the silence, she was aware of them enfolded by silence, held there, together, in silence. He puffed his pipe. She turned away, she looked away, into the night, in silence . . . She was very sleepy. Suddenly, very sleepy. Something, very heavy, painful . . . in her.

. . . He was there. He had arrived that morning, he had come on the boat that morning. He had come straight to her. She had seen him, making his way up the path. She was excited to see him, but also ashamed. She felt the shame. He was before her. He was handing her something. A letter. One she had written. He said to her, "Why did you write this?" She opened it. She started to read it . . .

"I didn't write that—"

"What, Janet?"

Awake, and the voice for her, aware of the voice for her. She sought the voice, holding on to it . . .

"I don't know—"

"You wrote it."

"I wrote it?"

"You said so—"

. . . said so. When had I said so? My breasts said so. Oh, white breasts, say so. Circle, softly, circle, and say so. Darling, say so. Oh so. He said so. A voice said so. When did the voice say so? . . . Earth. Endure. They deface it. Change it. It endures. Outlasts them. All, all, outlasts them. And receives them. Finally, somehow, somewhere, receives them. Briefly, climbing out of her, walking over her, triumphing over her. So briefly and then—returning. Ever. Return . . .

*. . . turn, swiftly, dazzle them, beauty, my beauty . . .
now, slowly, enchant, slowly, white beauty . . .*

. . . who said so . . .
*. . . She was a little girl. She was with her mother, in the
rose garden. They were walking, slowly, about the rose garden. It was beautiful, all in bloom, in the sun, in bloom. The
fragrance about them, all about them. Wonderful roses. All
color roses . . . Drifting . . . through them . . . the fragrance . . . belly . . . Her mother's belly . . . She averted it
. . . She didn't want to look at it. Something in it. She knew,
something in it . . . Her eyes, looking upon it, would penetrate it, destroy what was in it . . . Must Not Destroy What
Was In It . . .*

"*Signore—*" she said, quickly.
Crescent patterns, streaking, high and across the sky,
bursts of light falling . . .
"Fireworks, Janet."
He said, calmly to her.
She watched them. They burst high up, they fell away, in
all directions, brilliantly, alive in the night sky . . .
She turned to him.

---------------------------------58

Where the days? Days. *What were days?* She knew nothing of
days. Time, passing, touched her, lightly brushed her. One
long day. *Eternal day . . .*
Hers.
Only . . .

She rose early, and eagerly. She looked out at the new day.
Her day. She read a while. She walked. They had breakfast.
They talked, laughed, over breakfast. Always they talked. She
loved to talk. She loved to hear him talk . . .
Occasionally, he would go away. She hated that. But he
came back, usually the same evening . . .
She would ask him sometime, "Where have you been?"

He never answered.

She could have murdered him, not answering.

She didn't, though. She only sulked, shot beastly looks at him, a whole evening, sometimes . . .

Time, urging her . . .

She was saying something about Degas to him. A young dancer, practicing, *sur les pointes,* lovely, about to turn, the mist of her dress, turning . . .

A long while he listened. They were in the parlor. There was the music. Her lovely music.

"Would you haved liked him to paint you?"

She smiled, delighted at that.

"Oh, of course! Yes!"

"As whom, Janet?"

She hesitated.

"I don't know," she said, "I hadn't thought of it."

She paused. He was watching her in the pause. She was afraid. She knew the pause . . .

"Just as myself," she threw out. "Probably."

"Not in role?"

"No. I don't think so—"

"If he wished to?"

She said nothing.

"Your last role?" he suggested . . .

She said nothing. She sat, quietly, looking away from him, within frightened, trying to veer from it . . . time, holding her, slowly enfolding her . . .

"What was your last role?"

Calmly, casually.

Dropping into her.

Hurting her.

She said nothing. She reached for a cigarette. She held it . . .

"Don't you remember?"

She tried to light the cigarette. She struck a match but did not light the cigarette . . .

The match, in an ashtray, burned itself out.

She held the cigarette . . .

She heard the music.

Out of time, here, the music . . .

Her eyes on him.

"They've told me."

And on him.

"I don't remember . . ."

She thought of the young man. She thought, *go to the young man* . . .

Signor Armandi, saying nothing, turned away now, leaned his head to the music, slightly, and looked out, into the night now . . .

———————————————————————*59*

"My God!"

Roscoe, shaving, said that aloud. He was thinking of— England. The fuming would not contain itself. He had been back some three months now, but he couldn't forget the place. He loathed it. It had become a fine focal point. He thought, wistfully, of dropping a few on them, not too many, just enough to—

"Blow the whole goddamn place to Kingdom Come!"

He uttered . . .

Too bad, he thought, the Germans never got in there. They would have straightened the bastards out. And how. Got them the hell on the ball, silly bastards, stiff, lazy bastards. They would have shown them!

"By God, they'd have shown them!"

He blurted out, thrusting his face close to the mirror.

Fine job.

Just one small nick.

"What the hell . . ."

He muttered . . .

Everyone was in a turmoil about Janet, Roscoe found out. She had—completely disappeared! They hadn't heard in months! Last trace was Genoa. Since then—*mystery*. Roscoe was sick of it all. Ellen had something to play with now, and she really went at it. Half her time on the phone "helping" the search, other half consoling dear Linda. Yes, real fun—for Ellen. Not Roscoe. He was so sick of it. Utterly sick of it. He had no part in it, and would have no part in it. He did learn though, via the grapevine, i.e., Ellen, all about any developments in the affair.

The other day, near the Senate, he had bumped into Roland. He had, among other things, put to Roscoe, "You think those damn Reds have orbited her?" He had only stared, he hadn't answered. He saw, or it looked like to him, the man was serious . . .

Roscoe was sick of it.

Thoroughly sick of it . . .

Ellen, moaning, "Why couldn't you have kept an eye on her?"

Goddamnit!

He thought.

"Goddamnit!" he said. "You want me to go back to the British? You want me to do that? I did what I could. Job to do, did that occur to you? I don't suppose that ever occurred to you!"

"Don't speak to me in that way!" she fired at him, picking up a delightful blue vase and hurling it halfway across the room at him. *What an arm!* He was not ruined for life by this because, adopting Emergency Special Hairtrigger Maneuvers, he smartly avoided it. It crashed behind him.

"You're nuts!" he yelled. "Absolutely nuts!" he howled, "You trying to kill me? You damn fool—That Could Have Killed Me!"

"*Get Out!* Get out of here! Get into your fool airplane and Find Her! Don't come back till you've found her. FIND HER!" She was out of her head, shrieking, and alarmed Roscoe. He was still angry, but he felt he had better calm her. Console her. Calm her. After all—what if she burned the house down? In such a state, bitch that she was, *anything* could happen. He moved toward her, bravely, nobly almost. He would calm her. He placed an arm about her, or, rather he tried to place an arm about her. It never got there. She spotted it coming and put an abrupt halt to its passage by winding up and delivering one straight and true punch, solidly, to his jaw. It sent him reeling, and finally, careening. He crashed to the floor, he lay there, sprawled in a heap, out cold, near the remains of the blue vase, delightful blue vase . . .

When Roland got home that evening, he headed straight for the lavatory. He had been through one hell of a day. A long conference with the coordinator of his investigators. Another with the investigators of his coordinator. And other stuff. All the stuff. He was tired. Fed up, tired . . . And no sign of Janet, to top it all. It had only been a suspicion at first, but now, it was beginning to look like a real possibility that the Reds had kidnapped her, and that she would turn up one day behind the curtain, a convert, appearing with one of their nationalized troupes or other. It irritated him considera-

bly, nay, *upset* him considerably. It caused sleeplessness, con-
stipation, and nightmares, in which he, Pillar of The National
Security, was the laughing stock of the Nation—and run out
of politics, to boot.

He muttered, straddling the commode with his ample back-
side, unleashing a horrendous salvo. It shook half the house,
reverberating. It pleased him, reassured him. He had been
slightly off form lately, slightly, and had been getting worried.
Now, he felt better. Uplifted! He felt the old power and glory
returning, he felt them in all parts of himself, surging. He
saw himself, Triumphant . . . He thought of Clarise. His enemies. He flushed the toilet . . . They were gone, in an instant, all of them.

"By God, that's a state of affairs!" he said suddenly.
"Trouble, trouble, more trouble, that's all it's ever been. *Ballet stuff!* God, I *told* them! Long time ago, hell, I sure *told
them.* This tops it all. The fools, they should have stopped
her! That's it, they've never stopped her! If I'd have known—"

He unleashed another broadside and felt even better. A
truly tremendous surge of confidence raced through him.
Who could beat him?

"We'll find her! By God, we'll find her!"

The Senator heaved a long sigh and relaxed now. He was
happy, comfortable, supremely relaxed now . . .

Mr. and Mrs. Hunter were discussing the day's events.

"Absolutely ridiculous," she observed.

"Dear?" he queried, half-asleep.

"You're not listening! You haven't been listening! Have
you heard *one* word I've said?"

He opened an eye, peered at her.

"What was I saying?"

He opened both eyes.

"What?" she demanded.

"My dear—" he ventured.

She glared at him.

She burst into tears.

"I want my dear girl!"

Mr. Hunter, observing her, said warily,

"There now—"

"You don't care! You've never cared! *You* got her into Ballet! It was *you!* You caused *everything!* All that—*and everything!* You fool! Your music! You and your music! You
ruined her. Your hours and hours with her— *What Did You
Do To Her?* Damn your music! She could have been a sweet

girl, a nice, normal girl. What did you *do* with her?" She paused, sobbing quite loudly now. "And Carl! *What about Carl?*" The sobbing got louder. "Do you *remember* Carl?"

The sobbing was very acute now, and Mr. Hunter, distressed, awaited the moment. He prayed he would know it. It would take all his highly refined powers of judgment, plus the prayer, to know it. He would move cautiously toward her, murmur to her, stroke her, *so gently* stroke her. And, if all went well, eventually—Cuddle her.

"*Oh!*" she shrieked, at his first touch.

He backed away, quickly. Had he misjudged the moment? He was appalled, yet—resigned to his fate. *Anything* could happen now!

"So—*Now You Touch Me! What do you want? My Body?* Animal! Are you hot? *You Animal!* Are you *so* hot? Tear off my clothes! ASSAULT ME! Go on— *Go On*— Assault Me!"

Mr. Hunter, baffled, held his ground. He tried cooing,

"There, dear—There there, dear—"

"THERE NOW!" she screamed, throwing her nightdress off.

She stood there, before him, naked, her eyes closed, trembling, white and naked . . .

Ellen and Clarise met for lunch.

They didn't do this often, but the urge had taken them.

"I don't know what you think of it," Ellen was saying. "Is it too sheer?"

"Oh, El, I don't think so. Whatever makes you think so?" Clarise responded.

"It certainly didn't look sheer on the model. *Those models!*"

"Aren't they?"

They giggled. Their drinks came.

"Here's to everything."

"Long may it!"

Ellen took a long sip.

"So, you don't think so?"

"I assure you."

"All right. I believe you."

She sighed, took another sip.

"I wanted to get a swimsuit. Do you need a swimsuit?"

"Why—matter of fact I could do with one. They've just got some marvelous beach jackets in, by the way—"

"Foamback jerseys?"

"That's right."

"Aren't they sweet!"

"I like the hyacinth blue—"

"Isn't this drink nice—"

"Oh, it goes right down—"

"Hyacinth?"

"That's right."

"Sounds lovely."

"*Sexy!*"

They giggled.

Their lunch came.

Clarise said, "Will they find her?"

"I hope they find her!"

"So do I. I certainly do hope they find her."

"Roscoe's very upset about the whole thing. Poor Roscoe. He did his best over in England. His very best."

"I'm *sure* he did. How is he now, dear?"

"Much better. Only a tiny concussion, nothing more, really."

"He must be more careful."

"It was a fall-and-a-half. I keep *telling* him."

Their eyes met over the lunch table. Ellen turned to her food, quickly. There was danger of giggling . . . hysterical giggling.

She sighed, conquering it, "I must find a new hairdresser. Isn't it *awful*, dear?"

Clarise inspected.

"Oh—it looks quite nice—"

"I can't get the sides right! Look, they're supposed to be swaying—that's what it should be, *swaying*—"

"Well—hmm—I see— No, I can't say it's *swaying*—"

"Exactly! What good's the place? It's supposed to be swaying! It's *Not* swaying!"

"You're right, El—Definitely—certainly *not* swaying—"

"I'm giving up the place! I'm certainly not ever again going near that place!"

"Definitely, not swaying—"

"*Swinging!*"

"That's it! *Swinging!*"

"Swinging! Swinging!

"John Carlton," Hamilton said. "Had a hard day?"

The Judge eyed him.

"Pretty rough, yes."

"Thought so."

"On top of everything, this Janet thing has taken the wind out of me. I'll say. Right out of me." He sighed, wearily.

"Yeh, well take it easy, John boy. They'll turn her up soon. She's probably shacked up with some smooth Frenchie or Wop, ha ha, wait and see. Ol Roland will find her!"

John Carlton didn't like that, but Hamilton rolled on, unperturbed, "Yeh, you'll all be surprised soon. Will *you* be surprised?"

"Evidently you won't be."

"Hell no! I *know*, bud!"

"Do you, *bud?*"

Hamilton laughed, slapped the Judge on the back.

"Take it easy. Just take it easy! Not going to send me up for that are you, Judge?"

"My boy—"

"Ho boy!"

"One day—you're gong to go too far—just a teeny bit Too Far—"

Hamilton suddenly was sober.

"John, listen, can I say it?"

"Say it."

"What's she always meant to you? How come she's always meant so much to you? I mean, a smart guy like you—"

The Judge didn't answer.

Hamilton went on, "I mean—listen—*that ballet crap*—now John, listen— *A bunch of crap*—I mean it. It ruined her! My God, all those weirdies in it—John, listen boy—Sure, O.K. she was big stuff— So What? It *ruined* her!"

The Judge said nothing. He just was too tired to lock horns today with Hamilton, supreme *agent provocateur.*

But somehow he couldn't leave him. Somehow, today, he had a need to be near him. In any event, how often did he see him?

He ventured, finally, "Aren't you working today, Hamilton?"

"Hell no, not the rest of the day. Closed the shop and that was that. How about that?" He paused, surveying John Carlton. "Want to go for a spin? You havn't seen the new little beaut, have you? German! C'mon. You look pretty low!"

The Judge sat there, feeling indeed *mighty* low.

Hamilton said, suddenly, "I know just the thing for you! Let's go down to the Tramps—"

The Judge blinked an eye.

What was he speaking of?

Where, Hamilton?"

Upwind gave a hearty laugh, thumped John Carlton again. "Ho Ho! You're behind, man! You're falling behind up on that chair, Judge! Listen, it's the greatest! Most of us do it—what a lift—Terrific!"

John Carlton stared at him. He raised an eyebrow. Vaguely, the smell of something obscene drifted—

Some new—

Perversion!

"What are you talking about, Hamilton?" he asked, cautiously.

"Tramps! *Trampolines!* You know *Trampolines!* C'mon, we'll take a run to the Center—"

"Center?"

"Trampoline Center? Good God, John, you amaze me—and you a judge. My God, John, no Tramp cases before you? I've had a few and let me tell you!"

John Carlton hadn't. Though, now, thinking of it, he certainly could see possibilities . . .

He sighed, diverted, bemused, and curious. Indeed curious. He thought he had seen it all. But—once again, the buggers had done it. Always, as always, one jump ahead of him. He reflected. If he went with Hamilton, he knew, there was a good chance he might shake off his rotten depression. He was certainly attracted by that idea. On the other hand, here he would be risking his life. He wondered if he should go to that extreme. He mulled it over. Was it worth the risk? His curiosity urged him. Perhaps he could actually—*control* Hamilton. He succumbed to it . . .

"All right," he sighed, moving off with Hamilton toward the bright, shiny vehicle.

"Great, Judge!" Upwind hooted, crawling behind the wheel of the vehicle.

"Now, *remember,*" John Carlton began, his voice sucked away by the roar of the blast-off and immediate acceleration of the vehicle to 95 miles per hour . . .

"Pretty good, John, *huh?"* Hamilton yelled, "Four seconds flat from zero—*and now Watch This*—"

John Carlton tried to say something.

But Upwind had moved a little lever which seemed to ignite another engine. With a roar and an amazing surge the car shot forward. The speedometer, John Carlton noted, read 125 mph.

A sudden memory, the last little session he had attended, flashed before him . . .

Had the man—

"How's that? Huh? Pretty good, huh?" Upwind, gleefully.

"Hey—*Hamilton*—" John Carlton shouted.

"Yeh, John?"

"What's The Speed Limit Here?"

"What, John?"

"SPEED LIMIT—"

"Ho, *Hell, John*—could hit *one-fifty*— *Easy*—at least— WANTA SEE?"

"NO, *Fool*, NO! THE SPEED LIMIT—HERE—WHAT'S THE LIMIT?"

Hamilton glanced at him, then burst out laughing.

"WHAT THE HELL DO I KNOW? *Do I know? You* Ought To Know! Jesus Christ, if anybody—*John Boy*— Hey— TELL ME!"

John Cartlon, sighed, crossed himself—not that he was a Catholic or, truth be known, an adherent to any Faith. It just struck him, at this moment, as the thing to do. He had so often seen it done . . . He sat back, closed his eyes, and prepared.

After all, a voice within assured him, *it'll just take a second.* One little second. Won't feel a thing. Fireball. Ground Zero . . .

So long, everyone . . .

"John! *Ol Buddy!*"

Someone was tugging at him. He dared not open his eyes.

"John—Ol Buddy!"

John Carlton came out of it. He was aware they had come to a halt. Was it Upwind tugging at him? He still dared not open his eyes.

Upwind's voice, clearly "John— Hey— *Come on, Ol Buddy!* Here we are! Come on, up and out— *Up*, Buddy!"

Was this Heaven?

He opened his eyes.

Upwind, tugging at him.

John Carlton moaned, moved, managed somehow to get out. He was very wobbly and walked along tamely, supported by Hamilton. Wherever he was leading him . . .

Trampolines. All about him. Outdoors. Dozens of them. Big fairground, sort of. Crowds of people, milling among them. On the trampolines, two, three, sometimes six at a time, bouncing, leaping, high in the air, landing, rebounding, up, down, up now . . .

"Boy! He's Good!" Hamilton shouted admiring a particularly nimble Trampolinar before them. "Watch His Footwork!"

They did, then walked around more. The Judge was fascinated. He had come back to life—he felt Quite Good! There were even old ladies bounding around on the things! A whole new field of Jurisprudence seemed to open up before him, vast vistas of heretofore unimagined possibilities—he had a swift phantasy of himself writing the first major treatise on it: *Tramps—A View and Review* . . .

Hamilton said, "Ho—let's go—here's one—"

He was on it in a flash, after buying the tickets. It took a while to haul the Judge on, even with the use of the special steps.

Upwind was soon bounding, happily. The Judge, flopping and falling, rolling, just couldn't find his feet. Upwind went higher and higher, and John Carlton, watching him, was alarmed, astounded. He was achieving truly prodigious heights. He drew the admiring attention of even this hardened crowd, now gathering about his Tramp.

He slowed down after a while and helped the Judge get started. He got him on his feet and gave him some pointers. Soon, both were bounding rather smartly. John Carlton was having fun!

"So—you think they'll find her?" he asked Hamilton, as they came face to face at the apex of an upward bound.

"Sure! They'll find her! She'll Find *Them!* Hey—John—what do you say— Ain't This The Greatest?"

"I Hope They Do!" the Judge answered.

And up and down, up, down . . .

Hamilton, suddenly, "I'll tell you a good one—"

John Carlton, "Go ahead—"

"Operated on some—old lady this morning—been coming to me—for years— Claimed she had— Cancer— Convinced of it—I couldn't find anything— She begged and begged to *"get it out of her"*— Finally, to get rid of her, what the hell —I decided to open her—not *Do* anything, understand— *Understand Me?*"

"This morning?"

"Yeh—this morning—and now I'll tell you—"

"Go ahead, Hamilton—"

"She Had It!"

"Is that right—Ham—"

"Yeh, Right! All over, inside her, Did She Have It!"

"My God! Will she live, Ham?"

"Hell No! Don't know— What kept her— Going! Can you Beat That?"

"It's a—good one—all right—"

"Dandy!"

"You didn't know—Eh?"

"Who Could Have—Known?"

"By Damn—"

Up, down, up and down . . .

"Tired?"

"No, no, Hamilton! It's— Refreshing— Really—"

"Told you— Didn't I?"

Down, rebound . . .

"Hamilton—is that fellow— Still Suing— You?"

"Who, Judge?"

"The fellow— Wrong Leg fellow—"

"We settled—"

"Rough, wasn't it? Pretty rough— Eh?"

"Was I to know? They set him up for me! Damn nurse— *Those Damn Nurses,* John!"

"So now—"

"No Legs."

"Rough, Ham—"

"Could I Help It?"

Now, at the top of the steps, a gentleman appeared. He was perhaps forty, and smiling. He stood there.

"Mind if I join you?" he queried.

"How many?" Hamilton countered, rebounding.

"Four of us."

"Males?"

"All but two."

Hamilton smiled.

"All Aboard, then!"

The party climbed on and soon six Trampolinars were happily bounding.

"Say—" said the gentleman, on a downbound, "aren't you Doc Upwind?"

"One and only—"

"What Do You Know! You don't know me!"

"Can't say I—"

"Dexter! Farnsworth Dexter! You snipped out my gall bladder—four years ago—Remember?"

"Why— Uh— Well— *Yes!* I Remember! Sure, I Remember! How are you?"

"Not too Bad— Been away— Must come—see you—"

"You Do That—"

"Everything seems O.K. though— Kidneys—heart—stomach—bowels— *Say!* My Bowels—"

"Farnsworth!" A woman was shrieking—

She had lost her balance and was tumbling over and over on the floor of the Trampoline, a bouncing doll. She had tripped up some of the others, who fell and in turn tripped up all the others, and now all flew like tenpins, in a heap,

tumbling, and soon—screeching, squealing, one tangled heap
there.

John Carlton lay at the bottom.

They were all laughing and shouting, happily, one tangled
heap. John Carlton fought hard to breathe. A woman's breast
was pressing against his mouth. He sighed, half-suffocated,
loving the breast, suffocating him . . .

———————————————————60

*. . . Smell of woodworking. Delicious sweet smell of wood-
working . . . They had a wonderful shop set up for him. He
spent a lot of time in it. Made all sorts of things . . . She
looked in at him. He looked up. The dark eyes, on her. Her
heart, jumping. Warm, jumping. He was making a figurine of
some sort, she couldn't tell what it was, still too early. She
stood, watching him . . . She was wearing a pink dress,
white ruffled hem, her hair loose, long, light brown, her
lovely hair . . . Going out soon, she had to go to the city,
someone to see there about the new school . . . She watched
him working. Steady scraping, rubbing . . . Pretty. So Pretty.
She knew, she felt it . . . All Pretty . . . She waited, watched,
a long while. The car was waiting. She knew the car was
waiting. That was all right. Let it be waiting . . . "Carl," she
whispered. He looked up again. "Carl"—and silence . . .
Now, in the silence, long, long moment of absolute silence,
their eyes were upon one another . . . held there, immured
by the silence . . . She moved toward him. He did not move.
Her hand touched his. His eyes still upon hers . . . Dark,
lovely eyes, upon her . . . Her hand caressed his gently . . .
Her face next to his, warm face touching, caressing his . . .
warm breath, sweet breath, brushing his ear . . . She took his
hand, she moved it, toward her . . . she placed his hand on
her breasts, inside her dress, she had unbuttoned it . . . his
hand on her warm breast, fondling her breast . . . His hand
thrilled her, warm, loving hand, thrilling her . . . She sighed,
pressed close to him. She kissed him. He held her now, kissed
her. She leaned with him, back, back . . . with him . . .
whispering, now whispering, her eyes closed, his hand about
her, caressing her, stroking her . . . lips to his, whispering, to
his lips, moist lips, seeking, whispering . . .*

. . . Fine fineries . . . warm, white flesh, my flesh . . .
under *the fineries. . . .*

*. . . magic branch, touched by it . . . awake, a ghost, out
of the tomb . . . temps levés . . . gently, series of . . . ara-*
besque *. . . turn now . . . yes . . .* en tournant *. . . yes . . .*

*. . . Moments, gazing in on themselves, seeing only them-
selves, turning, over and over . . . There, the moment, minute part of moments she held the moment . . . Desperately,
trying to hold on to the moment.*

*. . . Time, locked away, somewhere . . . where was time
. . . how had time . . . there . . .*

*Permanence. Nothing. Absolutely, nothing. Motility. Pre-
doomed, predawn futility. To immotility. Nagging nugget.
Tug. Indifferently . . .*
"What are you thinking?"
The voice caressed her. The voice held her. It reached out
and held her.
"I want peace."
A silence. Touching the silence.
"What sort of peace?"
"Real peace."
"Can you find it?"
Looking out, over the silence—
"When you talk to me—"
Halting, abruptly . . .
She looked at him. In late afternoon sun, turning away
from the gentle sun, she saw him. He held his pipe. He was
looking across the bay . . .
Late afternoon sun, sinking slowly . . .
Dusk. They watched it. Aware of dusk, now, upon them . . .
She said, suddenly, *"When did I get here?"*
No answer. She knew there would not be an answer. It
made her angry, but she didn't protest. She turned away . . .
"The young man—" he said, finally.
She said nothing.
She sipped her coffee.
"What can you remember?"
"I don't remember," she replied, quietly . . .

. . . Four bells, one after the other, slowly, echoing through all time, for her . . .

. . . gravel path, leading somewhere. It would lead her there. She knew it would lead her there. Open plain. Astonished. Nothing, just bare, open plain . . . where was it . . .
. . . Guitar Boogie . . .

"You feel he loves you."
She heard that, only.
"Sometimes I feel that," she answered, finally.
"When did he last write?"
She looked at him.
"Didn't I tell you?" She paused, looked away—"I thought I told you."
He said nothing.

---61

. . . His eyes were two daggers trying to penetrate her. She sought to evade them. She could not. They dug into her. They hurt her. She felt the pain grow. It spread through her. She tried to move. She wanted to move out of there. She could not. Suddenly, she felt the pain was his pain, he had put it into her. She cried out, feeling his pain, and angry, resenting the pain. Why should he do that? Why should he be allowed to do that? She moved toward him. Slowly, painfully, toward him. Touch him. She would touch him. Put it back in him. Where it belonged. Just where it belonged, In Him. Ever, forever, ever and ever. In Him . . .

She awoke.
It was morning.
She turned her head, looked out the window.
The calm sea . . .
"The Princess," she murmured.
. . . pale moon, circling, she reached out and checked the circling, her hands held the circling . . .
"Who was the Princess?"

"I'm a Princess!" she told him . . .

. . . *Candelabra. Exquisite glass shimmering in fine light, divine light. Oh divine light! Here, look now. Fairlylike diamond and crown from Chaumet emphasizing soft grace of simple coiffure (oh coiffure) by Lintermans. My Dear: Lintermans! Smooth—sophisti—I say—would you say— Let me Say—SAY! Sophisticated . . . René Goujean style, dear, swirling ever, jewel clip and forward-placed chignon and two jeweled bar clips and holding rope of hair and back in place of Hey Mace . . .* MACE! *I say . . . mace . . . sweet ears, dainty ears, sweet dainty white ears, brown eyes, lovely mouth, warm mouth . . .*

CADWALADER

i say
cadwalader

elegance
sweet summer

elegance . . .

_____ 62

She smiled. "Didn't I mention the Princess?"

He listened.

"Lovely woman, really! Lovely young woman! Also, can dance quite well. Really, quite well. I've stayed with her often. Awfully nice person, *signore,* not too far from Rome." She paused, observing him. *"How I love Rome!"*

He looked at her.

"She really can dance?"

"Oh yes! Not professionally, understand me— She wouldn't hear of it! *La Principessa.* My goodness! *My Principessa—"*

"Did you teach her?"

"What could I teach her?"

A smile. Pause.

"You knew her—"

"Long time. Such a long time."

"I see," he said now.

What, signore? She wondered . . . She thought of the Princess, wondering . . . Why hadn't she seen the Princess? She must run up, see her . . . Sylvia, one night . . . *filmy overskirt, mimosa rose print, silk, so nice* . . . The Princess *came up to them* . . . *cara* . . . *Sylvia* . . .

"I love it in Italy! I love it so much in Italy!" she said now, suddenly.

"Why don't you stay here?"

. . . She was with the Princess. Turn, cara, *now,* sur les pointes, *good, so good,* arabesque, cara . . . *She was holding her, gently, showing her . . . murmuring to her, What a fine figure, you have,* mia cara . . .

"Has he been here?"

"He hasn't been here . . ."

. . . lovely Princess . . . white lovely Princess . . . she caressed her . . .

"Would he stay here?"

She lingered.

"I haven't asked him . . ."

She smiled. She curled up.

"Perhaps I can get him to stay here . . ."

. . . She soared, in the white light . . . lovely, alive . . . soaring white beauty in white light . . .

. . . oh pussy . . .

. . . rosebud tips of my white breasts he loves my white breasts . . .
"My breasts—"
"Yes."
"Do you want to see my breasts?"
No answer.
"They're very lovely—"
"I know."
"Why not, then?"
He didn't answer.
She pouted. She sat, and pouted . . .
"Did he see your breasts?"
He asked, now.
"He saw them."
She answered.
"Both your breasts?"
She stared at him.
"When did he first see your breasts?"
"What did you mean?"
No answer.
They were looking at one another. She was waiting. She was sure he would answer. She wanted an answer . . .
"Who are you?"
She asked him.
"Who was he?"
He answered . . .

. . . masked angels sweeping on in silent flurry . . . she turned sur les pointes, she stood still . . . arabesque . . . she moved . . . quickly . . . round and round . . . glissade . . . away from them . . .

"He loved my breasts—"

. . . like a martyr, he came to her. She held him close. She kissed him. She felt his arms going about her. She kissed him. In the moonlight, on fire, she was kissing him . . .

"Both your breasts?"

Odile *. . . in no way part of* Odile *. . . run from her . . . dazzling . . . treacherous* Odile *. . . Away From Her . . .*

"Yes! Of course!"
. . . her foot struck something. It was caught. Something had hold of it. Cold, heavy, primitive. It held her. Powerfully. Indifferently. In the darkness, she struggled. She could not move. It moved. It was moving, upward. She was aware of it working its way upward. Slowly, relentlessly, upward. It would destroy her. She was horrified, helpless, aware: destroying her . . .

"BOTH MY BREASTS!"

She hurled at him . . .

64

Sylvia . . .

Brute man. To know what he feels, in that instant: *shaft sinking into feminine softness.* Receptive, open, soft softness. *Oh body.* Exquisite body. *To Know.* God, *my body.* Do I Know? Fearful moment. Brute, brute moment. Knowing, sensing, seeing the round thing, round long hard thing, *Oh Thing,* darling, moving toward you, *Oh Darling,* ever toward you, *Yes Darling,* touching you, hot throbbing velvety thing touching you, probing, *Brute Thing,* slipping, pushing into you, seeking the core of you, Deep Deep, *very core of you,*

So Deep, lunging, *Oh Deep*, Plunging, *in you*, In You, Go Deep, lovely thing, *Horrible Lovely Thing*, ecstatic thing, Suddenly Erupting Thing, Stupid, Stupid, *Stupid Thing*, oh god, *Brute Thing*, my god, *Loathsome Thing*, good god, *Loathsome Lovely Thing*, MY GOD . . .

. . . *dear Sylvia* . . .

"Do you remember?"

She heard him. She looked up, and over at him.

In slacks, her legs draped over the arm of the chair, she pulled on her cigarette . . .

"I can't remember."

. . . *développé* . . . *slowly* . . . *my dear* . . . *lovingly* . . .

"The music?"

. . . *turn now* . . .

She didn't answer.

"Was it Paris?"

"No. I'm sure. Not Paris."

"You were in Europe—"

"Yes—"

"London?"

"It might have been London."

"You don't remember?"

A pause.

"I don't remember!"

Suddenly, fighting the tears trying to break out of her . . .

. . . *Tommy, Marge, Diane, Bob* . . . *others* . . . *there were others* . . . *one by one they dived into the water. They were naked* . . . *In the boat they had gone to the Point. The bay, calm, beautiful in moonlight. Diane near her. Diane's breasts, lovely, in moonlight* . . . *toward the others. She swam toward the others. They were swimming in a circle, in the warm waters, round and round, slowly* . . .

. . . *white breasts* . . . *oh darling* . . . *my breasts* . . . *my darling* . . .

"It might have been London . . ."

. . . *He sat near a window* . . .

65

Time, lost in itself, knowing only itself, on, and on, for itself . . .

. . . She wore a white dress, fluttering, pretty white dress. Little girl. She was that little girl. Her father was there. He was smiling at her, now, talking to her. She followed him into the music room . . . They sat and listened, a long while. . . . He talked to her about the music. She asked questions. Many questions. He answered them . . . sun-filled room, great windows, looking out onto the grounds . . . she was smiling at him . . . far, falling away, smooth lawns, tall, strong trees . . . the lake, to the right of her, graceful, curving . . . the waterfall . . .

"Who was Bernice?"

The question hung there, startling her. When had she mentioned her? She tried to recall. Beyond recall. She didn't care . . .

So snug in the parlor. She was in her favorite deep chair in the parlor. Early evening. Traces of light, far off, still lingered. She watched the light.

She said to him, finally, casually, "Did I mention her?"

"You mentioned her."

She turned to him.

White-haired old man.

. . . lovely man . . .

"When did I mention her?"

No answer.

"Why don't you answer?"

No answer.

"I could kill you. I could absolutely *kill* you, when you don't answer!"

No answer.

She fell silent, she stared at him, a long while.

"Who was she?" he asked again, quietly.

"My choreographer." She paused, glaring at him. She was

204

quite angry at him. "My friend, my teacher," she threw at him . . .

"Was she with you?"

She turned from that.

She didn't know how to answer that . . .

"You're very angry with me—"

"Of course I am!" she exploded.

"I know you are . . ."

"I love her," she said at last.

"When did you last see her?"

"Before I came over. In New York."

"Was she with you?"

Again, silence. She watched the moon now, in silence. She smoked her cigarette, slowly. He was watching her . . .

"How was she?"

"Fairly well, I thought." She paused. "Overworked, as usual, I also thought."

She smiled.

"Did she know him?"

"Who?"

"Carl."

The hand halting, the hand holding the cigarette halting, before her, still, absolutely still, halted. The smile was gone. She saw the smoke rising, curling . . . She turned away, finally . . .

She saw Vesuvius.

Erupt for me!

Naples.

The lights of Naples.

Her eyes on the lights of Naples . . .

. . . Odile, *what is love to you* . . .

"Does he love me?" she asked, faintly.

"Who?"

She heard it. She fell back from it, veering a long way away from it, peering, only out at him . . .

"He's dead now,"

She said to him . . .

Time, whose patterns assume clarity suddenly, fatally . . .

Time, the metamorphosis of desolate violence into ravaged silence . . .

Vile Time . . .

Killing us.

. . . Down the stairs. Full moment, only. Known to her, fully, only. Evening. Sweet, silent, warm, caressing. Gentle breeze through the great windows. From the lake, touching her . . . Music. She heard music. She walked toward the music . . .

. . . His room. She stood before it. She would knock on the door . . .

"He'll let me in—"

"Who, Janet?"

"He's in there—"

"Where, Janet?"

. . . near him. She touched him, her hand over his face now, white, warm hand, caressing his face . . . she whispered to him, bending to him, brushing her lips over his forehead. She took his hand, urging him up from the chair . . . his eyes, upon hers . . .

"Signore—"

. . . long, curving staircase. Lovely staircase. Her mother, descending, slowly. She carried something. She saw she was carrying something . . .

"Who are you?"

No answer.

"Why don't you tell me?"

No answer.

"You're a lovely man—*I love you*—I love it here, I could absolutely stay forever here— But you're so stubborn! So incredibly stubborn! I could scream. Shall I scream? *Stubborn!"*

A moment, silence.

He turned now, looked at her through the silence.

"You know. I've told you," so quietly.

Friendly smile.

She sat there, furious, observing the smile . . .

"No one knows where I am. I've completely disappeared from the world." She paused, touched her hair, turned to him. "Marvelous, isn't it?"

No answer.

"Not even Sylvia! I'm awful. That is awful. I should write her . . ."

No answer.

"Don't you think I should write her?"

Coyly. Softly . . .

"Months. Months and months. It's been *months*—hasn't it?"

She murmured now . . .

. . . *her mother joined her on deck. They were near the Bahamas. Tomorrow, they would reach the Bahamas. Her mother spoke, she heard the words, softly spoken, drifting to her. She stared into the night, silent, hating the words drifting to her . . .*

—rather lovely . . . *moon* . . . lovely . . .

Shrouded silence . . .

—Carl's really enjoying himself

—*Isn't he*

Abruptly, breaking the silence . . .

"I thought you wrote him—"

She looked at him.

"You said you had written him . . ."

_____68·

Days. Moments . . .

Whose were the moments?

. . . They had brought that colored band down from the Inn. They were good. Oh good. We jived all night, almost. In the mountains that summer it was cool and brilliant. I was seventeen. We were having a wonderful party. This fellow came up to me, and he seemed like rather a nice fellow, and we danced. Then, as we were standing aside after the number,

—Just how rich are you, Jan girl?

The question staggered me. I may have been a bit drunk but honestly it staggered me. And the way he asked it! Where had he come from? I'd never thought about it. Who ever thought about it? I stared, but didn't answer. I didn't know what to answer. He laughed. Looking at me, in the night light, on the terrace, amid the music and dancing, he stood there, laughing at me . . . He went away, finally. I never saw him again . . . It was the first time I ever thought of money. What was money? He disgusted me. He spoiled the party for me. I found out later he was from the town nearby, his father "ran a chain of dress shops," or something. He ran something. One of the Radcliffe girls had brought him along. She had a crush on him. This quite terrific crush on him. I wondered why. My god I sat there, wondering why . . . I never felt quite the same about Radcliffe after. Ever after . . .

. . . my wonderful practice room in our place in the mountains . . .

. . . I spent quite a few summers there . . .

*. . . A cello. A piano . . . She was alone, she danced, before
the mirror. Lovely, exquisite, in the mirror . . .*

*. . . The cave, darkness. In the cave, golden ornaments.
She feared the cave, hated it. Yet, drawn to it. For there was
laughter. From within the cave, inane laughter, cruel, intrud-
ing upon her, searching out the tenderest parts of her, hurting
her. She would enter the cave, carefully avoiding the ornaments . . . destroy the laughter . . .*

"Will you go back to him?"

She heard that. She didn't know where it came from, but
she heard that.

She looked at him.

She turned, slowly, away from him.

She found her drink, she sipped it. She cuddled up in her
chair . . .

*. . . she leaned back, beautifully, back, touching time,
very core of it . . . en attitude, now, before the mirror . . .
arabesque . . . pirouette . . . sur les pointes, now . . . arms
arched above her head . . . turn . . . turning . . . slowly . . .*

"Will you dance again?"

It ended . . .

Suddenly—

All ended.

She sat up in her chair.

"Bernice was there."

"What happened?"

"I couldn't move—"

"What happened?"

"I fell—"

"Where?"

"That was the end of it."

She turned to him.

Silence. Looking across the silence.

"It was London . . ."

He asked her, calmly,

"When did Carl die?"

She turned from him.

"*When?*"

She hated him.

"Before that—" she whispered.

"How long before that?"

"Long, *long before that* . . ."

Her voice gone, falling away—

The sway . . .

. . . *late day, warm, late summer day . . . she had
returned from New York. She would spend a month here. So
glad to be back. Company had toured, she had been a great
success, everywhere . . . acclaimed, everywhere . . . She
would see him. So glad to see him. First long absence from
him . . . She brushed by her parents. They had greeted her,
chatted with her . . . So tired, she told them, must rest, absolutely, she told them . . . Upstairs. Maid carrying her things.
Hallway . . . Down the hallway. She told the maid to put the
things in her room . . . Hallway . . . Heart skipping . . . so
nice you're back . . . The maid left her . . . Down the hallway . . . His room . . . She was outside his room. She stood,
listening a moment. Her heart, only . . . She rapped on the
door, lightly. No answer . . . She touched the doorknob . . .
gently, she turned it . . . pushed the door . . . she was smiling . . . it swung open . . . "Carl" . . . softly . . . Slowly,
the door, there, swinging open . . . "Carl" . . . so softly . . .
She stood still. He seemed not to be there. Not much light.
Curtains, partly drawn. She took a few steps forward. The
smile was gone. She looked about, uneasy . . . all about,
slowly, suddenly so uneasy . . .*

"Where was he?"

. . . *to her left, she saw him above her, near the window,
just to the side of the window . . . A chair, overturned, near
him. Faint breeze coming in now through the window. It
turned him, slowly, so slowly . . . barely . . . and icy ham-
mers, suddenly, a million of them, beating within at her . . .
She felt the scream, only the long piercing scream . . . His
eyes, upon her, out of another world, now, in the turning,
tearing her world . . . She staggered, fighting the scream,
fiercely, she assaulted the scream . . . the struggle raged,
tearing her . . . it would tear her apart, she felt it . . . She
tried to move . . . There was a roaring . . . She was falling,*

*into the roaring . . . A chord, suddenly. She heard the chord.
Low, mournful, somewhere . . . Desperately, she clung to
the chord . . . Before him . . . turning . . . She stared at
him . . . Her eyes closed. She backed away . . . Her hands,
rising . . . slowly, aware of her hands, rising . . . above her
head, arching, fingertips just touching . . . barely touching
. . . she turned, she was turning . . . slowly, sur les pointes,
with the chord, turning . . . circling now . . . circling,
slowly circling . . . about him . . .*

"Within you—"

She stared at him.

"You danced, and danced—you kept him alive—*magically*—"

Her eyes would not move from him.

"Within you."

She sat there, cigarette in her hand, unlit.

"London. One night, long afterwards—*he died,* within
you—"

She heard the voice—

"You were aware of his death—*within you*—"

"One night—" her own voice.

"Do you remember?"

"Giselle—"

"Was it *Giselle?*"

"London—"

*. . . enchaînement . . . skim, birdlike now . . . entre chat
quatre . . . the music . . . en diagonale . . . my music . . .
right foot trembling . . . petits battements . . . soar,* Giselle
. . . avant . . . soar, now Giselle *. . . music . . .* Giselle
. . . the music . . .

"You fell—"

"I couldn't move—"

"He was dying—"

"Darkness—"

"Carl was dying—"

"All, darkness—"

"Within you, dying—"

She stared at him.

She heard him—

"And other things. There, already. Attacked things, *dead
attacked things,* bits and pieces, dead things—"

She heard him—

"Parent things." He paused now. *"And Carl now. Dead
now.* Dead things. Within you. Bits and pieces, mutilated,
these things—"

. . . try now . . .

All now.
. . . so hard to move now . . .
"Bernice—"
Her voice.

. . . I can't move at all now . . . Try now *. . . not at all
. . . Try,* try again now *. . . The music. Bernice, close to
her, urging her, touching her . . . She tried to follow . . .
She couldn't follow . . . A heaviness, within her, pressing, all
through her . . . Holding her . . . Heaviness, hanging,
within her . . . deep . . . within her . . .*
Hearse.
Black hearse *. . .*

*. . . She struck her, suddenly, a desperate fury directing
her, suddenly alive in her . . . She lashed out at her . . . Her
face was bleeding. She stared at the face, she loved, needed
the face . . . It was bleeding . . . She turned, fled . . . She
ran, aimlessly, into the night . . . Her footsteps, hearing
them, in the night . . .*

The house.

*Quickly, quietly, into the house. Flowers, great masses of
them . . . Hyacinths, near the waterfall. They had stood near
the hyacinths. She saw the hyacinths. Turning, in the turning,
whispering, in the turning, caressing him near the hyacinths
. . . Her mother, in black, near her. Her father. John Carlton . . . They would be coming out. Soon. She had come
out. They were coming out . . . She watched, numb, barely
breathing . . . They were out, carrying their burden, they
were out, making their way to the hearse with their burden
. . . Bright burst of light, a sound, one . . . and falling, to
the ground, falling . . . her mother's voice . . . calling . . .*

70

She tried to go to bed. She was on her feet. He helped her . . .

They reached her room. He helped her to bed. She lay in her bed, looking up at him. She lay quietly, staring at him. The moonlight. Her breathing. Barely, she heard her breathing . . .

"I'll go to him—"

He stood there, looking down at her.

"Do you think I can go to him?" she whispered, suddenly.

He said nothing.

She said, finally, very quietly, *"In me*. All over Europe. *Things have been put into me . . ."* She paused. "I let them be put in me . . ."

"Magic things," she heard him. "Magic restoring things," She listened, hearing him. "They would bring back the dead things, parent, Carl things," he paused, standing there, *"in you.* Dead, torn things, bits and pieces, *murdered things*—make them whole, put them together again, magically, *alive again—"*

"In me—"

"Within you—"

"Long, hard, round things—"

"Magic things—"

"Lovely warm things—"

"Restoring things . . ."

Silence.

She stared at him . . .

She murmured, "I'm going back to him . . ."

He said nothing. Her eyes closed. He leaned over her. She

was aware of him, leaning over her . . .

He watched her.

For a few moments, before leaving the room, he stood there, watching her . . .

71

She went to Rome, she was going to catch a plane back. She felt good, her life seemed to have purpose again. *Direction.* So good, having direction. Signor Armandi. Warmly, she thought of him. So warm, with her. Within her . . .

Wonderful man, really. So grateful. She would come back to him. She would bring Fred back with her. He would love it! Wouldn't he love it!

Italy, wonderful, fabulous place . . . *My place!*

A lovely day. The sun shone brilliantly and the sky was blue. A fleeting wisp of cloud, here and there, no more. Nothing more!

She sipped a cool drink at the airport bar. She heard music. Wonderful Italian music . . .

The waiter. She smiled at him . . .

The plane, a jet, roared down the runway and into the air, lifting itself gracefully, effortlessly, climbing, ever climbing, beautifully. She felt the climbing. She felt herself pulling away from earth. Free, if only a short while, of earth . . . Through her window, as the plane banked now, she saw the city. There, the Tiber, winding its way through the ancient place, marvelous ancient place. Silent Tiber, witness of centuries of history—tragic, comic, indifferent—here, all unfolded, before it. She thought of that history. Dates. Names. This very spot. *Here.* She smiled . . . *There* . . . She thought of her history . . . Mandolins, delightful melody. She heard them, loved them . . . *Sylvia.* She saw Sylvia. She closed her eyes, thinking of Sylvia . . .

She had a book—a Turgenev novel—Signor Armandi had given it to her . . .

When she got to New York, she thought, she might see Bernice. Tell her the news—that's all. *That was all.* What else? *Gone.* That was all. *Gone.* A longing . . .

"All gone," she said, aloud.

"Beg your pardon?" a voice asked, beside her.

Janet smiled. She felt so foolish. She turned to her fellow passenger.

"I'm sorry. I was thinking aloud."

The woman chuckled, "That's all right. We all do that, don't we, sooner, I mean, *sometime*—or other."

"Yes."

"Enjoy your trip?"

"Yes."

"First time over?"

The woman was smiling. Warmly, smiling. Perhaps late fifties. Plump. Janet liked her. There would be some—trite conversation, she knew. But—it didn't matter!

"No."

"Mine neither!" she chuckled. "Arnie and I come over often. Great, isn't it? We just love Rome. *Roma!* Ah—Venice! Wonderful Venice! We never get tired. As many times as we've done it—I tell you—" She paused. "Is this your first trip?"

"No," Janet, politely, re-informed her.

"Oh, I asked that! Didn't I ask that? I'm sorry now. Age. It's age, I guess. I'm getting there. No doubt about it! Yes, really getting there." She leaned slightly to Janet, "Take for instance what happened to Arnie—my husband, Arnie—"

She paused. Something seemed to have crossed her mind.

Soon gone.

"He threw a little tantrum just before we were due to come over. I don't know why! You know how—ha ha—old men get. *You'll know!* Anyhow, he said he didn't want to go yet. That if I wanted to go I should go by myself and he would meet me later on. *Later on!* He had a *"few things to do!"* Ha Ha, oh Arnie, things to do . . . *What had he to do?* Oh, well, I agreed. I came over. My friends in Rome were expecting me!" She paused. "And, well, do you know what subsequently *then happened?*"

Janet couldn't imagine.

"No," she said.

"Well," the woman chuckled, "I got over here all right—but—when the time came for him to join me—" She laughed now. *"He got on the wrong plane! Ha Ha! Honest, honey, the old fool, The Wrong Plane!"* She really was laughing now. "He wound up in—*Los Angeles!* Imagine? All the way from—New York! Oh ha ha! *Arnie!"*

Janet, smiling faintly, said nothing.

The woman worked through her laughter. Good, long laugh there.

At last she settled down.

She stared at Janet.

"So that's why I'm going back so early. I've got to fetch him." She paused, leaned closer to Janet, "That's the way the English say it. Did you know that, honey? *Fetch-him.*" She sat back again. "Well, he returned to New York via Chicago. Sore? My God, *Sore!* He wouldn't move from there. What a cable he sent me! Those cable girls must still be blushing!"

She sighed.

"So I'm going back for him." She paused. "I've got to! Only way now to get him over here! I've learned my lesson. The Duffer! Ha Ha! *Ol Duffer.*"

Janet sat silently . . .

"Rome! Italy! Oh, my Italy!" the woman said, "What did you say your name was?"

"Sylvia."

"Sylvia! What a nice name—*Sylvia!* Is there Italian in you?"

"No."

She had to smile now.

"I'm Bertha Morris, and I'm from Long Island."

She sat back again, after the pronouncement.

"Amazing people, aren't they? What were they—sixteen years ago? Think of it. *Sylvia, just think of it!*"

Janet thought of it.

Bertha Morris, sighing, continued, "Of course, they have—like us—their *Southern Problem*—"

She turned to Janet again.

"You know, Sylvia, it's the Dark Ages down there. Honestly! Have you been there? *Honestly!* And Sicily—*my God*—Don't Mention Sicily!"

She sighed again.

"Che sole, though—"

Janet, sleepy now, heard the voice . . .

"Paradiso!"

And then, near her, "Sylvia—do you mind if I ask a personal question? Excuse me—were you sleeping? Aw, I'm sorry—I didn't realize you were sleepy—"

"It's all right—"

Janet murmured.

"Can I ask you?" Bertha Morris, "Do you mind if I ask you?" her Bertha Morris, *"Are you on the stage, dear?"*

Very close to her.

"The stage?" Janet queried, stiffening, slightly.

"Are you an *actress,* dear?"

Closer.

"Oh, no. My heavens. No."
Janet, smiling . . .
Bertha Morris leaned back now.
So disappointed now . . .
Janet closed her eyes.
She slept now . . .

_____72

She took a train to St. Louis. She just didn't feel like flying.
She loved a train. She was very excited. She sketched little
scenes in a notebook. She gave them sweet little captions.
"Marry me" . . . Then, little poems. Dear little poems.
About love . . . She sketched the steps and movements for a
scene from *Swan Lake*. That ballet was in her mind now
more than any other . . .

She fell asleep. She dreamed she was watching a play of
his. He was her husband now. There were people, all about.
She was staring at the stage. She saw nothing. She heard voices
though, bizarre, a cacophony of voices. They conveyed no
meaning to her. They were coming from the stage where the
play was unfolding. *Supposedly unfolding.* She saw nothing . . .

She awoke, abruptly. The dream disturbed her. She took
two little pink capsules from a bottle she had acquired in
New York. Soon, she felt better. By the time the train pulled
into St. Louis, she had forgotten it . . .

Lovely bath, she lingered a long while, sweet, scented bath
. . . She lay in the bath, caressed by the water . . . she
touched her breasts, white and warm, lovely . . . she smiled
. . . she saw her breasts . . .

Slim dress, with a spiral frill. She looked wonderful in it.
Delightful new color, dusty orange. Perfect. She was perfect
in it. She turned, before the mirror, loving herself in it . . .
Lovely white arms, neck . . . She smiled, happy and warm,
loving her dress . . .

She whispered, "He'll love it—"

She sat at the dressing table to put the finishing touches to her makeup. She smiled at herself. Her lips, a lovely light red. She loved her lips. *Warm, lovely lips.* She smiled again, lingering over her smile, loving it . . .

Lashes. Mascara. Dark. Just a bit. Darker.

. . . lovely eyes, my eyes . . .

She powdered herself a bit more. She extended, very slightly, the line of her eyebrows. She fluffed her hair and brushed it, so lightly . . .

She saw her face.

She smiled again, loving her face . . .

Nostrils, arching, pretty quarter-moon nostrils . . .

. . . he loves my face . . .

"I'm not old," she whispered, "My God—*am I old?*"

She smiled, daintily touching her nose . . .

She got up now, looked at herself in the long mirror.

. . . his hands over satin . . .

So pleased.

She tried to recall—Had she ever been so pleased?

She couldn't.

Really . . .

He would be coming. He had acknowledged her wire. She had also found a message from him when she arrived at the hotel this morning. It would be soon. The phone would ring. His voice. She would ask him up.

Her heart leaped, thinking of it . . .

She looked about, admiring the furniture. It was funny, really, she thought, how fine pieces of furniture sometimes found their way into hotel rooms . . .

Heart beating. Aware of her heart beating. *Swan Lake.* Its principal theme going through her. Odette, in the wings, awaiting the moment . . .

The theme, suddenly, saddening her . . .

The phone.

It woke her.

Her head had slumped forward, a heaviness upon her. She could not resist it. Things had darkened . . .

Sudden rush of blood in her, upward. Heart thumping. She was hot, shaking . . .

"Hello?"

"Jan?"

"Hello, Fred!"

"How are you?"

"Darling! *Oh, Fred!*"

"Shall I come up?"

"Come right up—"

"This is some place—"

"Like it?"

He had hung up, as she now did, gently. She stood before the phone, looking down at it, trembling, trying to control her trembling . . .

. . . *her hand caressed me . . . saved me . . . in the wings she caressed me . . . save me . . .*

. . . *Corps de ballet, before her . . . white, lovely . . . lovely in white . . . Shimmering, muted music, the waltz, pulsating urgently . . .*

She moved at last.

She crossed the room, to the mirror. She sat at the dressing table, before the mirror . . .

The doorbell.

Her heart jumped. She rose quickly. Fleeting, dotted grayness, white-grayness. She walked to the door.

He was there.

"Hello! Welcome!"

His face was tanned. He looked well. Young, and well.

They stood there.

"You look beautiful, Jan," he said, at last.

"So do you!" She smiled at him.

Neither moving.

"Come in—" she said, finally.

She led him into the room.

"Beautiful hotel, Jan," she heard him say . . .

She looked at him.

Seated now, and talking a stream, aware of herself talking a stream.

". . . two days later, Fred. You can't imagine the giddy time I've had of it. Have I lost weight? I'm all propped up with vitamins and stuff. *How are you?*"

Silence.

"When did you last write me?"

There, the silence.

Cigarettes . . .

The moment tightening. Aware of the tightening. She felt she might scream in the tightening . . .

Blue smoke, hovering.

Casually hovering . . .

"I'm all right, Jan."

She fought the tightening . . .

"I actually didn't think I'd be here. Did you ever, really, expect me to be here? It began when I met this wonderful old man—*wonderful*—in Italy—I stayed for a while at his place in Capri—"

Silence.

He looked at her, then away, pulling on his cigarette.

"So—" she said. "What are you doing?" And, quickly. "How's the play? Have you finished the play?"

No answer.

Before her, puffing his cigarette, not answering . . .

"Fred—" she began. tremulously.

He was looking at her.

He was looking right at her.

A wire, high up, tight, ever tightening . . .

"I can't do it, Jan."

Silence.

Hovering . . .

High, high on the wire, looking down from the wire . . .

The leap from the wire, and falling, hurtling, reaching out now, desperately, seeking something, anything, grasp, hold on to, stop the fall . . . Years, exhumed, rushing up at her . . . Whiteness, gray, cold whiteness . . . Sounds . . . Would be. *That would be . . .* Her voice—

"I—"

Holding now—

"I'm going to be sick."

She tried to rise.

She saw him.

He was sitting there.

She saw him, clearly, glasswork splintering, falling, all about her, she heard the falling . . .

"Jan—"

Before him, tugging at him, a fire leaping and driving in her.

"What? What do you mean? *Tell Me What You Mean!* Will You?"

If time owned its moments . . .

"Talk to me! I've come halfway round the world to talk to you!"

He was rising, he stood before her.

"Jan—don't scream—don't do anything—"

"My God—"

"Listen—"

"Oh My God!"

"I couldn't write it to you. I had to see you and say it to you—"

"Say it to me!"

He waited, she saw him there, waiting . . .

He said to her, "It would end us."

"No—" she whispered.

"Both of us—"

"No!"

"I know—*now I know*—"

"You don't know!" And *"What do you know?"* And "Who's got to you? Tell me—*You Tell Me*—"

"No one."

Silence.

His eyes on her.

She stood there, in silence, letting him look at her . . .

She said, finally, quietly, "You've a new girl. Young, sweet romantic girl—"

"No, Jan."

Abruptly, *"What,* then?"

Silence. Watching him now in the silence. Part of his silence . . .

His voice, "Jan—"

She stopped it. She was near him. She reached out and touched him. A desperate warmth surged in her. She wanted to tell him, she was murmuring, telling him,

"I love you . . ."

Watching him.

Ever, watching him . . .

He stood silently, before her.

"Listen—"

Nothing more . . .

He was turning, moving away, she saw him. She held him. She was before him, looking up at him.

Footsteps, muffled, in the hallway, faint whirring, stirring, sounds of the night, far night, out of night, this night . . .

Only.

Her hand slipping from him. Aware of it, slipping from him.

She was frightened, suddenly.

He was backing away. She saw him, slowly, backing away. His face. Her eyes upon him. Her face . . .

She was standing in the middle of the room. She heard his voice . . .

Hand descending, slowly, arc unseen, unknowing, movement, moment, delineating itself for itself, unknown . . .

At the door. She saw him at the door . . .

Lips, soundless, moving.

He was looking at her. His eyes never strayed from her . . .

. . . *white rustle* . . . corps . . . *about her* . . . *swaying* . . . *lovely white* corps . . . *around her* . . .

"Good-bye, Jan—"

Barely, reaching her . . .

She was alone.

_____73

The room, suspending itself . . .

Awake. She knew she had slept, or lain in a numb stupor, for some time. *Numbness.* She saw the table lamp. *All numbness.* She sat up, slowly, trying to dispel the numbness.

Long silver thread, spun out in stillness, night, her stillness. Shadows, about her. She saw them. They surged, devouring themselves, about her.

She tried to stand. Barely, she did so. She made her way to the mirror.

Dress. Her dress. Lovely dress. Breasts. *My lovely dress—*
"No!"

Uttered, suddenly, softly, her breath carrying it through open lips, red, lovely lips. A scream dying. Falling, within, and dying, moments focusing themselves, hovering, revolving . . . Before her. Eyes on the figure before her. Reflected, eyes on themselves now, the image blurring eyes, burning . . .

Drawn face before her, lines, crossing away from her eyes, wet by her eyes, for her . . .

She saw the eyes.
In the mirror, a long while, she stared at her eyes . . .
"*Italia*—"
Her voice, finally . . .

She drifted to bed.

The night was melting away.
She reached out and felt the night melting away . . .